The Conquest of

Lonnie Dolan

By
Harold H. Milton

Llumina
PRESS

Requests for permission to make copies of any part of this work should be mailed to:

Janice L. Blanton

376 Canterbury Road

Bay Village, Ohio 44140

ISBN: 978-1-62550-265-0

978-1-62550-266-7

Printed in the United States of America by Llumina Press

Library of Congress Control Number: 2015918233

Dedicated to

Orville B. Blanton

and his Daughter,

Janice Louise Blanton

The Conquest of
Lonnie Dolan

Chapter 1

The Birds and Bees

"*I*'ve just got to make love, real man-like, to that high-stepping little filly one of these days, or bust a gut trying," Lonnie Dolan mentally promised himself every school day as he covertly and speculatively ogled the trim, five-foot-two figure of the new teacher at Point Fountain grade school.

Lonnie was in his middle teens. He was tall and well built, with handsome features, dark eyes, wavy brown hair, and a winning personality. His father was a coal miner, and Lonnie had never lived anywhere but mountainous West Virginia.

Since this was his last year of elementary schooling, he had hoped to concentrate on his studies and make the most of his eighth-grade year, but Lonnie had made that decision before he met Carrie.

The summer before, he'd spent six weeks with an uncle and aunt on their farm below Elkins, and his whole outlook towards the opposite sex became permanently altered. Until that vacation, girls, to Lonnie, were just people. Nice to have around, but nothing to get excited about. All that changed. His mind now was largely occupied with one of the oldest and most fascinating games the world had to offer—namely, the conquest of the female by the male.

Carrie West was blond, beautiful, and diminutive, a perfect specimen of well-developed young womanhood. Within hours of their meeting, she informed Lonnie that she was really in the know when it came to the facts of life. Girls of sixteen and younger should have more fundamental things on their minds than helping their mothers with the housework, Carrie maintained. Their primary objective should be to attract boys. All else was secondary.

Two days later, she arranged for them to go fishing by themselves the following afternoon, and to take a picnic lunch. When Lonnie expressed surprise that she wanted to go on a picnic in the middle of the week, she smiled sweetly and said she would be awfully disappointed if he didn't go with her. She promised to try real hard to be entertaining, if he did. Swallowing his objections, Lonnie told her he would be happy to go fishing and picnicking with her.

It was July, and the day was hot, but no sooner had they reached the deep pool of water where Carrie said the big fish hid than her behavior underwent a transformation. It became quite obvious to Lonnie that fishing was the farthest thing from Carrie's mind.

"Let's go swimming," she said eagerly, a roguish smile curving her ripe red lips.

"I can't," Lonnie stammered. "I ain't got any swimming trunks with me."

"So what?" she laughed, and a light of girlish wickedness danced in her big, innocent-looking blue eyes. "Who said anything about swimming trunks? You've got skin, haven't you?"

"Yeah, but—"

"Come on then, fraidy cat. I'll bet I can get undressed first and beat you into the water."

As Lonnie stood rooted to the spot in open-mouthed wonder and embarrassment, an unbelieving thing transpired.

With a trilling little laugh, Carrie unbuttoned the print dress she wore and pulled it over her head. Her cotton slip and lace-trimmed panties followed the dress to the ground in the twinkling of an eye.

She wore no brassiere, not that she needed any. Her breasts were perfectly developed and stuck straight out like the two halves of large orange. Her pink nipples were as big as ripe cherries. Dropping his bug-eyed stare below the luscious fullness of her breasts, Lonnie noted her slender waist approvingly. Her well-rounded hips and beautiful, contoured legs claimed their fair share of his fascinated attention.

Carrie laughed again. Stepping out of her shoes, she tripped up to him daintily. She threw her arms around his neck, stood on tiptoe, pulled his head down, and claimed his mouth with a pair of lips that were as soft and sweet as a baby's cheek, but as hot and demanding as only a woman's could be.

She pressed her lovely, nude body tightly against his overalls and kissed him again. Just before their lips parted, Lonnie felt the hot lance of her tongue in his mouth.

"What about the fish we're supposed to be trying to catch?" he gasped, his blood on fire.

"Pee on the fish," she giggled, winking at him and giving her round buttocks a tantalizing wiggle. "We've more fascinating things to do, big boy."

Before Lonnie could collect his wits, Carrie whirled out of his feverish grasp and ran to the edge of the pool. She waded into water until it came to above her waist then began splashing around.

"Get undressed and come in, Lonnie baby," she called. "If you don't, I won't let you do to me afterwards what I'd planned on us doing. We can have oodles and oodles of fun this afternoon. So don't you be a ninny and spoil my plans."

"But suppose someone comes up the creek and catches us?" he quavered, his overall half off.

"Don't be silly," she laughed. "I've lived here all my life, and nobody comes up to this hollow until squirrel season. That ain't for three months yet. Please, hurry up. I'm getting impatient."

His face flaming scarlet, Lonnie complied. He seemed powerless to do otherwise. When he entered the pool, she was down at the lower end, splashing around and singing to herself, but she turned and began paddling towards him.

They met in the deepest part of the pool. The water was slightly roiled. When Carrie stood, just her head and part of her shoulders showed. The rest of her body was cloaked by the murky water.

She moved close to Lonnie and wrinkled her nose playfully. She reached out and drew herself to him. Once again, her hot, wine-sweet mouth found his and clung to it as though she was drowning. With a gasp, she released his lips, took his two hands in hers, put them on her full, rounded breasts, and squeezed them just a little. Another clinging, hot-mouthed kiss followed. Carrie slid one of his hands down through the water, past her slender waist, and to the exciting bulge between her beautiful legs.

"Fondle me down there," she whispered. "And please, don't be scared or easy about it, either. I'm sixteen now, and I've been wearing rags between my legs every month for over three years. Don't worry, Lonnie honey, I'm as much a woman now as I'll ever be."

When Lonnie began doing as Carrie requested, she pulled his head down and whispered into his right ear. He blushed scarlet, and she smiled intimately up at him. She laid one of her hands against his nude body, at the waist, and began inching it downward. The instant her hand made contact with that for which she was searching, Lonnie gasped, in spite of himself.

"Ah," she whispered, delighted. "Gosh. Oh, gee. I can tell by what my fingers are wrapped around that you're more man now than boy. I'm glad for us both."

With brutal force, Lonnie caught her to him. At his whispered request, she shook her head, kissed him once again, and then turned toward the creek bank.

"Not here in the water, sweetheart." She smiled. "Too cold, and we couldn't get in the right position. Let's go on up the creek a little ways. I know a good place for what we've got in mind. It's nice and mossy. We can have more fun doing what we're thinking about when we reach that spot than we could here in the water. Come on. It'll only take a minute to get there."

Carrie led the way out of the pool and picked up the lunch basket they'd brought. Slipping her wet feet into her shoes, she scooped up her clothes. She smiled up at Lonnie and walked upstream a hundred yards or so. Wordlessly, Lonnie splashed along behind.

They came to a fork in the stream and a small jack oak-covered ridge sloped up between the channels. Carrie slipped out of the creek and up the gently sloping ridge a little ways. A perfect sod of thick, springy, green moss grew on a level spot. It looked cool and velvety. Carrie set the lunch basket on a rock nearby and lay down on the moss. Then, looking up at Lonnie, she held out her arms to him.

"Come lay with me, kind sir," she urged. "Let us explore the wonders of nature."

"You're awful pretty lying there," Lonnie whispered as he sank down beside her. "But if I let myself go and harm as much as one hair on your head, your paw would hang my hide on the fence, and I couldn't blame him for it, either. Please, put your clothes back on. I'm not a man grown, yet I know how it feels to ache all over from wanting to make love to a girl."

"Forget Paw, and Maw, too, for that matter. As far as I'm concerned, they'll never know a thing that went on between us."

"You could get in the family way, Carrie. You're old enough to have a baby, and I'm old enough to make one for you. And there's another thing to consider. If I gave in to what I'm wanting to do so bad right now, I could be jailed for rape."

"Hush your mouth, silly boy," she admonished, pouting prettily. "I'd have to make a complaint against you first, which I ain't about to do. I like you, Lonnie Dolan. Like you a lot. I'm fairly in a lather from wanting your love so badly."

"What about your maidenhead?" Lonnie gasped, his eyes devouring her nude loveliness. "Paw once told me that girls get messed up when they let a boy have his way with them the first time. If I ruined yours, I'd be in one hell of a fix. Why, Paw even said—"

"Horse manure," she spat, disgusted. "Stop worrying and shaking all over, and let's get started. I want to play like I'm a new bride, and I want you to play the part of an excited bridegroom. Forget all about this getting knocked-up stuff, too. Mom always takes a good swig of turpentine after Paw tops her. At least, she says she does. When I get home this afternoon, I'll take a good swig of it. That is, if you stop pussy-footing around long enough for us to do anything exciting."

"Are you sure you can depend on this turpentine treatment?"

"It must do the trick. I'm going on seventeen, and I don't have any brothers or sisters."

"Neither do I," Lonnie said, wondering. "Maybe Maw uses something like that, too. She never said."

"She wouldn't tell you if she did, stupid," Carrie grinned. "Look, Lonnie, honey. You can forget all about busting my cherry. It was busted wide open over a year ago."

"Did some feller pop your corn?" Lonnie asked, a wide grin replacing the worried look on his face.

"Sure did," she giggled. "It hurt some while he was doing it, but I loved every minute of our little get together."

"Tell me how it happened," Lonnie said.

"All right. It was like this. One day last May, while my parents were in town shopping, I began reading a love story in one of them romance magazines."

"What's that got to do with you losing your cherry?"

"Everything, silly," she murmured dreamily. "I got hot panties from reading about this boy and girl doing it every chance they got and how much they loved it."

"Yes, yes," Lonnie urged impatiently.

She paused in her narration to French kiss him. "Be patient, lover boy," she said, smiling archly. "I'll tell you all about it if you lie down beside me and act as if you want us to do each other. Can't you see I'm trying to educate you about the birds and bees?"

"All right," Lonnie agreed, dubiously. "But if I hurt you down there between your pretty legs, don't blame me."

"I won't. Just lie down, relax a little, and enjoy yourself while we let nature take its course. There. That's better. As I was saying, I got hot panties from reading about that boy and girl. I was really in a lather. Right then, I honestly believe I could have screwed a snake if someone would hold its head so it couldn't bite me. Then it happened."

"Oh, hell," Lonnie swore, disgusted. "Go on, Carrie. Don't keep me in suspense this way."

"A knock sounded on the front door. It was a young fellow selling garden seeds. I felt all kinds of ways inside when I saw how handsome he was, and before I realized what I was doing, I had invited him inside. We sat on the living room couch, and I looked at the stuff he was selling. The magazine I'd been reading was lying on the floor before us. It was open to a picture of a man and woman lying in each other's arms, practically naked."

"Yes, yes," Lonnie said impatiently as she paused to kiss him in a way that left him gasping for breath.

"This young fellow looked at the magazine, then looked at me, and grinned. When he asked if I read those kinds of stories, I told him about the story I'd gotten hot panties over. He laughed and asked if anybody had ever made love to me like that. I said no, not that way, but I sure liked to kiss. That was how it started. I still get excited thinking about that day."

"Tell me, Carrie," Lonnie urged, his blood racing like fire through his veins.

"Before I realized what he was doing, I was in his arms, and he was kissing me. For just a moment, I was sort of scared. Then I went wild and began kissing him back. In just a little while, we were lying in each other's arms on the couch, and he was putting his hands all over me, especially my titties and between my legs. I loved every blessed minute of it. When he saw how excited I was, he took my panties off. I even helped him. I was eager for his love. Then we did it, Lonnie. We made love to each other like they do in the stories in these romance magazines."

"Did it hurt a lot, Carrie? Or did it feel real good, like everybody says it does?"

"It hurt some, but it was heavenly, too. While we were doing it, I wiggled all over the couch. I couldn't hold still. That alone goes to show you I was really enjoying it."

"Did he ever come to see you again after that?"

"Shucks, no, darn it. When he asked how old I was, I told him fifteen. He got real scared. He begged me not to tell my parents about what we had done, gathered up the stuff he was selling, and dashed out of the house like he was running for his life. He jumped into his car and drove off, lickety-split. I never saw him again, and I never told my parents about what he'd done to me, either."

"That bastard raped you, Carrie," Lonnie said.

"Nonsense," she murmured, looking at him with age-old knowledge shining in her big, expressive eyes. "He just busted my cherry, and I was more than willing for it to happen. Now are you still scared of ruining me for my wedding night?"

"I don't know what to say or think," Lonnie stammered, as he looked longingly at her lovely, nude figure. "Honestly, Carrie, I'm still afraid to do what you want."

"Don't be," she whispered. She clasped her arms around him tightly, gave a strong pull, and rolled on her back. Lonnie found himself on top of her. She spread wide her legs and squirmed. Since they were naked, this brought their sexual organs in contact with each other and in the right position. With another eager, wiggling squirm, Carrie accomplished her purpose. Nature had its way, and the sexual organs of the young lovers fused deeply together.

"Ah," Carrie exclaimed softly in blissful realization. "Please, oh, please, Lonnie darling, don't hold back now. I don't care if it hurts a little bit. Maybe it should. I only know that it's wonderful. That's it. That's the way. Let's work together, in harmony. Oh, Lonnie, I love you. I love you."

With wild abandon, on fire with the intensity of their union, Lonnie complied with his partner's instruction as best he could. He was in the grip of a sensation the likes of which he had never experienced. It flooded his body from head to toe.

Suddenly, Carrie caught at him with trembling hands. Uttering another little cry of bliss, she told him in a gasping whisper that something wonderful was happening to her. She was having an orgasm. Then nature exerted itself with Lonnie. He sank into her entwining arms, as weak as water, but gloriously satisfied.

With moist, hot lips, as sweet as new honey, Carrie kissed him again and again. He returned caress for caress, his fear and reserve gone, his budding manhood dominating.

During his stay at his uncle's farm that summer, he and Carrie went fishing together five times. Only once did they forego sexual relations. That time, Carrie was having her period. Even then, she insisted on lying in his arms, completely nude. She kissed him so many times, and so passionately, that his lips felt bruised for days afterwards.

To know such a girl as Carrie West was an education in itself. She insisted that men and women were destined to have sexual relations with each other, and only an idiot would argue otherwise. That was the most dominant law of nature, she maintained, and Lonnie came to realize that she was wise beyond her years.

"Remember all that, Lonnie, honey," she said as she kissed him goodbye the night before he left for home and school. "Every girl wants some man to want what she has between her legs. Don't ever let any one of them tell you differently. I know. I'm a woman."

"You're a woman, Carrie, baby." Lonnie grinned down at her. "A woman all the way. And I don't mean maybe."

"We may never meet again," she said softly, snuggling closer in his arms. "It's fifty miles from here to where you live, and my folks are talking about moving to Clarksburg this fall. Just bear in mind what Carrie taught you when you meet the next pretty girl you desire. Don't be afraid to ask her for it. She might act mad as a wet hen first, but secretly, she's glad she appealed to you. Nine times out of ten, if you keep after her for it, she'll eventually give in. Us women are built that way. Bye-bye now, Lonnie, baby. We had fun, didn't we?"

"We sure did," Lonnie agreed, kissing the soft, sweet lips she held up to him. "I was bashful as all get-out at first, but you was right all along. I wanted what you had the worst way, but I was too tongue-tied to make a play for it. I think I'll practice what you've been preaching to me with the pretty girls I meet. I might wind up with a few black eyes, but it's worth a try. Bye, Carrie. It was wonderful to know you. If I live to be a hundred, I'll never forget this summer."

As Lonnie ogled Betsy Blake, the new teacher of Point Mountain Grade School, he resolved to put into practice that which Carrie had hammered into his head. Carrie West was a woman, he told himself. She ought to know what she was talking about.

Thus, it was that at an early age that Lonnie Dolan launched himself upon a plan of behavior towards young women that would shape his future life into a most interesting and intriguing pattern.

Chapter 2

The School Teacher

On the first day she began teaching at Point Mountain Grade School, Betsy Blake insisted that all pupils address her by her given name.

"Boys and girls," she said, right after school had taken up the first day. "I'm happy to have the opportunity to teach you. I sincerely hope all of you will like me as much as I'm sure I'm going to like all of you. Feel free to bring your problems to me. I will do my best to help you. My name is Betsy Blake. Instead of asking you to address me as Miss Blake or Miss Betsy, I'd much rather just be called Betsy. Okay?"

The pupils took to Betsy right from the start. Some of the eighth-grade boys confided to Lonnie that they wouldn't mind tomming the new teacher, just a little bit. Lonnie felt the same way, but he kept his own council.

Betsy was nineteen. Her features were strikingly beautiful, and her head was crowned by an abundant mass of glossy brown hair. Her green eyes were wide-spaced. She was tomboyish, full of fun and the love of life.

As the school days came and went, she gradually entered into the pupils' games, until it was not unusual to see her out on the playground at noon, running and yelling while playing baseball with older boys and girls.

Betsy boarded with a retired miner and his wife, who lived about a half mile from the schoolhouse. Twice a week, her boyfriend, a dry-goods clerk from Webber Springs, came to pay court to the beautiful young teacher. His name was Hershel Jones. Hershel was frail to the point of emaciation. The drab suits he wore hung on him like sacks. His long, thin neck, bony features, horn-rim glasses, and balding head did not add to his manly appearance.

Lonnie was dumbfounded at the thought that a young woman of Betsy's beauty could be attracted to such a specimen. To his young mind, it seemed against the laws of nature.

"I wonder if that funny-book character ever tries to top her?" he mused. "If he does and succeeds, I'll bet she'd consider letting a feller like me get behind her panties. Carrie told me to ask if I wanted to receive. Guess I'll take her advice first chance I get and make a pitch for what Miss Betsy's got between them pretty legs of hers. It won't do any harm to try. The most she can do is turn me down and tell me to mind my own business."

Lonnie decided to use his job as the janitor of the school to help him conquer beautiful Betsy. Every morning after the weather turned cold, he tried to have the school house unlocked and a good fire going in the huge, pot-bellied heater by the time the first pupils arrived.

Often, Betsy arrived in ahead of the pupils, just as Lonnie was firing up the heater. He would talk to her about this and that, and if he could manage it, he'd swing the conversation around to where he could tell her how beautiful he thought she was, and how he hated it because he wasn't older.

"Why do you always say that, Lonnie?" Betsy asked one morning while Lonnie was bemoaning the fact that she was older by almost three years. "Don't you like me anymore?"

"Of course, I do, Betsy." He grinned. "But I sure don't like the way things are between us.

"What do you mean?"

"Aw, forget it. I'd only embarrass you, and you wouldn't understand anyway."

"Please tell me," she begged. "I'm here to help anyway I can."

"It wouldn't be right to tell you this," Lonnie demurred, hoping she would press the point. He wanted to see her reaction when he told her he was jealous of Hershel Jones and wanted to make love to her himself, even though she was his teacher and older.

"Now, Lonnie, I'll feel hurt if you don't share your troubles. After all, that's part of my job as teacher. I'm supposed to help solve my pupils' problems. Is this about a girl?"

"Yes, it is."

"Who?" she asked, moving close to him and placing one of her shapely hands on his arm.

"It's you, Betsy," he answered, looking into her eyes.

"Oh, Lonnie," she whispered, gazing at him, thunder-struck. "You can't be serious. You only think you feel that way about me. I'm terribly flattered, but please don't."

"But I do," he muttered, red-faced.

"So that's why you hate my being older than you?"

"Sure, but that ain't all."

"I don't understand," she murmured, giving him a big-eyed stare. "What else has got you worried, Lonnie?"

"It's that Jones feller that comes to see you every week," he growled. "I ain't saying that he ain't no good, but it curls my hair to think of you in the arms of that scarecrow, and him putting his hands on you and kissing you, and you kissing him back."

"But he's my boyfriend," she said, smiling. "Doesn't that make it right for him to hold me in his arms and kiss me, and me kiss him back?"

"Maybe so," Lonnie replied. "But I want to kiss you, Betsy, and hold you in my arms. You asked me, so I'm telling you how I feel. I want to make love to you, go 'all the way,' as they say in the storybooks. That's what's been on my mind since you began teaching here at Point Mountain."

"Lonnie, Lonnie," she whispered. Her eyes glowed. "You're only a boy in years, yet a man in body. And you want to make love to me like a man would. It that it?"

"Yes, Betsy, that's it," he said, laying a hand on her right arm. At his touch, a tremor ran through her body, and her beautiful face flamed scarlet. A moment longer, she gazed into his eyes. Then, bowing her head, she dashed to her desk and began fussing with some papers. Grabbing up the coal bucket, Lonnie stalked outside, his blood on fire and victory in his heart. Betsy had received his declaration of love better than he had hoped. In fact, Lonnie mused to himself, I believe it pleased her. Carrie said girls were built that way.

For the next two weeks, Betsy arrived at schoolhouse in the morning just before school started for the day. She was still her vivacious self, but whenever she addressed Lonnie directly, her eyes were veiled and her voice impersonal. Lonnie was very casual with Betsy, but her actions told him more than words could have. On numerous occasions, when he raised his head from his studies, he found her looking at him, a strange light shining in her lovely eyes.

"Maybe the thought of me tomming her appeals more all the time," he thought. "I sure hope so. It'd be heaven to do to her what I did to Carrie last summer. Betsy is prettier then Carrie and she's got a better shape, but I doubt she's any hotter between the legs than that little bitch was. If I could only get Betsy in my arms and kiss her a few times, I'd know better how I stand with her."

Circumstances placed Betsy in his arms sooner than Lonnie had expected. During the week of Thanksgiving, one of the school board members had a party at her home. Everybody in the community was invited. The hostess insisted, against Betsy's half-hearted objections, that the new grade school teacher be present. Betsy laughingly accepted the invitation, and that night, dances had been danced and refreshments served. The young people of courting age insisted on playing post-office. Betsy was forced into the game against her smiling protests, much to Lonnie's satisfaction. Hershel begged off, and chose instead to talk with the older men present.

Everyone participating in the game was given a number. As the game progressed, the young people called each other's numbers. Lonnie kept his ears open to hear the number Betsy had drawn. Eventually she was called into the darkened bedroom by a gawky boy of fourteen who had been called in before her. As soon as the door closed on her trim figure, Lonnie smiled and waited. As soon as his number was called, he intended to call Betsy into the room with him.

The doorkeeper whirled around and said the schoolteacher had requested number thirteen. Lonnie's heart leaped. Thirteen was his number. When he slipped into the room and closed the door behind him, he heard a gasp.

"Oh, Lonnie, it's you," Betsy cried softly. She came up to him in the darkness and placed her hands on his arms.

"Yes, Betsy, it's me," he whispered hoarsely. "You know how bad I've wanted you since the first day we met."

"I know, I know," she breathed.

"I won't though, if you don't want me to."

"Maybe I do want you to," she said. "Hershel isn't much of a beau when it comes to smooching, but I like it. Lots. Kiss me, Lonnie. Kiss me like you've wanted to for so long."

When he wrapped his arms around her, she threw her arms around his neck and raised her lips invitingly. As Lonnie claimed them, he thrilled to his toes. Her lips were soft as rose petals, but hot and searching. She worked her soft, sweet mouth onto his until it felt as though she was eating at his lips.

"Betsy, Betsy," he gasped, when she finally tore her mouth loose. "God above, but I want you. You've set me on fire. I can't go out there and face those other kids until I cool down some. My trousers are sticking out in the front as though I had a poker in my pocket."

"I feel the same way," she whispered against his mouth, "only it doesn't show on me. Please, kiss me once more, Lonnie, and then let me go."

Another devastatingly sweet and thrilling kiss followed. This time, just before their lips parted, her tongue lanced into his mouth, deep and hot.

"I've got to go. But first, Lonnie, promise me something."

"What?"

"Promise me you'll be a good boy at school when we're alone together. I can't help it if I wanted us to kiss each other. The important thing is for us to not let it go any further than that."

"No, Betsy. No," Lonnie whispered fiercely. "If I promised you that, I'd look and feel like an idiot. You're a wonderful young woman, and I'm a hot-blooded young man. I want very, very much what's inside your panties. There now. I don't care if you have me expelled from school for telling you that. I must be honest with you. That's how I feel, and that's what I want. And I can't help it if I feel that way about you."

"Lonnie," she cried, shocked. She turned to the door and left the room. Ten minutes later, she and Hershel bade everyone good night and departed.

From that day forward, Lonnie was more subtle in his campaign to conquer Betsy's charms. However, after they kissed so passionately at the party, she began arriving at the schoolhouse after several pupils were present. In the evening, she made it a point to grab her papers off her desk and leave the building on the heels of the last pupil.

Lonnie usually swept the huge one room of the schoolhouse after each day's classes. He brought in coal and dry kindling to start a fire in the pot-bellied heater the following morning. Experience had taught him that this was a good practice. On rainy, snowy mornings, all he had to do to get the fire going was rattle the ashes out of the stove, then apply a match to the dry fuel he brought in the evening before. Sometimes he was busy for a half hour or more, tidying up the schoolroom and getting things ready for the following morning.

As time passed, Betsy gradually changed her method of leaving the schoolhouse in the evenings. Lonnie wisely bided his time during those days, and soon they began exchanging casual remarks before saying goodnight.

Every Monday, her attitude towards him was different. When he thought on it, Lonnie concluded that Betsy's apologetic air was because Hershel Jones paid court to her over the weekend. Knowing how Lonnie felt about her, perhaps she suffered from a mild case of guilt.

Sometimes on Monday, she was downcast and moody, while she regarded him from the corners of her expressive green eyes several times during the day. Then she would be quite gay, and as talkative as a dozen young women ought to be. Too happy—as though she was covering her real feelings.

Four weeks went by. Still, Lonnie played indifferent and waited for the day when Betsy's womanly curiosity would demand to know why he wasn't giving her the rush act.

One evening, the week before Christmas, Betsy tarried longer than usual while getting ready to leave. As Lonnie swept around her desk, she moved from her chair and stepped out of his way, picking scraps of paper off the floor as she did. He winked at her and swept on, as solemn as a judge. Betsy walked back to her desk, sat down on its edge, and regarded him with a puzzled look on her beautiful face.

"Lonnie," she called softly. "Come here."

When he leaned his broom against the wall and came to stand before her, she stood up. She stepped close to him, placed her hands on his arms, and looked up at him, a hurt expression in her eyes.

"You're still angry at me, aren't you?" she said. "Christmas is only a week away. I've a present for you. It's all wrapped up. Doesn't that make you happy, even though you don't like me anymore?"

"Oh, sure," Lonnie grunted, without cracking a smile.

How lovely and desirable she was, but Lonnie knew that victory was his only if he played his cards right. Betsy Blake would be thrown completely off balance if she were ignored by a man she liked. Lonnie realized this was a part of her complex makeup and acted accordingly. He longed to sweep her into his arms and claim her sweet, upturned mouth with passionate, uninhibited kisses, but common sense told him that to give way just then was to lose out in his plan to conquer her lovely young body. Instead, he assumed an air of indifference, and even shrugged his shoulders as she looked up into his rock-hard face.

"Don't you like me anymore?" she whispered.

"What good would it do me if I did?" he growled in reply.

"Lonnie," she pleaded. "Be nice. Why would you snap at me?"

"Well, it's the truth, ain't it?"

"What do you mean?"

"Horse manure, Betsy. Don't act so dumb. I'm younger than you, and your pupil to boot, but don't play me for a fool."

"Oh, please," she cried, her eyes swimming in sudden tears. "I'd never do that."

"Oh, no," he scoffed. "You're doing it to me every weekend."

"I don't understand," she whispered tremulously then dropped her gaze. "How am I making a fool of you every weekend?"

"It's that Hershel Jones feller you're always lolly-gagging around with. That's how you're making a fool of me."

"I told you the night of the party, he's my boyfriend, and I'm his girlfriend. Doesn't that make his courting me right in your eyes?"

"No, it does not," Lonnie growled. He pulled her against him. "Look at me, Betsy. I just can't for the life of me believe that you'd let a scarecrow pimp like that feller kiss you the way I did that night at the party, let alone play with your titties and get into your panties. Do you let him do that to you, Betsy?"

"Lonnie Dolan," she gasped in a shocked whisper. "What a vulgar thing to ask a girl. Aren't you ashamed of yourself?"

"Never. I couldn't be. Especially not while I feel about you the way I feel right now."

"I don't know what's come over you. Why do you act like you do and talk to me this way?"

"I'm a man, that's why," he snapped, looking into her eyes. "Maybe still a boy in years, but with a man's body to feel. And you, Betsy, are a woman. A beautiful, wonderful one, too. Also," he continued, clutching her in an iron grip, "looking at that sweet mouth of yours, so close to mine, is setting my blood on fire. You know how badly I want to kiss you, don't you, Betsy, darling?"

"No, no, don't say that," she pleaded. But all the time, she pressed against him tighter. "I don't want you to kiss me. Please, believe me. I don't. I don't."

Even though Betsy pleaded with Lonnie not to kiss her, she brought her lips up close to his hungry ones. At last, with a ragged gasp, Lonnie swept her into his arms. Even in his impassioned state, he noted with satisfaction that she was every bit uninhibited as he was.

He bent his head, his lips found hers, and he opened his mouth just a little. Then, he began to caress her more emphatically. Her breasts were cushioned against him, and she moved her body in such a way that her breasts rolled against his chest. Unable to bear the tension longer, Lonnie withdrew enough to bring a hand between their straining bodies. He cupped it over one of her firm, round breasts and began to massage.

She tore her eager lips from his and caught at his hands on her bosom. A moment longer she let it remain there, then stepped back, and with bowed head, slowly disengaged herself.

"Lonnie, Lonnie," she cried reproachfully as she touched her fingers to her bruised lips and looked up at him with accusing eyes. "See what passion for each other leads to? We must never let this happen again. Next time, it might go beyond kissing. We're flesh and blood, Lonnie. Not stone. Let's not play with fire anymore."

"You're right, girl," he cried hoarsely. "I'm flesh and blood, all right. That's why I want you so."

"Goodnight, Lonnie," she said, turning away, her voice tear-laden. She put on her hat and coat and dashed out of the schoolroom.

Christmas and New Year's Day came and went, with the midyear vacation of two weeks. Betsy withdrew into her shell of reserve after Lonnie kissed her in the schoolhouse. She seemed ill at ease around him, and took to dashing out of school just as soon as she dismissed the last class for the day. Once again, Lonnie played the waiting game. This time, however, he did not have as long to wait for results. On Thursday evening, a fortnight after New Year's Day, Betsy again elected to stay a few minutes after school.

As Lonnie tidied up for the coming day, she appeared to be rummaging through some papers on her desk. Seeing her linger, he chose to sweep by her desk and the rostrum. He hoped she would find some excuse to start the ball rolling between them again. And if she did, he planned, if all possible, to take it from there.

Getting his broom and the dustpan, he walked up on the rostrum and began sweeping the floor with long, swinging strokes. It was wrong to sweep that way, and he knew it, but intuition told him that Betsy, once she noticed his sloppy work, would call his attention to it. That was exactly what he wanted her to do.

"Lonnie," she cried, exasperated, as he gave the broom an extra vigorous swish that sent the dust swirling through the air. "Is that the way your mother taught you sweep at home?"

"No, Betsy, it's not," he grunted. "I'm sorry. Guess I wasn't noticing what I was doing. My mind doesn't seem to be on my work tonight."

"A penny for your thoughts," she laughed, but her gaiety was forced. There was explosive tension between them, and she, being a woman, knew it.

"They'd be a bad buy for you at any price," he said. "I wouldn't want to cheat you."

"I really don't know what to make of you these days. Why are you so glum around me all the time? Why can't you and I get along like the other pupils and I do? Why must we be different?"

Instead of answering, he laid aside his broom and walked over to where she stood by her desk.

"Here's why, Betsy," he growled, sweeping her into his arms and crushing his mouth down on hers. She reciprocated.

As soon as he released her lips, she flung her arms around his neck and pulled his head down to hers. Her searching lips found his. When their tongues met inside his mouth, Lonnie felt all kinds of ways. Betsy Blake was all kinds of woman. She had everything he wanted, and he wanted everything she had.

Catching her up in his arms, he set her down on a corner of the desk and laid her back on it. When she divined his intention, she began to struggle and plead with him to release her, but Lonnie was not to be dissuaded this time. He had waited too long for this moment.

Reaching up under her skirt, he hooked his fingers in the waistband of her panties and gave them a vigorous yank. In a moment, they were off her and dangling in his hands. Lifting up her legs, he spread them apart, and pulling her towards him, stepped between them and unzipped his trousers.

"Please, Lonnie. Oh, please, let me up," she pleaded, as she strove vainly to disengage her legs from around him and get off the desk, but her frantic efforts were to no avail. "I'll let you kiss me all you want, and even let you play with my breasts, but don't do this to me. Lonnie, stop. Oh, stop. I might get pregnant. I could have a baby if you persist in this. Why, I could even—"

The instant his sexual organ made contact with hers, her protests ceased. With a soft little scream of pure ecstasy, she closed her eyes and began to harmonize with his movements. As he continued his movements, her breaths became ragged gasps. Then she began to plead with him to increase the speed of their gyrations. In their first all-out lovemaking, her former denials and refusals were as if they had never been. She was a woman being sexually satisfied.

"Lonnie, Lonnie. Lovable, darling, Lonnie," she exulted in a gasping, panting rush of breath. "Faster, faster. And deeper, oh, please, deeper. I didn't know. I didn't realize it could be so heavenly, so all consuming, so…Ah!"

As nature manifested itself to its fullest with her, she at last abandoned all semblance of self-control. She made violent wiggling movements and little animal cries and squeals of sheer, blissful enjoyment, giving herself over to the pleasure of the moment.

During the remainder of the school term, the young lovers enjoyed sexual gratification in each other's arms at least a dozen times. Most of the time, Lonnie was the aggressor, with Betsy protesting, at first, that they should not engage in so degrading a practice in the school in which she was teaching. But once they were in each other's arms, her response was never wanting. In fact, there were times when she seemed impatient that he spent so much time kissing her and playing with her breasts, instead of getting started with intercourse.

One evening in early March, as they were doing it on their hands and knees, Betsy became so excited, responsive, and demanding during their copulation that Lonnie was exhausted by the time they finished. While they were still in position, having not yet separated, she looked back over her shoulder, smiled, and wiped sweat from her brow. A funny, bewildered look was in her expressive eyes.

"Lonnie, darling," she whispered. "I don't know what to make of myself when I like it as well as I did just now. Do you think I could be a nymphomaniac?"

"Idon'tknowwhatyoumean." Hegrinned."What'sanymphomaniac?"

"A girl or woman who's over-sexed. One who likes to do it more often than might seem normal. Has it ever occurred to you that I might be that way? Do you think I might be a little abnormal from the way I carry on sometimes?"

"Heck, no, Betsy, baby," Lonnie scoffed, giving her a playful spank on her bare buttock. "You're as normal in every way as apple pie. What man wants to waste his time and energy on a woman who's about as sexy as a dead fish? Why, he'd be more ahead to find himself a fur-lined knothole. I wouldn't want you to be one little bit less anxious for it than you are. If you was, we wouldn't be having all this fun we're having, now that we understand each other."

"I'm glad you look at my uncontrolled carrying-on like you do," she said, slowly disengaging herself from him. "I was worried you'd think me a sexual manic."

"Not a chance," he laughed, playfully spanking her once more as she got to her feet and began rearranging her clothing, preparatory to leaving the schoolhouse for the day.

Six weeks later, after they had indulged in numerous sexual relations and various positions, Betsy confided to Lonnie that she was going to have a baby. At his shocked expression, she smiled and said bitterly, "Oh, don't look so shocked, Lonnie. My having a baby isn't going to be the end of the world for you."

"But what'll we do?"

"Nothing."

"Don't be silly, Betsy." He gulped. "I got you in the family way, so it ain't no more than right that I marry you."

"It would never work out, lover boy," she returned, a scornful look crossing her face.

"Why not?"

"You're actually only a boy yet, in years, and still in school besides. Then there's our ages to consider."

"What's our ages got to do with us getting married?"

"Everything," she replied listlessly. "There's almost three years difference in our ages, and all on my side. Have you forgot that you're three years younger than me?"

"No."

"Well, neither have I. If we married, you'd soon feel trapped, like you'd married an old hag. No, Lonnie. Marriage for you and I is out of the question."

"But darling," he remonstrated, though his heart wasn't in his argument. "Face facts. Having a baby is a serious business for a girl at any time, let alone when she is without a husband to stand by her side. It is just not fair to you to face this alone."

"Oh, don't act so guilt-stricken," she laughed without humor. "I've already figured a way out of this mess I let you get me into."

"How?"

"Hershel is going to be the scape-goat, only he doesn't know it. Last Saturday night, I encouraged him to get behind my panties. He was all excited at having broken down my defenses. After it was over, he got real serious and said we'd get married just as soon as I set a date. He was so worked up over what we'd done, that he swallowed my act hook, line, and sinker."

"Well, I'll be dog-gonned," Lonnie exclaimed.

"I know it's a dirty trick to marry Hershel while I'm with child from another man, but what can I do under the circumstances? When a girl's knocked up, it's no time to get squeamish about the methods she uses to get a wedding ring on her finger. Besides, Hershel has wanted to marry me since the first day we began going together. So here's his chance. I guess the prospect of having an illegitimate child haunts every girl who plays around before marriage. Some get caught, and some don't. I got caught. Hershel and I decided to get married the week after school is out for the season."

"Suppose he puts two and two together later on and comes up with the right answer? What then?"

"He won't," Betsy said, matter-of-factly. "He isn't the type to stop to figure things out like that. I'm glad he isn't. We'll do it tonight, Lonnie, for the last time. That is, if you still want to after what I've just told you. If we do, I suggest we make it interesting. Something to remember each other by, you know."

The evening before the last day of school, Betsy kissed him goodbye and wept while his arms were around her. Lonnie was unusually downcast himself, and words would not come to him to comfort her. When she turned and walked away, he felt he was losing something priceless, and indeed, he was. Betsy loved him, and she was carrying his unborn child.

Eight days later, Betsy Blake married Hershel Jones. The newlyweds went to the national capitol for their honeymoon. During their absence, the firm Hershel worked for in Webster Springs changed hands. As a result of this change, a completely new staff of clerks was hired for the store. Hershel lost his job, and the honeymooners did not return to Webster Springs. Lonnie never saw Betsy again.

Chapter 3

The Girl of the Forest

*F*or more than a month after Betsy Blake walked out of his life, Lonnie was very down at the mouth. He moped around without interest in anything or anybody. Finally, at his mother's suggestion, he took his twenty-two rifle and began tramping over the mountains. He hoped long, strenuous hikes through the woods could help him regain his easy-going outlook on life.

One Saturday morning in June, while the dew was still on the grass, he packed a lunch and started out to explore. His destination was a lofty wooded ridge that soared high in the sky, far across Elk River from where he lived on Point Mountain.

Noon found him a good five miles from home in unfamiliar territory. As he ate his lunch beside a spring of clear, cool water that gushed out of the rocks on the ridge, he contemplated turning homeward and abandoning his desire to explore the entire ridge. It seemed endless, and it was cloaked in places by huge patches of rhododendron.

Suddenly, a piercing scream shattered the forest stillness. Startled, Lonnie scrambled to his feet and looked all around. Again, the strange, thrilling cry rang out. Just then, a huge silver-grey hawk sailed over his head and lit in the top of a dead chestnut snag about a hundred yards out on the ridge from where he was standing.

Picking up his rifle, Lonnie began cat footing out the ridge. The scream he had heard was the hunting cry of the hawk. If he could, he intended to kill it. Huge hawks such as this were a deadly menace to all small game, such as squirrels and rabbits.

Coming to an open place in the underbrush, he paused and peered ahead at the dead chestnut. From where he stood, the hawk was exposed.

Raising his rifle, he sighted up the barrel. He was about to squeeze the trigger when the unexpected happened.

A rifle shot rang out with a sharp, stinging report. As Lonnie gazed at the hawk in open-mouthed amazement, it tumbled off the top-most branch of the dead chestnut and came fluttering down to fall in a dense copse of bushes a stone's throw ahead.

Lonnie dashed up to the fallen bird and poked it a couple of times with the muzzle of his rifle barrel. Then when no life showed, he bent to pick it up.

"Get your ass away from my bird, mister, and do it quickly."

Whirling around, Lonnie saw a dark-eyed young woman leaning up against a tree about twenty feet away. The repeating rifle she carried was held casually. However, even at first glance, he could see that it covered his middle section in a way that gave him cause for thought.

"Howdy, miss," Lonnie said, smiling, though he eyed the position of her rifle apprehensively. "Did you shoot this hawk?"

"I sure did. And don't you be trying to claim it. There's a bounty of a dollar apiece on hawk heads now, and I need that dollar the worst way."

"Have no fear, Miss," Lonnie said testily. "I haven't the slightest intention of swiping your hawk."

"Well, you couldn't even prove it by me," she snapped coldly. "Here I shoot a hawk, and when I come to pick it up, I find you bending over it with your hands practically on it. What am I to think?"

"Look," Lonnie suggested. "Let's get better acquainted before we accuse each other of stealing. Please, believe me. I had no intention of taking your bird. My name's Lonnie Dolan. What's your name?"

"Millie Denton."

"Live around here?"

"Slaty Fork."

"Gosh," he exclaimed in wonderment. "You're quite a hike from home, aren't you?"

"Far enough," she smiled. "I'm used to tramping these old hills, though."

As they talked, the tension eased out of the girl. At last, convinced that Lonnie meant her no harm, she sat down on a mossy rock and leaned her rifle against a tree by her side. Millie Denton was a fine figure of young womanhood. Beautifully tall, her long, slender legs were encased in a pair of tight-fitting jeans, which brought out the roundness of her hips and her slender waist most becomingly. She was attractive, with flowing, ebony hair framing her face. Ruby lips and white even teeth completed what, to Lonnie, was a picture of feminine beauty.

"Tell me about yourself," he said, wanting to know more about this lovely girl who tramped the lonely woods, miles from home, carrying a rifle, who obviously could shoot like a man.

"Really, there's nothing much to tell," she sighed, poking at the leaves underfoot with a stick. "I live over on Slaty Fork with Mom and Dad and my little sister. I passed out of the eighth grade a year ago. Last winter, I went to high school, but I don't think I'll go any more."

"Why not? A good education is a fine thing to have."

"I know that. And I wish I could force myself to go on. It's only that I can't make up my mind whether to slap the taste out of several of my schoolmates' mouths, or ignore their sly digs and get my education, regardless of how they tease me and call me an old man's darling."

"Why would they do that?" Lonnie asked. "It's not unusual for a girl to love her father. Most every girl does."

"It's not my dad they're referring to," she said bitterly, with downcast eyes.

"Do you want to tell me about it?" Lonnie asked softly. This lonely, lovely girl of the forest intrigued him. Already, he was visualizing how wonderful it would be to hold her in his arms and kiss a smile onto those ripe, red lips. He trembled at the thought of exploring the exciting swell of her rounded breasts, and wondered at what lay behind those tight fitting jeans. Yes, as Lonnie looked at Millie Denton, he pictured another conquest, and he resolved to do everything in his power to get her in his arms in all-out lovemaking.

"It's none of your affair," she said harshly. "To start with, I'd be damn fool to trust a perfect stranger and pour my sad tale of woe into his ears. Lonnie Dolan, do you think me a complete idiot?"

"Not at all. I only wanted to help you, if I could."

"That's a laugh," she said scornfully. "If my own mother can't help me, how can some fresh kid I never saw before come up with something? Forget that I mentioned my troubles."

"Are you trying to tell me that you really are in trouble?"

"Yes and no, if that means anything to you. Look, Lonnie, I've got to be hotfooting it for home. I'm glad we met, even if it wasn't under the friendliest of circumstances. Good-bye."

"Wait, Millie," Lonnie said, stepping up to her side.

"What do you want?" she inquired.

"Can't we see each other again?"

"Why do that? I'd only be poor company for you, and besides, Dad would fair take the hide off my behind if he caught me meeting a strange boy in the woods. My dad's got plans for me. And I do mean plans," she added, bitterness dominating her rich, throaty voice.

"Maybe we could go hunting or fishing together. How about that?"

"I love to fish," she said quickly, while a soft smile played around her mouth.

"Then that's what we'll do. How about us meeting in the woods again in a couple of days? Say, right here. Do you know of a good place to fish that ain't too far from where we're standing?"

"I know of a dandy place. It ain't over half a mile from here. And it's a place where nobody ever goes to fish. Too far back in the woods, I guess."

"Then, how about it? Do we go fishing, or are you going to kill off any chance we might have to be friends, even before we get to know each other at all?"

"I'll do it," she breathed excitedly, a laugh of pure joy bubbling up in her throat. "Heaven help me if my dad finds out, though. He'd just about be fit to be tied."

"Good. Do you come into the woods often by yourself?"

"All the time. It's only that I'm glum when I leave the house for tramp in the woods, and glum when I return. If I come out of the woods looking happy, my dad might get suspicious. He's funny that way."

"At least it's worth a try," Lonnie urged. "What do you say?"

"All right," she laughed. "Reckon it won't do any harm to fool my old man a little. The good Lord knows he ain't doing right by me these days. I'll meet you here day after tomorrow, at noon. That is, if it's a nice day and I can get away from the house without Dad following me. Good-bye, Lonnie. Bring a can of worms and some grub. We'll need them both."

During the next ten weeks, Lonnie met Millie Denton in the woods more than a dozen times. After the first fishing expedition, he began complimenting her good looks. At first, she only looked at him in round-eyed solemnity whenever he told her how pretty she was and how anxious he was to kiss her, just once, to see if her lips were as sweet as he knew they must be.

However, as time went by, she began making bantering remarks in reply. When he commented on how beautiful her face and form was, she accused him of telling all the pretty girls the same thing.

"Go along with you, Lonnie Dolan," she laughingly said one day as they were fishing and he was paying her high-sounding compliments. "Don't think for a minute that I can't see through that line of bull you're forever handing me. It's old hat. Why, I've been hearing the same line of malarkey from the boys ever since my titties were as big as bee stings."

As they laughed together, Lonnie bent his head and kissed her full on the mouth. She reacted differently than he had anticipated. Instead of reciprocating, she sprang up off the log they were sitting on and struck him a stinging blow across the mouth.

"You dirty son-of a bitch," she blazed. "Get fresh with me, and I'll knock half your teeth down your throat."

The blow was so violent and unexpected it bowled Lonnie off the log they were sitting on, and into the deep hole of water in which they were fishing. As he climbed out on the bank, dripping wet, Millie burst into gales of merry laughter.

"See what you got yourself into, smarty pants? Next time, ask permission before you kiss a girl like you kissed me just now. I don't like that kind of goings-on a little bit."

Fingering his bruised lips, Lonnie decided it was time to play the "absence makes the heart grow fonder" game with Millie, and straightway, he began putting it into operation.

Picking up his lunch basket and fishing pole, he turned away and started up the ridge in the direction of Point Mountain and home.

"Good-bye, Millie," he called back over his shoulder. "It was nice knowing you."

"Lonnie," she called after him. "Please, come back. I'm sorry I struck you and called you names. I didn't mean it. Believe me, I didn't."

But Lonnie walked faster, smiling. His experiences the winter before with Betsy Blake had taught him that a girl hates like poison to be walked away from by a man she likes. If she feels she has wronged the man in question, her repentance would be doubly sincere. That was exactly the reaction Lonnie hoped for in Millie Denton.

He stayed away from the fishing hole for two weeks. Then, one sultry day in late August, he decided it was time to see if he could contact

Millie Denton again. Just before noon, great white thunderhead clouds began pushing up out of the southwest. As Lonnie gained the crest of the high ridge on which they had first met, the low roll and boom of thunder sounded. It was a good half-mile to the fishing hole, and the shelter of an overhanging ledge of rock that jutted out of the mountainside.

Increasing his stride, Lonnie hurried on. When at last he descended the slope above the fishing hole, the summer storm was breaking around him in its fury. He ran through the spray of rain and darted under the sheltering rock just as a terrific bolt of lightning zigzagged out of the stormy sky with a deafening roar, like the blast from a ten-inch cannon.

Simultaneously, a scream of mortal terror smote Lonnie's ear. Swinging around, he peered into the gloomy shadows under the ledge at his back. Millie Denton stood within ten feet of him, her eyes reflecting her terror of the storm, her face as white as chalk.

"Why, Millie," Lonnie said, smiling at her. "What a pleasant surprise. I didn't know you were here. Are you all right?"

Instead of answering his questions, she dashed up to him and flung herself into his arms. Wordlessly, Lonnie folded her close to his chest.

"Oh, Lonnie, Lonnie," she sobbed. "I've missed you so. Forgive me for being so nasty to you the last time we were here. You do, don't you? Please, tell me you aren't angry at me anymore."

"Does it look like I'm angry?" Lonnie grinned, looking into her tear-filled eyes.

"No." She smiled happily. "I'm so glad you aren't. I've come here five times since that day you left and today this awful storm caught me. If you hadn't come back when you did, I honestly think I's died of fright. I'm deathly afraid of lightning."

"Are you afraid now?"

"Not anymore," she sighed. "With us here together, I don't care how much this old storm rips and roars."

Lonnie bent his head and kissed the inviting lips so close to his own. This time, her reaction to his kiss was far different. Stirring slightly in his embrace, she slipped her arms around his neck. As he removed his mouth from hers, she smiled into his eyes and whispered to him to kiss her again and again, only longer and more possessively.

This is my chance to try a French kiss on her, Lonnie said to himself. She might like it, and then she might balk at it like an unbroken filly.

Whatever the outcome, I'm going to try it. As my pappy always told me, one never knows until one tries.

When his mouth sealed her sweet, soft one, he worked his lips onto hers thoroughly. Then, opening his mouth just a little, he slipped his tongue into her mouth until it touched the tip of her tongue. Her eyes opened wide, but she made no move to withdraw. Instead, as he flicked his tongue in her mouth, she closed her eyes, clasped him tighter around the neck, and relaxed against him.

"Why did you kiss me that way?" she asked when he moved his mouth from hers.

"No particular reason." He grinned. "Did you like it?"

"Um, maybe," she replied, blushing furiously. "But ain't that sort of a nasty thing to do? This sticking your tongue in a girl's mouth. Has that kind of kissing got a name?"

"It sure does," Lonnie laughed. "It's called French kissing. It's not so nasty, Millie. Fact of the matter is young people do it all the time while they're courting. Some girls would rather kiss a boy that way than any other. And that's way they want to be kissed, in return."

"But why?"

"They say it's more intimate. More exciting. What do you think?"

"Oh, I don't know," she hedged. "One thing, though. When you kissed me that way just now, I felt it clean down to my toes."

"See what I mean? You did like it, only you're ashamed to admit it."

"No, I'm not."

"Want to try it again?"

"I don't know." She hesitated. "Promise me one thing. If we do, can I put my tongue in your mouth after you do it to me?"

"Sure can," Lonnie laughed, excited.

Millie closed her eyes and held her mouth up to his. As he sealed it with his own, she expelled her breath in a rush and pressed against him. As he inserted his tongue in her mouth, she began to tremble. Then when she, in turn, inserted her tongue in his mouth, it felt as though she was reaching for his tonsils, so deep and hot was her thrust.

"How did you like it that time?" Lonnie asked breathlessly, as she tore her mouth from his and hid her face against his chest.

"I'm ashamed to tell you," she whispered softly, a tremulous note in her voice.

"Did it hurt your mouth? If it did, I'm sorry."

"No, it didn't hurt me. At least, not in the way you mean."

"Then let's do it again," Lonnie urged. "If you're ashamed to tell me how you felt after we kissed, it must mean that you enjoyed it. Did you, Millie?"

"Yes, yes," she cried, leaning back in his arms and looking at him with eyes that were unfathomable pools. "But let's not kiss each   other that way anymore."

"Why not? I enjoyed it, and you said you did, too. I don't think I forgot to brush my teeth this morning."

"Kissing like that can be dangerous," she replied, solemn. "And I don't mean from germs, either."

"Aw, go on, Millie."

"It's a fact. A boy and girl could lose control from it."

"You're joking."

"I'm serious, Lonnie, honey. When you kissed me just now, I had the strangest feeling."

"Like what?" he asked, a broad smile on his face.

"Listen, and don't laugh," she whispered, hiding her face against his chest again. "I felt sort of tingly all over, on fire, when you stuck your tongue in my mouth the first time. Then the second time we kissed, I felt even more wacky."

"What do you mean, Millie?"

"I just didn't want you to stop kissing me, ever. I also wanted you to put your hands on my titties. And that ain't the only way I felt, to be perfectly honest."

"What else did you feel, darling?" Lonnie asked softly, as he kissed the top of her head and his blood raced like fire.

"Lonnie, sweetheart?" she murmured, snuggling even closer as the wind and rain roared outside the shelter of the overhanging ledge. "Did you ever see a bull and cow together when she's in heat?"

"Plenty of times," he replied.

"And did you notice how he would finally rear up on her and pop it to her real good? Also, how satisfied she always looked while she let nature take its course with them?"

"Yes, yes," Lonnie cried hoarsely, his heart beating as loud as the thunder that rolled and boomed overhead. "But for heaven's sake, Millie, what's that got to do with you and me?"

"Everything," she breathed. "That's how I felt when you gave me those French kisses. Now isn't that a terrible way for a girl to feel when she's being kissed?"

"I think it's wonderful," Lonnie said, bending back her head to cover her beautiful, flushed face and throat with passionate kisses. "How do you want to feel while I'm kissing you? Like an old woman?"

"I don't know," she said. "I've never felt this way in a boy's arms. Always before, I've been disgusted, but not now. Oh, Lordy, not now. Kiss me, Lonnie. Please, hold me tight, and kiss me. No more of that French stuff, though. It scares me. I'm afraid that if you keep that up, I'll become so wacky that I'll do something awfully wild and ornery."

While her lips were sealed with his, Lonnie casually put one of his hands on one of her firm, jutting breasts. At his touch, she began to tremble, and when he commenced to massage first one then the other, she tore her lips from his. With bowed head, she slowly disengaged herself from his arms.

"Lonnie," she said in a hurt voice, her dark eyes looking into his reproachfully. "You shouldn't have done that. I'm beginning to think the world of you, and it's heavenly to have you kiss me. But I won't have you pawing over me like I was a damn whore."

"Millie! Please, that's the last way I'd think about you. I'm only flesh and blood. Nothing else. I can't help it if you're beautiful and desirable. I want you so badly that I am a little wacky when your sweet lips act as though you want to eat me up. I'm seventeen, and I want the same things from a lovely young woman that any mature man would want. Just because I'm a boy yet in years doesn't change the picture any. I've got a man-size body to feel with and want with."

"I know, Lonnie, honey, I know. To be truthful, I feel the same way. I can see right now that we'd better call a halt to all this hot lolly-gagging we've been doing. If we don't, it's liable to get us into hot water."

Despite her resolutions to the contrary, three days later, Millie was once again in Lonnie's arms; also, contrary to her resolution, she not only kissed him numerous times in the conventional style, but also insisted he kiss her a few times the French way.

"I just want to show you, Lonnie, baby, that it doesn't bother me one little bit to be kissed this way, after all. I think it was the storm that affected me so strangely the other day. Not that slobbery, tongue-sucking kissing we were doing."

However, after two passionate, searching thrusts of his tongue, Lonnie felt her begin to tremble. Two more such kisses followed in slow, agonizing ecstasy. Then the unexpected happened. Tearing her mouth loose from his, Millie looked up at him with dark eyes and a blank expression. Then, with a low, moaning cry, she unbuttoned two of the buttons on her blouse and hunted his lips again. When they were looked together, with her tongue deep in his mouth, she took one of his hands in hers and slipped it inside her unbuttoned blouse, making sure that it cupped one of her warm breasts. She was not wearing a brassiere.

All that afternoon, until the sun had dipped far to the west, Millie lay in Lonnie's hungry embrace. Soon after she slipped his hand inside the front of her blouse, she unbuttoned it completely. At times, she sat up in his arms and pulled his head down so that he could kiss her luscious breasts and nibble at her protruding nipples. Whenever Lonnie did this, her breathing became thick and labored, and she clutched him to her so tightly that he was almost smothered by her sweet bosom.

"Take off your jeans, Millie, darling," Lonnie pleaded, time after time. But her answer was always the same.

"No. No," she panted. "I dare not. I dare not. If I did, we'd never stop till we went all the way. I'm afraid, sweetheart. I'm shaking like a bowl of jelly inside. If I took my jeans off, we'd lose control completely and act like a bull and heifer. I'm ashamed to admit it, darling, but I'd want us to act that way."

"Would that be so bad? So terrible a thing for us to do while following the dictates of our hearts? We're in love, aren't we?"

"I'm hopelessly in love with you, Lonnie Dolan," she whispered, pulling him to her breasts again. "And it'd be heaven itself to give myself to you. But I'm afraid. I'm scared sick at what might happen if I do."

"Of what, sweetheart?"

"I could get knocked up, have a baby. My dad would just about kill me for a thing like that. As I told you the first day we met, he has plans for me."

"Tell me about it, darling. I'll understand," Lonnie coaxed.

"No, honey. I'm too ashamed of it all. Let's skip all that and enjoy ourselves with what limited privileges I can permit you to take with me."

But Millie had neglected to consider the tremendous temptation involved when two young lovers hold their trysts deep within the concealing fastness of the forest.

Ten days after the day she first succumbed to the magic of French kissing, she again lay in his arms. On that day, she came to him with her eyes red from weeping and with black and blue marks on her face and arms.

When Lonnie questioned their source, she clammed up. Soon after he took her in his arms, the tension eased out of her beautiful body and she confided to him that she and her parents had had an argument the evening before, and her father had gotten rough with her.

"Maybe it was my fault," she muttered, but her dark eyes were full of rebellious fire. "Perhaps I shouldn't have told my parents last night that from now on, I intend to do as I please. Anyway, when I said that, Dad sure whaled the tar out of me. Now I hate him more than ever. Oh, why must parents be so narrow-minded?"

That afternoon, Millie insisted Lonnie kiss her exclusively in the French style. Shortly after their lips locked in their first kiss, she unbuttoned her blouse all the way and removed it. After a few ecstatic caresses, she gave a queer little laugh, and slipped out of her jeans and panties.

"Lonnie, sweetheart," she whispered brokenly, hiding her face against his chest. "I know I'm being an awful slut to do a thing like this, but I can't help myself. I love you so very, very much. If you still want to, I think we better make love to each other, all the way, while I can come to you. Slow at first, and be gentle. No boy has ever touched me like I'm going to let you touch me now."

After three exploratory attempts, with her helping as best she could, Lonnie made the first complete union of their sexual organs.

"Oh," she gasped as he began a slow, in-and-out movement. "It hurts, so good, so good. Oh, Lonnie, Lonnie. My darling, my lover. I love you. Give all of yourself to me. It's all right, honey. So don't hold back, even a little bit. I want all of you. I—Ah!"

That day marked the beginning of all-out love making between Lonnie and Millie. As time passed, she began to insist they perform the sex act in every conceivable way and position.

"These are our moments of love, Lonnie baby," she said as they went about the preliminaries, arousing fever-pitch desire in each other. "So let us enjoy them to the fullest while we may."

Once, while they prepared to copulate, he suggested that perhaps they should use protection against her becoming pregnant. However, a hurt expression came over her beautiful face, and tears welled up in her eyes.

"Aren't I good enough to take just as I am?" she whispered softly.

"I meant no insult to you, sweetheart," he hastened to assure her. "It's only that I want to protect you from becoming pregnant, if I can."

"I'm willing to take that chance," she said softly, creeping into his arms and beginning to kiss him passionately and possessively. "Just make love to me as nature intended, and I'll be happy. Won't you be, too?"

"Always, my love." He smiled, folding her close.

But Lonnie and Millie forgot to reckon with circumstances and human nature. On Labor Day weekend, he went to keep an appointment they had arranged the week before. But Millie was not there to greet him. Instead, a white slip of paper was weighed down with a small rock upon the spot where they had spent so many blissful hours.

With trembling hands, Lonnie picked it up, a premonition of bad news settling over him like a dark cloud. The note was tear-stained and covered with writing on one side. He began to read.

> *My darling Lonnie,*
>
> *When you read this, I will be a married woman and on my honeymoon. Now I can tell you what I've always been ashamed to tell before. I'm marrying the man my dad promised me to two years ago. He's a widower with two teen-age sons, and he's old enough to be my father. I hate him, but I'm becoming his wife, anyway. My folks are forcing me. Either that, or they lose their home. This man is well off, and my dad owes him a lot of money. So he's using me to pay his debt. I hope they both die tomorrow.*
>
> *I'm thankful that you and I was able to get to know each other, and was also able to make love to each other like we did these past ten weeks.*
>
> *It was heaven to me. Those moments we spent together, in each other's arms, will live in my heart as the most beautiful, satisfying time of my life.*
>
> *Forget me, my dearest, for that would be best. But should you ever think of me in years to come, remember this. I will always love you and wish you the very best this disappointing old world has to offer. Goodbye, sweetheart. May the Good Lord bless you, always. I'll love you till my dying day.*
>
> *Millie*
>
> *P.S. Today is my eighteenth birthday.*

With his heart dead inside him, Lonnie stumbled homeward. For the next three months, he lived from day to day, dreading each tomorrow. He vowed in his heart that he would never fall victim to another girl's charms. But that promise was made before he met Cindy Hamrick.

Chapter 4

The Sun Bather

During the spring of Lonnie's twentieth birthday, his father was forced to retire from mining because of ill health. Fortunately, however, he had managed to buy and pay for a home and bank a tidy sum besides. When his health would no longer permit him to work in the mines, he sold his home on Point Mountain, bought an eighty-acre farm in the Tygart River Valley, and began tilling the soil for a livelihood.

He also bought a span of mules. Lonnie had always been good at handling animals, and the elder Dolan began leaving the bulk of farming chores to him. That first summer on the farm, Lonnie put in an abundance of crops. Soon he was busy from dawn till dusk, tending them. The farm, and the responsibility of running it, was new to him, but he took to it as a duck takes to water. Many months had passed since Millie Denton walked out of his life, but his young heart still bore scars of the emotional upheaval. This was new and different, and he was glad.

For nearly three years, all he had to do to bring the memory of Millie flooding over him was look across the Elk River to the lofty ridge where they first met. When he did, he could picture her soft lips, dark flowing hair, expressive eyes, and luscious body as she lay in his arms and whispered her love for him. In those moments of painful reminiscence, his heart beat like a trip-hammer, and he felt sick to his core.

By working long, hard hours out in the open air, he eased the hurt and healed the scars in his heart. As the weeks slipped by and he toiled in the sun, wind, and rain far from the old homestead on Point Mountain and the sight of the wooded ridge with it's painful memories, he began to hope he might never again know the heights of bliss and the depths of despair a woman's love could propel him to.

Experience had taught Lonnie Dolan at a young age that love for a woman was painful and blissful. He quaked with fear at the thought of going through such an upheaval again, and solemnly vowed that love was a thing of the past. However, the powers that be had other experiences of the heart in store for Lonnie Dolan.

One blistering hot day in July, about three months after he and his parents settled in their new home, he was running the five-fingered cultivator through a new stand of corn on the upper forty-acre lot.

People by the name of Hamrick owned an adjoining farm. Occasionally, he saw their daughter Cindy out in the yard or garden when he drove the mules past their place. She always waved to him gaily, and called out a cheery greeting. Lonnie would drive on, his mind overflowing with thoughts of how a woman could get her way with a man.

Cindy Hamrick was a honey blond. She was twenty years old and very beautiful, with a body that took a man's mind off beauty and put it on other things. Cindy knew the power that beautiful chassis held for the opposite sex, and she played it up.

Lonnie first met her at a square dance two weeks after he moved into his new home. During the course of the evening, she let him know she was his next-door neighbor and expected to see lot of him in the future. She informed him shyly that she was a lover of the great outdoors, especially sunbathing in the nude.

"I just love that old sun," she giggled, smiling up at him as they danced the peek-a-boo waltz. "It does things to my body. Nice things, I think. Do you like the outdoors, Lonnie?"

"I love all forms of nature," he said as he grinned down into her blue eyes, "but mostly I prefer the female forms of nature."

"You dear boy," she breathed, hiding her flushed face against his chest. "We must talk about nature again soon. I believe you and I have a lot in common."

"I'm sure we have," Lonnie assured her. Thus was his introduction to Cindy Hamrick.

On this particular day, Cindy came up to where he was plowing corn carrying a small bucket of fresh, cool drinking water from their well.

"Hi, Lonnie," she called, coming into the cornfield as he was turning the plow about a dozen rows up the slope. "See what a good neighbor I am? I brought you a cool drink of water. Come and get it, or I'll pour it out."

Lonnie tied the mule to a small hickory tree, dashed down the slope, and grabbed the bucket of water out of her hands, a look of mock severity on his face.

"You wouldn't dare," he growled, shaking a finger under her pert little nose. "Why if you'd do a thing like that, as thirsty as I am, I'd be tempted to spank that round behind of yours."

"Lonnie," she squealed, pleased with his reference to the symmetrical beauty of her hips. "How you talk."

"As it is," he continued, "I think I should give you a big kiss in appreciation of your kind deed. Here I was, dying of thirst, and you came to my rescue."

"I was only doing my neighborly duty." She smiled. "I expect no compensation other than your thanks. However, if you insist, I'll be most happy to cooperate."

There it was. As complete and perfect a challenge as ever woman flung in the face of man.

Wiping the water off his lips, Lonnie swept her into his arms. She flung back her head, raised her mouth to his, and closed her eyes. Tenderly and expertly, he claimed her ripe lips with his own in a kiss that awakened the fire of longing in his breast. Her lips were rose-petal soft and as sweet as new honey.

"Lonnie, Lonnie," she whispered, as he released her and stepped back. "Where, oh where, did a plow boy like you learn to kiss like that?"

"I've read books on the subject." He grinned. "Did you like it?"

"I loved it," she breathed, looking up into his eyes. "Take pity on a poor girl and do it again."

Her mouth was full and ripe, warm with life, and so tempting. Lonnie pulled her into his arms and tasted that sweet mouth and the fire that smoldered within her. He felt her body mold itself to his, eager and excited.

"I like you, neighbor." She smiled up at him from the shelter of his arms. "Like you a lot. But I've got to be getting home. If we keep this up, things might get out of hand between us. Don't you agree?"

"Depends on how you look at it. Things might get much more exciting between us, Cindy, but I'd bet you my bottom dollar they'd never get what you could rightfully call 'out of hand.'"

"You're a naughty boy," she reproved gently. "Now you've got your mind below your belt. I can tell right now it's going to be nice having you next door."

"I feel the same way about you. Have you gone sun-bathing yet this summer?"

"Not yet, but I think I'll go tomorrow. That is, if it's a nice day or not quite as hot as it is today. I just want to get a good tan all over my body. Not be burned to a crisp."

"Mind if I come along?"

"Lonnie Dolan, I declare," she gasped, her baby-blue eyes wide with shock.

He could see that she was only putting him on. He suspected she wanted him to want to come along while she was sunbathing. He promptly told her as much, but not before he gave her another long, searching kiss that shook her to her pink little toes.

"Why the surprised look?" he asked, his face as empty of expression as a blank sheet of paper. "Remember the night we met at that square dance?"

"Yes," she murmured. "So what?"

"As I recall, you told me you loved to sunbathe in the nude. I recall telling you that I was a great lover of nature. Especially the female kind. I haven't changed, Cindy. I still feel the same way about females."

"And I still live to sunbathe in the nude." She grinned. Swinging around, she pointed toward a huge, flat rock about a quarter of a mile up the hollow. "See that big flat rock up there?" she asked.

"I do."

"The top of that big rock is my favorite sunbathing spot. It's a long ways back from the road, and I've never been disturbed up there yet."

"Going to use that big rock to sunbathe on again this summer?" he asked, a wide grin lighting up his face.

"I expect to. It's on your father's farm, but I don't imagine he'd care if I used it. Do you think he'll let me?"

"Of course, he would, so you need to ask, but what I meant was if you use that rock up there again this summer, and I'm around, you're going to have company."

"You mean you'd come up there and surprise me?"

"That's right."

"Suppose I had no clothing on?"

"That wouldn't make the slightest difference to me. I'd still come."

"Even if I was stark mother naked?"

"I don't care if you was lying up there as naked as a bird. I'd still come up on top of that rock."

"Would you look at my naked body?"

"Right at you and at everything you've got, from head to toe."

"Well," she grumbled in mock anger. "Before I go home, I've one thing to say to you, Mister Plow-Boy Dolan. "I dare you to set foot on the top of that rock while I'm lying there. Now smoke that in your pipe, you big wolf."

There it was again. Woman's inevitable challenge to Man. Lonnie gladly accepted that challenge, whole-heartedly and without reservation.

"I'll be there with bells on," he promised, with a devilish glint in his eyes. "Just try me and see, you sweet, lovely, delicious bundle of feminine charms. I dare you to go up there and peel off while I'm around. I won't rape you, but I'll do the next thing to it."

"That I've got to see and feel," she said, smiling sweetly. Picking up the water bucket, she slung it over an arm and began walking home. However, before she passed from view, she turned and waved to Lonnie and blew him a kiss. Waving back, he blew her a kiss in return.

He walked over to the mule, untied him, and resumed his cultivating, but his heart was not in it. Instead, his mind was on a gorgeous, blond siren, and his blood was on fire with desire.

For the next five days, the weather was unseasonably inclement, with cold rain and high winds slashing down out of the north-west in a way that had folk wondering where the summer had gone. On the sixth day, the clouds parted, and the sun shone feebly for a few hours. On the seventh day, however, the sun shone down out of a cloudless sky, as hot as ever, but with cooling breezes wafting up the valleys.

A fortnight after he talked with Cindy in the cornfield, Lonnie had occasion to be on that part of the farm again, mending fences. As he walked towards the hollow where the flat-topped rock was, he decided to see whether Cindy was there, taking advantage of the warm sun and cloudless sky.

He walked to the uphill side of the huge rock and scrambled to the top, but no nude young woman of gorgeous proportions did he find there. Instead, he found a white square of paper stuck in a crack in the rock. It was fine stationery, delicately perfumed, and contained a dozen lines written in a clean, precise, feminine hand. "Sorry I missed you. Even so, I enjoyed two hours of wonderful sunbathing and relaxation. I haven't decided yet whether to label you a wolf or a chicken who likes to sound like a wolf around the girls. Until I see you on the top of this rock while

I'm sunbathing on it, completely nude, I'll have to call you a two-legged wolf with feathers. From You Know Who."

Smiling broadly, Lonnie pocketed the note and continued on his way, but he made a mental note to check the big rock every warm, sunshiny day for the rest of that summer. Sooner or later, he would find Miss Cindy Hamrick on top of it, and when he did, he fully intended to partake of her feminine charms.

Three weeks passed. Lonnie faithfully checked the big rock every sunshiny day, but he never caught Cindy on top of it.

On several occasions, she was out on the front porch at her home when he passed. She always waved to him and flashed him a white-toothed smile. Lonnie suspected Cindy enjoyed the cat and mouse game they were playing, but he kept his own council on the matter and bided his time. Experience had taught him that things had a way of balancing themselves out, and so it was with Lonnie and Cindy.

One bright, warm, Saturday morning in early August, he drove a past the Hamrick residence with his parents on the way to Valley Head. As he came abreast of the white house, he drew rein. Cindy was out on the front porch.

"Hello, there," he called, drinking in her loveliness. She was wearing a halter top and very short shorts. "We're going into the Valley Head to do some trading. Want to come along?"

"No, thanks." She smiled, waving to his father and mother. "Daddy and I was in town yesterday. He took off a day from the mail route to shop, and he splurged. Bought me this outfit. Like it?"

"I think it's very nice," he answered, clucking to the mules. "Bye, now. See you later."

She came out to the road and called after them. "Oh, Mr. Dolan. I've a favor to ask. I'd like to use your big flat-topped rock up in the hollow for a couple of hours today. I want to go sunbathing on top of it. Do you mind?"

"Not at all," Lonnie's father replied. "Help yourself."

"Them calves in the pasture up there, do you think they'd be cross?"

"Heavens, no. They're tame as kittens. Just watch out for snakes. That's all you need worry about. Use the rock anytime you like. You're perfectly welcome."

"Thank you, so much, Mr. Dolan," she said happily, as innocent acting as a baby. "See you folks later. Have a good time in town, Lonnie. Thanks again. Bye, now."

So this is her way of rubbing it in, Lonnie mused as he drove on. She thinks she's going to get away with it, too. I think I'll pull a fast one on that little lady and outwit her. Five minutes after they passed Cindy's home, he handed the reins to his father, wiped his forehead, and made a wry face.

"Gosh, Dad," he grunted. "I feel bummy all of a sudden. I don't think I ought to go into town, after all. Pull up ahead there under that big walnut tree and let me out. I'd better hike on back home and take it easy for the rest of the day."

"You sure you'll be all right?" his mother asked, her face grave with concern.

"I'll be fine, Mom," he assured her. "I'll cut over the hill here and be home in ten minutes. Sorry I flunked out on you. Guess I've been working too hard lately, what with the haying and all."

"Probably so," his father agreed. "Take it easy today, Lon. Your mother and I'll be home by sundown. Never mind the chores. I'll do them when we get back this evening. You rest today. Get up, mules."

The first thing Lonnie did when he got home was drink two full glasses of whole milk with raw eggs in it. If he made contact with Cindy up on the big rock, he would need plenty of reserve energy. He packed three huge ham sandwiches, three large, ripe tomatoes with salt, and a half-gallon jug of cool water from the well, and then set out for the big, flat-topped rock.

He chose a roundabout route. He cut back though the hills, but it was almost eleven o'clock by the time he came down through the woods opposite the rock. He picked an open spot through which he could watch the huge boulder, and he sat down to wait. He pulled his cheap dollar watch from his pocket and laid it on the leaves beside him. More than an hour went by. Then, through the trees, Lonnie saw someone walking up the hollow below the big rock. It was Cindy Hamrick. His heart began to pound behind his ribs, and his blood became liquid fire in his veins.

As he watched, she climbed up on the huge rock, set down a small basket, looked all around, and then began disrobing. In a moment, she was completely nude, a beautiful, naked creature of soft flesh, with lustrous caramel blond hair spilling down over her naked shoulders like melted butter. Lonnie sat, waited, and watched as she spread out a blanket and lay down upon it, face upwards.

"I'll wait till that pretty little bitch gets settled before I move in," he said, picking up his watch and lunch. "If she ain't flagging, and I bet she ain't, will I ever pop her corn good. I just hope she's had her cherry busted by some other guy. If she has, and I get her hot enough, all she'll want to do is screw. And that's exactly what I want from Miss Cindy in the worst way."

Lonnie picked his way through the woods very carefully and cautiously then stood at the huge rock looking on her nude loveliness before Cindy realized anybody was within a mile of her.

"Oh, Cindy, baby," he called softly, grinning at her shocked expression as she swept the blanket over her nakedness and looked at him. "I'm here, and I'm coming to you."

"Lonnie Dolan," she exclaimed, and then then burst into a trilling laugh of delight. "You big fibber. I thought you were going to Valley Head, but come on up, you chicken-hearted wolf. I dare you to. I double dare you. I'm lying up here, stark mother naked, and I don't intend to put a thing on in the way of clothes. So there you are."

Lonnie scrambled up the side of the rock and sat down by her side. Her eyes flashed a challenge at him as he drank in her loveliness.

"Take me in your arms, lover boy," she coaxed. "I've something for you."

"What, sugar puss?" he asked, gathering her in his hungry arms and fondling her intimate places.

"Two hot lips and seven kisses."

"I've something for you, too."

"Oh, how nice," she bubbled. "What is it?"

"Two hot nuts and seven inches."

"Ah, just what I want and need. Why torture me with talking about it? Let's do something besides look at each other. I'm burning up, and not from the sun, either."

Her lips were bright red and wet. They parted slowly, and her tongue flicked over her white, even teeth, inviting Lonnie to take what he saw. Throwing her arms around his neck, Cindy raised her hungry mouth to his. He searched for her mouth and found it. It seemed to burn into his soul as her lips fused with his. He got a king-sized taste of the love she offered and gave it back with all he had. He crushed her winsome body to him until her breath came in short, quick, gasps. As Lonnie released his lips to French kiss her, she divined his intent and beat him to it.

Her tongue entered his mouth with an intensity that sent love and desire coursing through him like an electric current. Tearing her mouth loose from his, Cindy looked up at him and pleaded for all his love, as is a woman's way.

"Lonnie, Lonnie," she gasped, clutching at him with feverish hands. "Let's not waste any more time smooching. I want to feel it now. I want those seven inches you said you had for me. I want them. I need them, badly. I must have them, or I honestly think I'll explode."

"First, let's get off this rock," Lonnie suggested. "It's hotter than blazes up here now. By the time we get steamed up with the real article, we'll be fried like a couple of eggs. There's a nice, cool, mossy spot up in the woods there. Let's go to it. We'll be lots more comfortable there than here."

"All right," she conceded, jumping up and slipping into her shorts and halter. She put her pink silk panties in the small basket. "Lead the way. I'll be at your heels. I think we wasted too much time, as it is."

In ten minutes, the young lovers were prostrate again upon her blanket, completely naked, on a mossy little flat about three hundred feet up the wooded hillside. Huge white oak trees clustered around, making an ideal bower for a picnic, or lovemaking. The spot was secluded. Lonnie was sure he and Cindy could make love to each other there to their heart's content without fear of being disturbed by man or beast.

Once again, Cindy pleaded for Lonnie's love. He fondled her with expert hands intimately, massaging every secret spot on her beautiful body. She gave a great, ragged sigh and clutched at him. Soon her breath came in short, hot pants. At every movement of his hands, she twisted and squirmed.

"Oh, darling, darling," she cried. "I can't stand this heavenly hell you're doing to me one minute longer. If you keep it up, I honestly think I'll go out of my mind. Why not give yourself to me now, all the way? I'll just die dead if you don't. I want you so much. I need what you can give me. Why torture me longer? I'm ready for your love. You know I am."

At last, when Cindy was white-hot with desire, Lonnie swung up on top of her. She spread wide her legs. The moment he was squarely between them, she locked her legs tight together at the small of his back. Their sexual organs made contact and fused together, and Cindy became uninhibited in her response.

"Oh," she screamed in ecstasy. "This is it. This is it. Oh, I hope this heavenly feeling never ends. Work with me, sweetheart. That's the way. That's the way. If only we could...ah!"

Cindy's breath caught in her throat and she clamped her strong white teeth on the muscles of Lonnie's right shoulder. A deep groan of pain and bliss escaped Lonnie, and Cindy screamed a jumble of hysterical, unintelligible words.

The day wore slowly away, but to the lovers in the forest, the hours were as minutes. Three times that afternoon, they sought sexual gratification in each other's arms. Three times afterwards, Lonnie sank into Cindy's tender embrace, exhausted, satisfied, and completely happy. With honey-sweet lips, Cindy kissed him, and he returned her kisses with equal passion. Her firm breasts claimed their fair share of his attention. He fondled and kissed them until their nipples stood out, as firm and big as ripe cherries.

The young lovers separated in the cool of the evening. Lonnie cut back up over the ridge to get to his home, and Cindy tripped daintily down the valley towards her home, carrying her lunch basket and blanket, as pure and innocent as if she had spent the past several hours wading in a brook, instead of partaking in uninhibited lovemaking. The following week, and once a week thereafter that summer, for as long as the weather held warm, Lonnie held their love trysts in the woods above the big rock.

Cindy's regular boyfriend reminded Lonnie of Hershel Jones. He saw that Cindy's craving for sexual gratification could not possibly be satisfied by such a suitor. As soon as bad weather set in, he began to call on her one night a week. Cindy's mother frowned upon this double-dealing, but Cindy only tossed her blond head and continued on her merry way.

All of Lonnie's previous loves had been uninhibited where lovemaking was concerned, but Cindy Hamrick, blond, beautiful, innocent appearing, could devise more ways and positions for sexual gratification than any girl he had met in his life. As the weeks went by, with no apparent decline in her desire for his love, Lonnie realized that he'd found a girl who copulated for the sheer joy of the act and her own satisfaction.

Sometimes, when her parents were away for the day, she phoned Lonnie and begged him to come over and fix some little thing or other around the house. Several big-eared neighbors were always eavesdropping on the party line, hoping for juicy gossip, but Cindy was too wise to the ways of her neighbors to state the real reason she wanted Lonnie to come over. At such times, she was discretion itself, and on numerous occasions, even mentioned her boyfriend, Oscar Meeker, to Lonnie.

When he came to her, she shed her cloak of reserve like a garment, and if she could arrange it, she dashed into his arms, stark naked, insisting he carry her to her room and make love to her. Sometimes she had a spot ready for them before the fireplace. There she would lay, as sinuous as a cat, her hungry mouth fairly screaming to be kissed, and her full breasts begging to be fondled. Every part of her luscious body demanded attention in its own special way.

Gradually, winter gave way to spring. One day in April, Cindy casually announced, while she and Lonnie were making love at her home on a Saturday afternoon while her parents were away, that she and Oscar Meeker were getting married.

"Why the big rush, honey bunch?" Lonnie inquired as he kissed a bare breast and ran one hand between her thighs lovingly. "Aren't I keeping you satisfied as far as nooky is concerned?"

"That's just it, baby," she purred. "I believe you've done too good of a job with little old me."

"I don't understand."

"Well, the truth is, I believe I'm knocked up."

"You're joking," Lonnie blurted.

"Not at all, nature boy." She grinned, giving him a French kiss that made even his toes tingle. "Just review our actions over the past eight months, if you think I'm exaggerating. You and I have averaged intercourse twice a week during that time. We went all-out, too."

"Even if we did go all-out every time, as you put it, Cindy, darling, we had fun while we were doing it, didn't we?"

"We certainly did. Look, honey, I've let Oscar get behind my panties a few times this past winter. Even so, if I'm pregnant, I believe you're the father."

"Oscar could be the father, as well as I," Lonnie pointed out. "Any man, if he's virile, can father a child with just one jump at the right time. Surely you know that much about human nature, Cindy, darling."

"Oscar could be the father," she conceded, "but I'd be willing to bet dollars to donuts he isn't. When we made love to each other, I insisted you give your all to me every time you had your discharge. That way, I felt I was getting as much as you could possibly give me. Sometimes it was pretty sloppy, but I wouldn't have had it otherwise."

He whispered against her lips, "And I loved every sweet ounce of you for wanting it that way. It made me feel important to you."

"You have been, too, darling," she sighed dreamily. "Ever since that day last summer on the rock, you've been very important to my peace of mind and my bodily satisfaction."

"Look, honey. If you think I'm going to be a father, let's get married."

"It will never work out between us," she murmured sadly.

"But why not, for crying out loud? I could make just as good a father and husband as the next man."

"Sure, you could, Lonnie, darling, but you aren't ready for marriage, yet."

"I'm almost twenty-one."

"I know, I know, and some day, when you're old enough, the right girl will come along. You'll know it when you meet her. But not you and I, sweetie. We don't have any real, deep, lasting affection for each other. Our attraction has been ninety-nine percent physical. That's how it would always be. Once that was gone, everything else would go with it."

"Maybe you're right," he said soberly. "I hate to give you up to another guy. It'll hurt like pulling sound teeth."

"I understand." She smiled up at him, misty-eyed. "Don't feel too badly about it, though. The feeling you have in your heart for me now will fade. Five years from now, you'll have a hard time remembering what I looked like."

"Cindy, you shame me."

"It's fact. Young men of your age are the most unreliable, romantically, of any age in a man's life. All the physiology books teach it, and it's true. But look, let's not throw a wet blanket on our little party this afternoon. What say we make this our most loving orgy of all and have oodles and oodles of fun and thrills."

"Okay by me." Lonnie grinned, reaching for her.

Cindy and Oscar were married in April. Lonnie had never held the man in high esteem, but he felt real sympathy for him as he walked down the aisle in the church with Cindy on his arm. She wore white, a full veil, and all the trimmings, just as though she was a virgin bride. Lonnie marveled at the picture of sweet innocence she presented.

As he sat in the church in that bright afternoon in April, looking at Cindy's flushed, smiling face as she took her vows, Lonnie could not but think of the many times she had lain naked in his arms.

Shortly after their marriage, Cindy and Oscar want to Pittsburgh to make their home and fortune. Lonnie did not see her again for many years. By then, Cindy had gained considerable weight, and only faint traces of her former beauty remained.

Chapter 5

The Davis Twins

The following summer, death struck Lonnie's family. On the fourth of July, his father passed away, the victim of a heart attack. By early fall, Lonnie's mother, who was several years younger than his father had been, began receiving suitors. At first, he thought it was just one of those things that happen in a widow's life and did not take his mother's courtships too seriously, but as time passed, he realized that his mother was intent on filling the vacancy left in her life with another man.

In December of that year, his mother remarried. The man she wed was a large-framed Irishman with flaming hair and a temper to match. As the winter passed, Lonnie saw that he and John McVay were not going to hit it off. Everything he did or said seemed to displease his stepfather. When his mother began aligning herself against him, Lonnie knew he had to find a home elsewhere. In the spring, he hired out to a dairy farmer by the name of Davis, who lived over on the head of the Gauley River. Sixty miles separated him from his mother and blustery, ill-tempered John McVay, and he was glad.

Sam Davis and his wife had one married son and twin daughters, eighteen years of age. Physically, the two girls bore little resemblance to each other. Otherwise, they were as alike as two peas in a pod. Each liked the same things, and each disliked the same things. They preferred the same type of clothing, and Lonnie was informed that each, on more than one occasion, had been crazy about the same boy.

Of the sisters, Marlene was the prettiest, but Maxine was whistle bait in any man's language, too. Their young bodies were in the full bloom of young womanhood. Seeing them in halters and shorts was enough to make even the most hardened male stop for a second look.

The sisters took to Lonnie from the first and began vying for his attention. This he liked immensely, and he began to look forward to the day that he could make love to one, or both, of the sisters. His bedroom was on the second floor of the Davis residence, between the sisters' bedrooms.

The first chance he had, he oiled the hinges on the bedroom doors, so that they would glide open and shut without a whisper and with the slightest effort. Weeks passed, and Lonnie bided his time. Every chance he got, he played the sisters against each other.

The twins helped with the milking, especially in the evening. As time passed, they fell to teasing Lonnie about the number of teats he pulled every day. They told him he ought to be ashamed of the liberties he took with the poor cows.

"Would you like to be a cow, Lonnie?" Marlene asked one evening as they milked cows in adjoining stalls in the barn.

"I don't think so," he chuckled.

"Why not?"

"My reason is simple enough, if you really want to hear it."

"I certainly do," she persisted, womanly curiosity in her voice.

Leaning around the end of the stall, Lonnie whispered, "Promise you won't tell a living soul."

"Cross my heart and hope to die," she whispered back, her eyes wicked with desire for a smutty story.

"Okay. I'd hate like sixty to have my titties played with every night and morning and only get one piece of nooky a year. Wouldn't you feel the same way, Marlene?"

With a squeal of mirth, Marlene slid her off her milking stool and kicked her legs in the air. Lonnie was shocked, but delighted, to see that she was not wearing any panties.

"Boy, but that was rich." She dimpled. "I don't blame you for not wanting to be a cow, Lonnie. I don't think I'd enjoy being one, either. I know I wouldn't if I was going to be short-rationed on the nooky. Haha. That sort of thing could take the joy out of living, right?"

"Sure could."

"Can I tell Maxine the cow joke?" she asked as they finished milking the two cows and moved on to fresh ones.

"I'd much rather you wouldn't. She might not understand and tell your parents I was trying to get fresh with you."

"Maxine wouldn't do that."

"But can't you and I have this little secret?"

"Of course, we can."

"Good. I'll tell you something else if I have your promise to keep it yourself."

"I promise." She giggled. "Gee, but this is exciting. Is it another joke?"

"No, Marlene. It's about you," Lonnie said. Everything he was about to say was a complete fabrication.

"What about me?" she asked softly, getting up to stand beside him with her hand on his shoulder.

"Maybe I shouldn't tell you this, but I will. The fact is, Marlene, I dream about you almost every night. Want to know what we're doing in my dreams?"

"Yes. Oh, yes," she whispered, running her fingers through his hair. "Please, tell me. Am I beautiful in your dreams?"

"Like an angel right out of heaven itself. Mostly, I dream I'm holding you in my arms and kissing you an awful lot. You seem to like it, too. I remember that part of my dreams real plainly. You kissed me a lot and made me promise not to tell Maxine about us. Aren't dreams cruel, though?"

"I don't understand what you mean," she said, still running her fingers through his hair.

"I'm awfully fond of you, little brown eyes," Lonnie said with a grin as he furiously milked away. "It was wonderful to dream of holding you in my arms and kissing your sweet, soft little mouth, but I guess that's as far as it can go between us. Only dreams and nothing more."

"Look, Lonnie. Don't you think I might enjoy having you kiss me? After all, I'm a red-blooded young woman, and you're a handsome young man. What could be more natural than for us to want to kiss each other?"

"I'm only the hired man," he said, sadly, bowing his head in perfect humility. "You're the boss's daughter. That should tell you where I stand. Let's not kid ourselves, baby."

"Silly boy," she laughed softly, kneeling beside him. "Faint heart never won fair lady."

She threw her arms around him and bent his head back. With a beautiful smile upon her lovely face, she bent her head slightly and claimed his lips with a mouth that was hot, alive, and grasping. A week later, she kissed him again while they were milking. This time, he held her in his arms for just a moment, but that moment spoke volumes. Once again, her mouth was fiery hot, and acted as though its owner was trying to drink him down. She molded her body to his while they kissed, trembling but eager.

"Marlene, baby," he whispered against her lips. "You're so sweet, so lovely, and so very, very desirable. I'm only flesh and blood. Only the hired help. But I want to make love to you, all the way. I can't help it. Honestly, I can't. That's how I feel about you."

"Shhh," she said, kissing him again in the French style. "I feel the same way about you. Maybe we can do something about our need for each other before too long. I'll think about it. Go on and do your milking. I've got to go to the house and change my panties. During that last kiss, I got so excited I wet them a little. Oh, but I'm a bad girl."

A few days later, it was exceedingly hot. That night, Lonnie lay in his bed without any clothes. About midnight, he dozed off to sleep. Hours later, something woke him. At first, he couldn't make out what it was then he realized that someone had entered his room. He heard his door close softly and someone moved towards him in the darkness.

A shaft of silver moonlight came in from the only window in the room. As Lonnie watched and waited, Marlene Davis stepped into the moonlight and paused a moment. She wore a flimsy nightgown that covered her to just below her hips. As he watched, she stretched her arms over her head like a goddess of the night then slipped out of her nightie and dropped it to the floor. A moment longer she paused in the moonlight, her beautifully contoured breasts heaving. Then she came towards the bed.

"Lonnie," she whispered. "It's Marlene. Are you awake?"

"Yes," he whispered back. "Why did you come to me?"

"I wanted you tonight like you've been telling me you wanted me. Are you angry I came?"

"Darling of my dreams," he cried softy, leaping lightly out of bed and taking her in his arms. "I love you, I love you." He kissed her warm, dewy mouth until she sighed happily and relaxed against him.

In a moment, they were prostrate upon the bed. There was something feral about the way she moved against him, into his eager embrace. As their sexual organs fused, a strange little cry escaped her, and she clung to him for dear life. When he commenced in and out movements, she became an animal who made whimpering noises until he stopped them with his mouth. She clawed, clung, and wiggled in a mad frenzy of cooperative motion until her breath caught in her throat and it was over.

That was the beginning of Marlene's midnight visits. Eventually, he persuaded her to stay in her room and let him come to her. This she agreed to do, reluctantly.

"Anything to please you, sweetheart," she said. "Only don't make your visits too far apart. I'm red-hot for what you've got between your legs, and I don't want to be kept waiting."

"I understand, darling. Please, oh, please, don't breathe even a word of what we're doing to Maxine. She wouldn't understand how we feel about each other. Perhaps she'd tell your parents. Then I'd have to leave."

"Don't worry," she promised, clutching him to her fiercely. "I won't tell a living soul about us, especially not Maxine. We've always liked the same things. It wouldn't be any different about this. She'd want to share you with me, which I would never permit. You're mine, Lonnie,   baby, and only mine. And I'm yours."

As time passed, Lonnie became more and more friendly with Maxine. Eventually, he shared things with her that he swore her to secrecy on.

"I know it might sound narrow-minded of me, Maxine," he said one day as they were weeding and suckering corn a third of a mile from the house, "but I've got to know I can trust you."

"You can trust me with your darkest secret, Lonnie Dolan," she said as she wiped sweat from her beautiful face with a big, red bandana. "I'll guard your secret with my life, if necessary."

"Please be serious with me. I am with you."

"I'm as serious as if I was in church," she declared, straight-faced. "I won't blab anything you tell me in confidence. The way I look at it is, if you tell me something in confidence, I'll keep it in confidence. Fair enough?"

"That's fine, as far as it goes," he said, pausing in the shade of a tree to rest. "But suppose something happens between us?"

"Like what?"

"Well, suppose I was to take you in my arms and kiss that sweet, inviting mouth of yours. How would you feel about keeping quiet then?"

"I don't see as that would make any real difference."

"Yeah, you say that, but if it was to happen, you'd high-ball it right to Marlene and tell her, wouldn't you?"

"Not if you didn't want me to. Marlene is my sister and a wonderful girl, but I know her. She'd get jealous, and if you didn't treat her the same way, she'd run to Mother and blab her guts out. I'd blow my stack, and hell would be to pay."

"That's what I mean. So you see how it would be smart to keep everything that happens between us to ourselves. Trouble is the last thing I want, Maxine, baby. If that was to happen, no doubt your daddy would fire me. Then I'd no longer be able to see you. I wouldn't like that even a little bit."

"Neither would I."

"Would you miss me if I was gone?"

"More than you know," she said simply, but her big, dark eyes told him plenty.

"Maxine!" Lonnie breathed, while shivers of secret delight chased each other up and down his spine. Things between him and Maxine were shaping up better than he had hoped. "To have you say that, with that look in your beautiful eyes, it does things to me."

"I'm glad," she murmured.

"Look, Maxine," he said as they worked their way into a corner of the cornfield, out of sight of the house. "Surely you know how I've felt about you ever since I came to work for your father. For all these weeks, I've wanted to take you in my arms and kiss your soft, sweet lips. Would you be angry with me if I did it now?"

"I think I'd like that very much," she whispered, moving closer to him and waiting expectantly. "It would make me happy."

He took her in his arms. Her lips met his, and she clung in a way that was positively sinful. When he would have released her, she made a little sound and flung her arms around his neck then plunged her tongue into his mouth as far as it would reach. Still she clung to him, her hot, demanding mouth tight against his.

"Maxine, darling," Lonnie gasped, when she released his lips. "That was the most wonderful kiss I ever received."

"Glad you liked it," she grinned happily. "Your part was satisfying, too. Tell me, hired man—where, oh, where did you learn to kiss like that?"

"I just kissed you the way I felt. I didn't know it was different in any way."

"It was positively heavenly," she breathed excitedly.

"Then you enjoyed it and aren't angry with me?"

"I loved every blissful second of it. I honestly will be mad at you if you don't take pity on me and do me a favor."

"Anything your little heart desires that I'm able to do."

"Kiss me again," she pleaded, slipping her arms around his neck. "French kiss me like I did you a moment ago."

"So you like French kisses, eh? Some girls don't, you know."

"Sure do." She wrinkled her nose at him. "Kiss me good this time. I want to feel it clean down to my toes. Only blue-nosed girls object to French kissing. I don't think my nose has turned blue yet. At least, I hope not."

As Lonnie claimed her soft, sweet mouth with his, he began to work his lips onto hers and tremble. A she strained against him with all her might, he opened his lips a little and plunged his tongue into her eager, waiting mouth several times. She clung to him like a drowning person, her eyes closed, and her arms tight around his neck.

"Oh, but that was heavenly," she whispered when he released her. "I'm so happy. I wanted you to kiss me ever so long. I've got to hurry home now, though."

"Why the big hurry, honey? It was wonderful to kiss you. I hope it will happen again soon. It's so nice to be here with you, alone, just us two and the corn."

"I've got to go." She giggled, blushing furiously. "When you French kissed me so thoroughly, I lost control and wet my panties. Aren't I silly and awful?"

"You're a little princess, that's what you are, and I love every sweet ounce of you. Be a sweetheart now and don't tell Marlene or your mother, or anybody, about us. They wouldn't understand."

"I won't breathe a word about us to a living soul," she promised, turning away and running towards the house.

That was Lonnie's introduction to Maxine Davis's intensity. Thereafter, he made the most of every opportunity that presented itself to take her in his arms. Sometimes it was in the fields; sometimes it was in the house or the barn while she helped do the milking, but wherever it was, Maxine always slung herself into his arms and kissed him so passionately and thoroughly that his head whirled like a schoolboy's afterwards.

"I'm crazy, just crazy for you, Lonnie Dolan," she said one evening in August as he kissed her in the barn. "If something doesn't happen between us besides kissing, I honestly believe I'll explode before another week rolls over our heads. This is torture, wanting you all the time like I do."

This was the break Lonnie had been angling for.

"There is a way we could have each other every time we desired," he offered hopefully. "Perhaps you wouldn't consider it. There's another way, only I'm ashamed to mention it. You'd get mad at me if I did."

"Tell me," she pleaded. "If it's anything short of rape, I might consider it."

"We could get married."

"Lonnie, are you proposing to me?" she asked, a queer little catch in her voice.

"I guess I am," he stammered, his heart in his throat for fear she would accept him. However, if he was ever to get behind Maxine's panties, he had to play some long shots.

"I'm deeply honored, Lonnie," she sighed wistfully, "but I couldn't possibly marry you, or anybody, right now."

"Why not? You're free, white, and eighteen."

"That's just it. I'm still under my parents' jurisdiction, as far as the law is concerned. You see, Dad and Mom has plans for me and Marlene. They're hip on the idea of us getting college educations. So, since we're only a little past eighteen, I guess we'll have to do as they say for three years yet."

"What about my other idea?" Lonnie ventured. "Don't you want to hear it?"

"I certainly do." She smiled and kissed him as though she would never let go. "If you're able to collect your thoughts after that kiss, I'd like very much hear your other plan."

"Let me slip into your room tonight when everybody's asleep. Say at about two in the morning."

"Lonnie!" she cried in shocked surprise, her lovely face flushing scarlet.

"Forgive me," Lonnie pleaded, watching her reactions with eagle eyes.

"It's all right." She grinned. "I know it sounds awful, but to be honest, I've thought of it, too. Let me turn it over in my mind for a few days. I'll let you know, one way or the other."

Inwardly elated, Lonnie continued with his milking. Three days later, as they passed each other doing the evening chores, she paused by his side, smiled at him, and said, "Come to me tonight."

That night, at midnight, he eased out of his room and visited Marlene for one hour. Fortunately, she was having her regular monthly period, and they could not indulge in sexual relations. Of that, he was glad, since he was going to Maxine as soon as he could leave Marlene, and he was thankful he could go to her with his sexual powers at full force, instead of depleted. When he departed, he paused at his door long enough to open and close it softly, in case Marlene was listening to hear him enter his room. He had never given her cause for jealously, but knowing girls as he did by now, he knew she wondered if he desired her twin sister. She had hinted as much on more than one occasion.

When he noiselessly entered Maxine's room, he heard a gasp from the bed. He eased over, sat down on the edge, stretched out his right hand, and whispered her name softly.

"Maxine, sweetheart," he said in a hoarse whisper. "I'm here. Are you awake?"

"Yes," she answered hesitantly, touching his hand. "Take me in your arms, darling. I'm scared."

"Don't be," he soothed, gathering her fragrant, warm body in his arms. She wore a filmy nightgown much like the one Marlene had worn the night she came to him. Silky panties with lace ruffles cloaked her buttocks.

Slowly and tenderly, he caressed her. As her passion for him mounted, he put his hands on her full, firm breasts.

"Ah," she whispered tremulously after he had held her in his arms for several minutes, kissed her, and fondled her intimately above the waist. "Please take my nighty off and kiss my breasts." She snuggled him to her and trembled like a frightened fawn while he kissed and nibbled her breasts. Then she threw herself back upon the bed. "Take the rest of my clothing off," she ordered. "Promise you'll be gentle when we give ourselves to each other for the first time. You will, won't you?"

"I'd kill myself before I'd hurt you even a little bit, honey. That's the way I feel about you, so have no fear."

"I love you, I love you," she whispered, her breath coming in ragged gasps as he expertly massaged her every secret place. "Oh, please, sweetheart, don't torture me any further with those heavenly things you're doing. Please, let's give ourselves to each other now, all the way."

Gently, but firmly, Lonnie made the union of their sexual organs. Maxine gasped, a sharp whisper of breath, and clutched at him. When he began withdrawing and reinserting, she became so uninhibited he was afraid someone would hear them. At the onset of her climax, she choked down a scream. Pulling his mouth down to hers, she kissed him with wild abandon, murmuring her love for him. Then nature exerted itself with Lonnie, and he sank into her eager embrace. He was exhausted, but happy and satisfied as he kissed her sweet, hungry mouth.

For the next few weeks, Lonnie was hard put to keep the sisters sexually satisfied and still maintain his secret relationship with each. There were times his knees fairly rattled together when he walked, but if he could hold out until the twins left for college in mid-September, he would have a respite from their demands, and he could recuperate before they came home for the holidays.

The last week they were home, before they left for college, was the most demanding. Each insisted he visit her every night. One night that week, he pleaded illness. But the next night, the winsome sisters were after him, as feverish as ever. The day they left for college, each kissed him shyly in front of her parents and each other. They gave each other a queer look, and a mysterious light sprang up in their eyes.

"Bye, Lonnie," they whispered, tears in their voices. "See you in November, at turkey time."

Chapter 6

The Hired Girl

A week after the twins left for college, Sam Davis hired a girl to help with the housework, milking, and other chores. Hilda Webster was the typical hired-girl in all respects except one: her physical appearance. She was neat and clean, the Davises complimented her on her industriousness.

Hilda's most outstanding trait, however, was not her beauty or good nature, nor was it her jutting breasts, flowing dark hair, or rounded hips. It was her legs. Hilda's legs were endowed with symmetrical beauty, but they were streamlined and curvaceous, as well. In fact, her legs possessed what is known in modeling circles as "the third curve."

As the days passed, Lonnie got better acquainted with Hilda. He found her very likeable and exciting. Sometimes she played checkers with him before retiring for the night. She even went to a movie with him in Camden, ten miles away. Lonnie borrowed his employers' pick up, and they laughed at the noise the truck made and enjoyed themselves tremendously.

Hilda had a suitor left over from her last place of employment. Hiram Kessel was a slow, plodding farmer who appeared much older than his thirty years. His thinning brown hair, bulging black eyes, and permanent stoop did not add to his attractiveness. It soon became apparent to Lonnie that Hiram was only a stand-in until a fellow came along who was better suited to her tastes in men. He decided to try to fill that void in her life temporarily.

Hilda was beautiful and vivacious. As the weeks passed, he kidded her about Hiram's attentions, and she retaliated with appropriate quips, tossed her dark-hair indifferently, and went about her duties.

"How about that Hiram feller of yours?" he asked one evening as they did chores. "Does he treat you like he should?"

"I don't understand what you mean," she replied with a puzzled look.

"I mean, does he show you enough attention?"

"In what way?"

"Like loving you up, that's what. A beautiful young woman should have plenty of hugs and kisses all the time. I think it's essential to your development. Does he see that you receive your fair share of cuddling?"

"That," she snapped with flashing eyes, "is none of your damn business."

"I know that, Hilda." He grinned, pleased at her spirit. "But I'm asking anyway. Does he neglect you?"

"I wouldn't tell you, Lonnie Dolan, if I never got kissed," she cried. "And I think you're awful for talking to me like this. I could hate you for it, you know."

"Forgive me, Hilda," Lonnie said, apologetic. "I didn't mean to hurt your feelings. I had no call to open my big mouth like I did, and I'm sorry. I only know that if you was my girlfriend, I'd hug you and cuddle you, and kiss that soft, sweet, little mouth of yours until you begged for mercy. Even then, I doubt very much I'd let up on you. That's all I meant."

"It's all right, Lonnie," she whispered, her face going red then white by turns. "I know you meant no offense. You needn't apologize. I've been kidded about Hiram before."

"But I do apologize. Your personal life is none of my business. Hiram is all right, I'm sure. Honestly, I couldn't blame you if you was so angry you'd never speak to me again."

"Forget it," she whispered again, a strained look in her eyes. "Hiram isn't the most exciting beau in the world, but at least he's a beau. That's more than some girls have got."

"I understand." Lonnie nodded, solemn. Inwardly, though, he was delighted. Hilda was ripe for a kiss, but he was determined that she make the first move. As he looked into her eyes, he would have wagered his life that before many more days, she would be in his arms.

"I must be about my work," she said softly, turning away. "Maybe I'll play you a game of checkers this evening after supper, if you want."

"I'll be ready and waiting." Lonnie grinned.

One evening, about a week later, Hilda was silent after supper and retired earlier than usual. The bedroom she occupied was the one formerly occupied by Marlene. Lonnie had to pass it on the way to his room.

An hour after she had gone up, he excused himself and climbed the stairs, his heavy work shoes making clomping sounds with every step he took. As he neared the entrance to her room, she opened the door and walked toward him. The hall was shadowy. Just as he was about to speak and pass on to his room, she stumbled. The next instant, she was in his arms, her arms around his neck, her face upturned to his.

"Lonnie," she whispered, but she made no move to disengage herself from his arms.

"May I kiss you?" he whispered.

"Yes, oh, yes," she gasped, raising her lips to his and closing her eyes.

Her mouth was fresh, sweet, and soft. A warm glow radiated from her luscious body and encircled his being. When he released her lips, she looked up at him a moment before moving. Then she tightened her grip around his neck, pulled his face down to hers, and claimed his lips in several passionate kisses. After that outburst, she remained in his arms, but uttered not a sound. Then she disengaged, dashed into her room, and softly closed the door.

That weekend, Hiram did not appear for his customary Saturday night date with Hilda. He phoned, saying he was sick and promising to come see her the following weekend. Lonnie asked Hilda to go to a movie in Camden instead. A beautiful smile came over her face, and she accepted.

On the way home, he pulled the pick-up off the road into a shadowy lane and cut the motor. Taking Hilda in his arms against her wide-eyed, voiceless protests, he kissed her conventionally and in the French style until she fell against him, gasping.

"Lonnie," she cried brokenly. "Why did you do that to me?"

"Did I hurt you, Hilda?"

"No, oh, no," she moaned. "But after the way you just kissed me, I'll never be satisfied with Hiram's kisses again."

"I'm sorry. I didn't mean to upset you," he said. He tried to take her in his arms again, but she fought against it.

"Please, don't. Oh, please, stop." She pulled herself out of his grasp. "I'm scared, Lonnie. I'm awfully scared and shaky feeling."

"What the heck is the matter with you?" He laughed as she backed into the corner of the seat away from him. "I meant you no harm. If my kisses frighten you that way, I won't do it again."

"You don't understand. I'm scared, but not in the way you're thinking."

"What goes, Hilda? I thought you wanted me to kiss you. Now I don't know what to think."

"I do, I do," she cried, covering her face with shaking hands.

"Then why are you acting this way?" Even as he asked the question, Lonnie knew why Hilda was so upset. The French kisses he had given her affected her the same way they had affected Millie Denton, and like Millie, she was at a loss to explain her unfamiliar reactions.

"It was those kisses when you put your tongue in my mouth," she said tearfully. "They tore me to pieces. When you did that, I felt all sorts of unexplainable ways."

"Did you like being kissed that way?"

"I loved it."

"Good. Now tell me how you felt when I was kissing you that way."

"Like a bad girl."

"I don't understand. Tell me about it." He reached over and stroked her glossy hair gently.

"I wanted you to kiss me like that forever. I wished that I was in your arms without a stitch of clothing on and you was doing things to me that I was just aching for you to do. Am I a bad girl, Lonnie, for feeling that way?"

"Certainly not," he told her empathically. "What you felt was a perfectly normal reaction to being in the arms of a man who's kissing you like I did. I felt the same way."

"Oh, Lonnie. Did you?" she asked in surprise.

"Yes, I did, Hilda. I'm not ashamed for wanting you. Now you know how I feel. I hope you're not angry about all this kissing business."

"I couldn't be," she whispered happily. "Take me home, please. The way I feel inside now, I couldn't trust myself to let you touch me again. I'm afraid I might lose control. I'd feel awfully ashamed afterwards, if I did."

"You're beautiful and sweet and wonderful," he said happily, his heart leaping. "I'm powerless to stop wanting to make love to you, all the way. After all, I'm only flesh and blood, not stone. And you're so desirable, so exciting."

"Please. Please. Start the truck, and let's go. My heart's playing leapfrog, and my head's whirling. Don't say any more. I'm flesh and blood, too."

When they arrived at the Davis farm, Hilda jumped out of the truck, bade him a hurried goodnight, and dashed into the house. When he climbed the stairs and went down the hall to his room, he paused at her door. It was closed tightly, but he could have sworn he heard muffled sobs within.

For the next few days, Hilda avoided Lonnie as much as she could. She was so moody and downcast that Mrs. Davis inquired if she was sick. When Hilda replied that she was all right, only in low spirits, Mrs. Davis rolled her eyes knowingly and said that perhaps she would feel better when she saw Hiram again. Hilda was noncommittal and went about her work with a long face.

The following evening, she again helped Lonnie at the barn and appeared very like her old self. However, when she gave him a direct look, her eyes were veiled.

"What's wrong, Hilda?" he asked as they began milking.

"Nothing," she whispered, refusing to look at him.

"If I've offended you in any way, I apologize."

"Please, don't say that, Lonnie. You've always treated me wonderfully."

"Then what is it?"

"I'm making a difficult decision. That's all I'll tell you," she said softly, picking up her stool and pail and moving to another cow.

That night, she again retired before Lonnie did. As he clomped past her room in his heavy shoes, she quietly opened the door and flung herself into his arms.

"Lonnie, darling," she gasped in a trembling whisper, raising her lips to his. "Kiss me like you did the night we went to Camden. Put your tongue in my mouth, too."

"Hilda, Hilda," he whispered against her sweet, dewy mouth. "Are you sure you want me to kiss you that way? Remember what it did to you the other night."

"I can't help it if I'm acting foolishly or unwisely. I only know I want it more than I can say. Don't torture me. Do it now."

Without waiting or asking further questions, Lonnie claimed her mouth with all the gusto he could manage. She began to tremble. When he plunged his tongue into her mouth, she whimpered and clung to him frantically.

"Good night, darling," she gasped. With a muffled sob, she tore herself out of his embrace and moved to reenter her room.

Lonnie detained her with an arm around her slender waist. "Be mine tonight, Hilda," he pleaded. "Be mine, all the way."

"Lonnie, darling," she sobbed softly as she clung to him. "I want to so badly. But I can't, I can't. If I did, I would be no better than a whore. My mother would disown me if she ever found out. Are you sure you want me so much?"

"More than I can say."

"Be patient, my darling," she sighed, offering her lips to him again. "The way I feel tonight, I won't say it won't be soon. My body is crying from need of your love."

A few days later, Hilda was quite talkative and gay after supper. Before excusing herself for the night, she and Lonnie had a slam-bang checker game. Hiram had been to see her the evening before. As she climbed the stairs on the way to her room, Mrs. Davis looked after her, a knowing smile on her face.

"Hilda seemed happier since Hiram came to see her. Don't you think so, Sam?" she asked her drowsing husband.

"Oh, sure," he grunted then sank back into his after-supper stupor.

"What do you think, Lonnie?" Mrs. Davis persisted. "Can't you see a difference in her?"

"I think you're right," he mumbled, trying to appear absorbed in his hunting magazine. He was aware of Mrs. Davis's attention to Hilda's good spirits, but he didn't want to show it.

The evening dragged. At about ten o'clock, Lonnie rose from his chair, stretched, yawned, excused himself, and announced he was going to hit the hay.

"Good night, and sleep tight," Mrs. Davis said pleasantly, as he climbed the stairs to his room.

"Good night," Lonnie grunted in return. "See you in the morning."

As he passed Hilda's room, he paused and listened, but no sound came to him through the heavy oak door. Shaking his head in disappointment, he continued on to his own room.

The October night was unusually warm, with a big, round moon that shed its light upon the sleeping countryside like a blanket. A shaft of light mowed a swath across the floor of Lonnie's room. Stepping into the mellow glow, he began disrobing. Soon his clothes were piled at his feet. Stretching and yawning again, he turned toward the bed.

Hilda's voice was a gentle whisper from the velvety darkness.

"You look wonderful without clothes on, Lonnie."

He froze in amazement, and there she was, standing in the moonlight. She wore a silk nightshirt open all the way down the front. The moon shone brighter, and its light made a pattern of intriguing shadows over the firm sweep of her breasts as they peeped out from behind her nightie.

She slipped out of the filmy sleeping garment, and dropping it to the floor, stretched her arms above her head. Like a pagan moon worshiper she stood, her body a nude shimmer as it absorbed the light coming through the window. She bowed her back and made every curve of her beautiful body stand out in sharp relief. Then, relaxing into a sultry pose, she ran her fingers through her lustrous hair and slowly moved toward him.

"You're beautiful, Hilda," Lonnie gasped. "Positively beautiful."

As he took her in his arms, she sucked in her breath. Trembling like a frightened child, she clung to him.

"I had to come to you tonight, darling," she whispered. "After that disgusting evening with Hiram yesterday, I had to have your love, all the way. Do you think I'm a bad girl to come to you like this?"

"You're an angel right out of heaven," he said joyfully, folding her sweet body in his arms and moving toward the bed.

He fell backward on it, with her on top of him. Her mouth came down slowly, with warm, soft, parted lips. Her tongue dipped deeply into his eager, waiting mouth. He ran his hands up the center of her back, and she shivered deliciously, making small sounds in her throat. All the fear, reserve, and misgivings melted away until she was nothing but a warm, sweet, beautiful female animal. Her mouth was an alive, demanding thing.

As their sexual organs made contact, she cried out softly in perfect ecstasy. Then the darkness closed in around them like a blanket until it exploded and left them lying there, tired and close, kissing each other with lips that were dewy with love, whispering about the tomorrows to come and the nights they would spend in each other's arms.

After that, there was hardly a night went by but Hilda spent part of it in Lonnie's arms. Some nights, she wouldn't use her room at all, except to muss up the bed. Lonnie marveled at what an accomplished actress Hilda was when the occasion demanded it. When others were around, she maintained an air of complete indifference, seeming to care not a whit about what Lonnie did or said.

However, at night, in the privacy of his room, she was a different person. In those hours, she shed her cloak of reserve. Clutching him to her, she fairly smothered him with kisses and fondled him lovingly from head to toe. When they had sexual relations, she gave way to complete abandon. She clawed, bit, panted, gasped, and moaned at climax in a perfect frenzy of passion and love. When Hiram came courting, Hilda put on a glad air, but as soon as she could conveniently shoo him away, she did. Then she would climb the stairs to her room, hurriedly undress, dab a little perfume on her nude body, slip into a filmy nightshirt, ease out of her room and into Lonnie's, and in a very few minutes be locked in his arms.

The twins came home from the college Thanksgiving week. Lonnie had foreseen this, and he tried to get that week off from work without success. He would be in for a rough time with three females with hot panties on his hands, and finally, he decided to play ill. However, it was practically impossible to convince an amorous young woman that he was unable to indulge in sexual relations when he was locked in her eager, demanding embrace. Fortunately, the situation worked out. Hilda shared Marlene's room, so Maxine was the only one of the three girls who had free access to his room that week.

"It's awful nice and exciting to be back in your arms again, Lonnie, baby," she sighed happily, after they had reached their climaxes the first night she came to him. "But you didn't act like you've been pining for nooky these past two months. You didn't act eager for me at all."

"I'm tired, sweetie-pie, that's all. Just tired."

"Oh, yeah?" she giggled knowingly. "I'll bet it's not the kind of tired that comes from hard work. I sized that wicked-legged Hilda up this afternoon after we got home. She's quite a dish. I'd bet my bottom dollar that you know what it's like to be between them burlesque-show legs of hers."

"Maxine! How you talk. Hilda's a nice girl."

"Oh, sure. I understand. So am I. Even so, I like my nooky. Don't act surprised. Us girls up at the school have our moments with the male students. We don't get a chance too often, but once in a while, we sneak a boy into our rooms at night. It's exciting and good when we do."

"Suppose you get caught at those shenanigans? Would the dean expel you?"

"Hardly. He would take the hide off our behinds with a blistering reprimand and loss of privileges, though."

"Let that be a warning to you girls with hot panties. Play it smart. Be a good girl and come home with that sheepskin." Lonnie reached down and lightly pinched her bare buttock. She squealed and pulled his mouth down to hers for a searing French kiss.

On the last night of her holiday week, Maxine came to him again, her body hot as a flame, quivering whenever he touched her. She tried to pump him about his relationship with Hilda again, but Lonnie was noncommittal.

"Tell me the truth, Lonnie, baby," she coaxed, her body feverish with desire. "Hilda has been hauling your ashes, hasn't she?"

"If she has, wouldn't I be a fool to give our secret away?"

"Guess you would at that. It's all right, though. Have your fun. Only don't break it off in her. She strikes me as the marrying kind. Who could blame her, with a papoose on the way?"

"I'll watch my P's and Q's," Lonnie replied, grinning into the darkness. Drawing Maxine close in his arms, he fondled her breasts and the other intimate places of her warm, young body until she panted anxiously for his love.

When she eased out of his room in the wee hours of the November morning, Lonnie was so sexually exhausted that he felt as though desire would never come to him again.

Slowly, the long winter passed, and as the months slipped by, Lonnie began to impress upon Hilda that Hiram Kessel was better husband material than he was. At first, she wouldn't listen to a word, but as time passed, and Lonnie persisted in pointing out the good points of the plodding farmer, her resistance began to crumble.

"Lonnie, darling, I want to marry you," she sobbed in his ears more than one night as she lay naked in his arms and gave him her beautiful body to have and love as often as he desired.

"I understand, Hilda, baby," he soothed, "but all we have is physical attraction, and you know it. Other than that, we're not suited for each other at all."

"You don't know how a woman feels when she loves someone like I love you and has given her all, like I have to you. Losing such a person makes a woman feel as though she is losing a vital part of her body. Her heart feels broken."

"I'm only thinking of what's best for you in the long run," he tried to explain. "You're beautiful and wonderful, and I think the world and all of you. But Hiram is far and away the better man for you. Please, believe me."

Hilda married Hiram Kessel in mid-April. After the simple ceremony, they drove back to the Davis farm to pick up Hilda's things. Lonnie shook hands with the newlyweds and offered his congratulations, but he felt like seven different kinds of heel at the condemning flame in Hilda's eyes.

"Goodbye and good luck, Lonnie," she said softly, a tremble in her deep, throaty voice. She stepped to his side, kissed his cheek, and whispered, "I'll always love you."

"The best to you both," he muttered past a strange tightening in his chest and a mist in his eyes. Giving Hilda up had hurt more than he cared to admit.

However, in the weeks following his separation from Hilda, Lonnie was thankful that that chapter of his tempestuous life was behind him. Everything began to pall on him at the Davis farm. He had to leave. Too much had happened during his employment with Sam Davis. He needed new places and new faces. Spring had come, and the urge to move on hit Lonnie like a ton of bricks. He was powerless to resist the call.

A month later, before the twins came home from college for the summer, he made up his mind. The next day, he notified his employer that that would be his last week. On Monday morning, he hit the road for Richwood, sixty miles away. The following evening, at sunset, he stopped at a neat, two-story farmhouse a mile from the city limits to ask for a drink of water. Reverend Jeremiah Woods was the name on the mailbox.

When he hailed the house, a tall, lean man, sixty years old or more, stepped out on the porch, followed by a blond-haired, blue-eyed, young woman of unusual beauty.

"Welcome to my gates, stranger," the grey-haired man boomed, his voice ringing deep and clear as a bell. "Come, set yourself down, and rest. Then please step inside and sup with us."

"Thank you, sir," Lonnie said gratefully, appraising the blond. "I wonder if I could get a drink of water."

"Indeed you can, young man. Esther, fetch a fresh bucket of spring water and a dipper. Now, tell me, son. Whence come ye, and what is your destination?"

"I came from up beyond Camden, and I'm going to Richwood to look for a job."

"Good, good. Looking for work, eh? Son, perhaps the good Lord directed your steps to my humble abode. You're looking for a job, and I'm looking for a responsible young man to take over the farm work while I'm away spreading the gospel. Know anything about farm work?"

"I've never done any other kind of work," Lonnie answered truthfully, accepting the dipper of clear, sparkling water the blond girl offered. When he thanked her, she blushed prettily and gave him a white-toothed smile.

"You're welcome, I'm sure," she murmured, setting the bucket of water on the porch and sitting on the steps.

"Excellent," the old man boomed again. "A farm boy looking for a job. Bide with us, son. I'll pay you well for your labors."

Lonnie was too tired and hungry to say no, so thirty minutes later, he was seated at the dining room table, enjoying a hearty meal and talking over the terms of the employment.

"Preacher Woods," he said, after they finished eating and retired to the coolness of the front porch. "I accept your offer. If at any time you're dissatisfied with my work, I'll seek employment elsewhere, with no hard feelings."

"Excellent. Excellent," Reverend Woods cried heartily. "Here's my hand to bind our agreement and cement our future friendship. My daughter will fix you up a room at the head of the stairs. I think you'll like it here, young man. We'll do our best to make you feel at home. It'll do Esther a world of good to have someone her own age to talk to, and it'll do me good, too. By the way, you haven't told me your name yet."

"Lonnie Dolan."

Chapter 7

The Minister's Daughter

Jeremiah Woods was a gaunt man with thinning, iron-gray hair and tragic eyes. For more than twenty-five years, since long before his wife ran away with another man, he had spread the gospel. Since that tragic day, eighteen years before, he and his daughter, Esther, had stayed on in the old family homestead, with the assistance of a maiden sister as housekeeper. A week after he began working for Reverend Woods, Lonnie knew the man's life history, from beginning to end. Sarah Woods, the spinster, supplied all the details.

"He's hip on religion, that brother of mine is," she declared one day out in the yard where Lonnie was mending the fence. "It's warped his life. Esther's mother left because of it. His blind adherence to a creed drove her away. Daisy Woods was as beautiful a woman as ever the sun shone on, and she loved him. He began accusing her of being fast and loose with other men practically on their wedding day."

"Was she?" Lonnie asked.

"Not at first. However, as time passed and Jeremiah kept harping about her 'sinful beauty,' as he called it, her bright smile, and her hospitable manner, the idea eventually took root. That brother of mine was so wrapped up in spreading the gospel that he couldn't see he was driving his wife into the arms of another man. When he woke up, it was too late."

"Look, Aunt Sarah," Lonnie said, "you shouldn't be telling me all this. It's none of my business. I'll listen and keep my mouth shut, but tell me about Esther. Has she inherited her mother's roving eye?"

"It's hard to say. Jeremiah keeps an awful tight rein on Esther, but I believe she'd be boy crazy if she had half a chance. I feel sorry for that poor girl. There isn't a thing in this whole wide world I can do about it, though."

"I don't see why not. You can set her straight on some of the facts of life, can't you?"

"Sure, but it wouldn't do any good. That's something every girl has to find out for herself."

"I find Esther beautiful. She's exciting to be around. Has she any boyfriends?"

"Not a one," Sarah said sadly. "Several boys tried to pay court to her, but Jeremiah made it so miserable they gave up in disgust."

"Do you think he likes and trust me?" Lonnie asked, dropping a new post into the hole he had just dug.

"I'm sure he does. I seen it the evening he hired you. Court Esther, Lonnie, but don't do her dirty. She's just aching to have a nice young man like you hold and kiss her. I know what I'm talking about. She's confided her feelings to me ever since she was a baby. Besides, I was a young woman once myself, and I know what one wants. I might look like a dried apple now, but I was pretty in my day."

As the days passed and Lonnie became more at home in his new employment, his estimation of Esther Woods grew. She was twenty and vibrantly alive. Her five-foot-two figure was an artist's dream, and her tawny blonde hair spilled down over her shoulders. Her eyes were two violet pools, and as she got better acquainted with Lonnie, they began to sparkle every time she saw him.

Her room was on the second floor of the Woods home, down the hall from Lonnie's. She retired earlier than he did, and often he heard her moving around in her room when he came upstairs to bed, hours later. Sometimes there was a light in her room until after midnight. Lonnie presumed she was reading on the nights she sat up late, and one night, he decided to peek through the keyhole into her room to see what he could see.

He slipped out of his room like a shadow, and crept noiselessly to her door. A light shone under the door. Kneeling down, he fastened an eye to the keyhole and looked inside. His breathing quickened and his heart hammered.

Esther sat at a small dressing table, reading a magazine, but she was completely naked. As Lonnie watched, spellbound, she took the magazine in her hands and idly thumbed through the pages. On the cover a beautiful, half-nude girl was locked in the arms of a man, obviously her lover.

Suddenly, Esther lost interest in the magazine. Laying it aside, she picked up a comb and began grooming her luxurious hair. He feasted his eyes on her lovely shoulders, with their soft curves of hidden muscle. Swinging around on the stool, she faced the door and shook her head until her hair swirled in shimmering waves down her back.

Esther Wood was very beautiful. Her breasts were firm and inviting. The rest of her was delicious and exciting. Slowly, she rose from the stool and stretched with the feline grace of a cat. She was a picture of loveliness, her hands cupping her luscious breasts and matted blonde hair cloaking the V between her thighs, drawing his hypnotized stare like a magnet. She walked to the window and stood before it a moment, then bent and blew out the oil lamp on her dressing table. A great round moon was sailing high that night. Its light came through the open window, silhouetting her figure.

As Lonnie watched, his blood running like fire in his veins, she stretched out her beautiful arms, as though reaching to embrace the moon. Then she let them sink to her sides. A moment longer she stood before the open window, turning this way and that, before passing out of his line of vision. When he heard her climb into bed, he silently rose and crept back to his room.

Until almost daylight, he lay on his bed, wide awake, his body feverish with desire. When he did drop off to sleep, he dreamed he was pursuing a temptress along a shady wooded path. In his dream, he was almost exhausted when she ceased running and lay down on a mossy spot. As he sank into her arms and tasted her sweet love, his body felt as though it was exploding. When he woke, he realized to his embarrassment that he had had a wet dream.

Then after, Lonnie always peeked through the keyhole into Esther's room before he retired, especially if there was a light shining under her door. Every Sunday, he went to church with the Woods and sat by Esther. Her father most always preached the sermon, but occasionally, a visiting preacher brought the message.

One Sunday, about a month after Lonnie went to work for him, Jeremiah Woods preached on the evils of a faithless woman. His strong, full voice rolled over the congregation like a condemning tide. As he talked, his eyes glowed like banked furnaces every time they rested on his daughter.

"There are times I think my father hates me," Esther said to Lonnie the following week as she helped him weed the garden.

"What makes you say that?" he asked, pausing to look at her.

"Maybe I shouldn't tell you this, Lonnie, but there's a sore festering in my father's mind. My mother ran away with another man when I was two years old. Daddy's never gotten over it, and I doubt he ever will. Now that I'm grown up and look so much like my mother did, all the bitterness in Daddy's heart seems directed at me. I guess I remind him of the past and the woman who left him."

"You have my sympathy, Esther. All I can say is that if your mother looked like you, she was a beautiful woman."

"Aunt Sarah says I'm the living image of my mother," she murmured, blushing furiously.

"Care to tell me about it? Your family trouble, I mean."

"All I know is that Daddy's obsessed with religion. It's like a disease with him."

"Go on," Lonnie encouraged.

"From what I've been told, my mother was very beautiful and full of life. She loved nice clothes, and lived for the few sweet things my father said to her, like how pretty she was, and how much he loved her. Aunt Sarah said when other men complimented Daddy on his lovely wife, he'd wait until they were alone together, and then he accused her of being unfaithful."

"How terrible for a man to have such a fixation. I'll be glad to listen if you'll tell me the rest."

"My mother and Daddy began arguing a lot, almost every time they came home from church. Eventually, Daddy got so worked up that he refused to sleep with my mother. That was the beginning of the end between them, so Aunty says. Aunt Sarah says my mother was very passionate, in more ways than one," Esther whispered with downcast eyes and flushed face. "When Daddy shut her out of his bedroom, it did something to her that only another man's arms could make up for. Eventually, such a man came into her life. In time, she ran away with him. Aunt Sarah always said if Daddy had been as good in bed as he was behind the pulpit, wild horses couldn't have dragged her away from him."

"Physical love is a very important and powerful factor between a man and his wife," Lonnie said. "Some authorities on the subject claim it's the most important bond between a man and woman. They say a woman is happy and content as long as the man in her life desires her body, and vice versa. How do you feel about all that, Esther?"

"I think it's essential, too."

"Did you study sex in school?"

"As much as they'd let me. Daddy always kept a close watch over my studies while I was in school, and he tries to keep me from reading any romantical magazine."

"Do you get to read any of that type of magazine?" Lonnie asked, remembering the publication he saw her reading in her room the first night he peeked through her keyhole.

"Every one I can get my hands on," she grinned. "I have several hid in my room right now, only Daddy don't know about it. He'd fairly raise the roof, if he did. Don't tell on me, Lonnie."

"I won't breathe a word," Lonnie promised. "Do these love magazines say that physical love is important between a man and a woman if they are to have a happy, well-adjusted life together?"

"Indeed, they do. And Aunt Sarah agrees with them."

"Do you agree?" Lonnie persisted.

"I think it's most important force in the world," she whispered, her face going red and white by turns. "I also agree with Aunt Sarah. If my daddy had been a man with my mother and had given her the physical love her body craved, she would never have left him."

"Does he know you feel that way?"

"I'm not sure, but I think he does," she replied.

"I'm sorry it happened, Esther. Maybe your father will change his outlook one of these days."

"I doubt it," she said sadly, as she pulled up a large ragweed and threw it on the pile of weeds she and Lonnie had collected. "Daddy is much too set in his ways."

"What about you? I've been here over a month, and not one young man has come calling. Don't you have any boy friends at all?"

"No, not any," she replied tragically.

"Why not, for crying out loud? You're the right age to have a dozen young fellows parked on your doorstep. What's the matter, Esther? Don't you like boys?"

"Sure, I do. Only Daddy thinks I might have inherited my mother's 'wild streak,' as he calls it. He discouraged every boy that tried to   date me. He even ordered some away. Now none comes around. They all avoid me as if I have the plague."

"Do you like me?" Lonnie suddenly asked.

"Yes," she whispered, "but what has that got to do with my lack of boyfriends?"

"It could have plenty to do with it. I like you too, Esther. Ever since that evening your father hired me, I've thought you was one of the most beautiful girls I've ever met. I still think so. I want to court you, very much. Do you think your father would let me?"

"Please, don't ask him," she cried, tears springing to her eyes.

"That would be the honorable thing to do."

"Daddy would never see it that way. He'd jump to the conclusion that you desired my body, and he would drive you away."

"Would you miss me if I had to leave?" Lonnie asked.

"Yes, oh, yes," she said. "It'd be unbearably lonesome around here without you, Lonnie. I think I'd be tempted to run away myself."

"I want to court you, Esther."

"Do you, really?"

"Yes, I do."

"Why?" she asked, her violet eyes searching his.

"I just do, that's all. From the first, I've wanted to hold you in my arms, kiss your sweet, inviting lips, and have you kiss me in return. I'm only human, and you're so beautiful and sweet and desirable."

"Lonnie!" she gasped, her hands touching her flaming face. "I didn't know."

"Well, you know now," he said gruffly. "That's the way I feel about you, and I'm not ashamed to tell you."

"You want to kiss me and hold me in your arms," she said wonderingly, as though she couldn't believe it.

"What's so funny about that?" he demanded. You're a damned beautiful woman, Esther. And if you think I am kidding, I'll take you in my arms right now and kiss that sweet mouth of yours a dozen times. I'll do it even if your father fires me. I think you're wonderful."

"I've got to go help Aunt Sarah with supper," she said suddenly, fright coming over her flushed face.

However, as she turned to leave the garden, Lonnie saw a pleased look in her eyes. She's happy that I desire her, he realized, as he watched her walk away. When she reached the corner of the house, she turned and waved. On impulse, he smiled back and blew her a kiss. Blushing furiously, she darted out of sight.

That night, Lonnie took another peek into Esther's room before retiring. She went upstairs about ten o'clock, and he followed thirty minutes later. All evening, she had avoided his eyes. After supper, when he asked if she wanted to play a game of checkers or go for a walk, she gave a faint excuse, grabbed up a Sunday school paper, and tried to act absorbed in it, but Lonnie was not deceived. All evening, he felt the tension every time Esther's eyes were upon him. She tried to act normal, but her lovely young body was as tense as a coiled spring.

A light was shining under her door when Lonnie went to his room. He peeked through the keyhole for another shock. She stood in the center of the room, facing him, completely naked, and looking at a magazine.

After idly thumbing through the magazine for a few minutes, she closed it and began to study its cover, with its picture of a beautiful Hawaiian girl wearing a grass skirt. The girl was standing in a sexy pose, her arms outstretched, her back slightly bowed, and her hips twisted at an angle that suggested the hula dance.

Esther laid the magazine on her dressing table. Then she struck the Hawaiian girl's pose. How easily her beautiful her beautiful nude body captured it.

She began humming a faint tune, swaying to it. As she swayed, she shook her upper body until her breasts quivered and surged like bowls of jelly. Her dance became more pronounced. Her hips wiggling like a fish on a line, she crouched almost to the floor. Slowly, she straightened up, wiggling and twisting all the while. Her back began to bow as she continued to spread her gorgeous legs. She stopped swaying and twisting, and gave her hips a forward snapping motion, like a burlesque dancer. Esther twisted and swayed, and shook her magnificent breasts, a look of abandon on her face.

After a few more turns around her room, she whirled over to her bed and threw herself on it. Her bosom rose and fell rapidly from the exertion of her dance. For a few moments, she laid motionless, despair settling on her face. Lonnie was amazed to see that she was silently weeping. At last, with a strange, choking cry, she reached over, cupped a hand behind the oil lamp, and blew it out.

Lonnie rose from his cramped position and silently crept back to his room. He was wet with sweat. The demonstration he had just seen convinced him to take the initiative with Esther Woods. She was starved for masculine attention. Lonnie vowed to see that she received her fair share of sexual gratification, even if her father fired him for his efforts.

"That sexy little bitch is red hot and needs attention the worst way," he told himself as he tried to formulate a plan, but he could not marshal his thoughts. "I'm going into her room one of these nights," he promised himself grimly. "And when I do, boy, oh boy, will I ever tom that well-stacked little chick."

Over the next three weeks, he got Esther alone several times. Each time, he told her how much he wanted to hold her and kiss her sweet mouth. She always smiled and gave him a non-committal, wide-eyed stare.

One rainy day, he was down in the cellar, rebuilding the shelves that held the canned fruits and vegetables. Esther was helping remove the canned goods from the shelves. He looked at her luscious figure, so close to him, and determined to kiss her then and there. He laid aside the saw he was holding and took her in his arms. She gasped, then looked at him questioningly, her violet eyes like dark, mysterious pools.

"Lonnie," she gasped. "What on earth are you doing?"

"Forgive me, Esther," he said. "I can't contain my feelings any longer. I've just got to taste that sweet mouth of yours. Being so near to you all the time and wanting you like I do is driving me right out of my mind. I've waited and waited for the right time to kiss you, you beautiful, darling girl, but the right time never seems to come. So I'm doing it now, even if you tell your daddy on me and get me fired."

For a moment, she struggled against him while Lonnie pulled her tighter into his embrace. He cupped a hand under her chin, turned her face to his, and bent his head to claim her ripe, red lips. She ceased struggling, closed her eyes, and laid her head on his shoulder. Her sweet, upturned mouth was inches below his hungry one.

As he sealed her lips with his, a tremor ran through her body, and she clutched at him with shaking hands. Again and again, he kissed her eyes, nose, cheeks, hair, and pulsing throat, and then moved back to her hot, waiting mouth. When he paused, she opened her eyes and looked up at him happily while a half-smile curved her beautiful lips.

"Do it again," she pleaded, slipping her arms around his neck.

"Did you like that?"

"Yes, oh, yes," she sighed. "Do it again, please."

"You're not angry?"

"Of course not, silly." She grinned.

"All right, here goes. I hope you like the way I kiss you this time." He joined his lips with hers and worked his tongue into her mouth several times in quick succession.

"That was heavenly," she cried. "And that putting your tongue in my mouth. Was that ever the berries. It gave me the strangest, sexiest feeling I've ever had."

"Was it a good feeling?"

"Oh, yes, and so exciting."

"Want me to do it again?" he asked, looking into her half-closed eyes.

"I'm afraid to let you."

"Why?"

"I'm ashamed to tell you." She giggled and ran one of her hands through his hair.

"Has that strange, sexy feeling you spoke about got something to do with down between your legs?" Lonnie asked boldly, remembering Millie Dolan and Hilda Webster.

She blushed scarlet and hid her face against his chest. When he repeated the question, she snuggled tighter in his arms and nodded.

"Tell me, Esther," he demanded in a whisper, "or I'm going to kiss you like that again."

"All right," she conceded, her face flaming red. "I'll tell you, but it's awfully embarrassing. If you kiss me and put your tongue in my mouth again, I'm afraid I'll pee myself."

"You darling little beauty." Lonnie chuckled and kissed her sweet lips.

"If that was to happen I'd have to go and change my panties. Then you couldn't be holding me like you're doing right now. Would you want that to happen?"

"No, sweetheart," he whispered fiercely into one of her pink little ears. "Now that I've got you in my arms, I think I'll just eat you up. You're so beautiful, Esther. So sweet and desirable, too. I want to utterly possess every wonderful thing about you, from the top of your lovely head clear down to the end of your pink little toes."

"I'm happy you find me sweet and beautiful, but what you speak of can never be."

"Your father again?"

"Yes. He'd never permit you to court me. Sometimes I believe he's afraid that if he lets me have a boyfriend, I'll be happy, and not miserable like he is all the time."

"Some parents have very narrow-minded ways of treating their children. Then they wonder why the boy or girl up and leaves them at the first opportunity."

"Daddy's like that. He's as set in his ways as a rock. Maybe he feels that by making me suffer, he'll ease his self-condemnation. I believe he's sorry for what he did to Mother, but he's too bull-headed to admit it."

"Do you ever hear from your mother?"

"No. When she left us, she dropped out of our lives completely. It's as though the earth swallowed her up."

"But what about us? Do you want me to quit my job with your father and get another one? That way, he couldn't fire me when I asked to court you. Maybe you could slip out at night and meet me. What do you say, Esther? Isn't there some way we can get together?"

"Only if I leave home," she said. "Mean as my poor deluded father is, I can't picture myself walking out on him."

"If you did, maybe he'd wake up and start treating you decent."

"I've got to go, Lonnie. I hear Aunt Sarah calling. It's time she and I got supper started."

Reluctantly, Lonnie permitted Esther to free herself from his arms. However, before he let her go completely, he bent his head and kissed her hungrily.

Later that same week, she was helping him store hay in the barn. They paused to rest for a few moments on a pile of hay on the barn floor, and he pulled her into his arms and again voiced his desire to pay court to her, but as before, she forbade him to say anything to her father.

"There's only thing left for us to do, then, if you want me to make love to you."

"What's that?" she asked, wide-eyed.

"Let me come to your room at night. We both sleep on the second floor. No one would ever be the wiser. Forgive me, Esther, honey, for suggesting such a thing, but it's the only way."

"Lonnie," she gasped, one of her sharply hands going to her mouth. "You insult me."

"No, I don't," he declared vehemently. "I've wanted to make love to you from the first moment I saw you. I've tried to point out all the ways to get together honorably, but you say no to all my suggestions. You keep telling me your father won't allow me to court you openly. Coming to your room late at night is all I've left to offer. If that sounds insulting, I'm sorry. I didn't mean it that way."

"That would make me no better than a common slut on the streets. No, Lonnie. No. Much as I'd love for you to court me, I could never do that. I've too much self-respect."

"Reckon there's only one thing left for me to do, then," he muttered darkly, taking his arms from around her and folding them across his chest.

"What's that?" she asked.

"Quit this job and clear out."

"Oh, please, Lonnie. Don't do that. Don't leave me. I'd miss you so much. I'd die of loneliness and heartbreak. You wouldn't want that to happen to me."

"I've no choice," he growled, stony faced. "You're forcing me right out of your life. I think you're wonderful, but what good does it do me to feel that way? No, Esther. I know when I'm licked. I might as well move on."

A heart-rending sob escaped her. With tears streaming down her lovely face, she laid hold of him with shaking hands. She pulled his face to hers and kissed him on the mouth with feverish intensity. Then she quickly got her feet and dashed out of the barn.

The following weekend, Sarah Woods retired at ten o'clock practically every night, and the preacher kept to his life-long habit. Within minutes of him saying goodnight, Lonnie heard harsh snores coming from his bedroom, which was off the living room on the first floor of the house. Reverend Woods was a sound sleeper and not easily wakened, which Lonnie knew well.

Esther had been very silent and moody since Lonnie told her he was going to quit his job. Even when he spoke to her, she was non-communicative. Often, Lonnie caught her looking at him with an odd expression in her big, blue eyes. He wondered if she was thinking over his suggestion. He decided to keep a closer watch on her nighttime activities.

For almost a week after Aunt Sarah left, not a flicker of light was seen under Esther's bedroom door when Lonnie went to bed. Then, on the sixth night, a beam of light showed. Lonnie crept to her room door and fastened an eye to the key hole.

Esther was naked again, doing another hula dance, interspersed with sexy wiggles. When she finally tired of dancing, she whirled over to her bed and threw herself upon it. Lonnie could take no more and threw the door wide.

At his sudden entry, Esther gave a tiny scream and clutched the sheets around her body.

"Lonnie," she gasped, her eyes very wide. "What are you doing in my room?"

"I've come to kiss you," he said hoarsely. He walked over to the bed, bent down, and suited action to his words.

"You've kissed me several times. Please go back to your room. What if Daddy finds you here?"

"He's sound asleep." Lonnie grinned down at her. "And I'm not through kissing you yet. Your lovely breasts would feel insulted if I ignored them."

"Lonnie, please take your hands off my tits," she whispered, her face flaming.

"Not till I've kissed them good. Will you hold still, or do I have to use force? They're so nice, round, soft, sweet, and lovely. I've just got to nibble them a little bit."

"Lonnie, I declare. That's enough. See how hard the nipples have become? They stick straight out. You've nibbled and nibbled. Stop it, I say."

"I've only began to make love to you, my sweet," he whispered, slipping out of his shorts.

He stood before her, naked, and she blushed to the roots of her hair and hid her face. When he grasped the sheet covering her and began pulling it away, she clutched it tightly, but her efforts were to no avail. With a quick jerk, Lonnie stripped the sheet off her.

"Oh, but you're beautiful, Esther," he said softly, looking down at her. "I've got to have all your love tonight. I've just got to, my sweet little blushing darling."

"Lonnie, that long stiff thing there between your legs, with the red head. What is it? And what are you going to do with it?"

"That's the old love-maker. You'll find out plenty fast what I'm going to do with it. You'll love what I do with it. Wait and see if you don't."

"Lonnie, Lonnie, if you do to me what I suspect you're going to do, you'll rape me. I'm a virgin."

"Calm your fears, honey," he soothed as he climbed into bed with her.

"Lonnie, what are you doing on top of me? Why are you spreading my legs so far apart?"

"Relax, sweetheart," he whispered, reaching down and kissing her. "Pull your knees up farther and spread your legs a little wider. Don't be afraid. Girls enjoy what we're going to do. Please, cooperate. I'll soon make it feel real good."

"Lonnie, please listen," she pleaded desperately. "If you push that big hot thing into me, I'll scream for Daddy."

"Shh. Don't act so silly. I didn't want to have to tell you this, but I know you crave and will enjoy this sort of thing."

"What are you saying? I don't have any boyfriends."

"I've seen you wiggling around in this room late at night, as naked as a bird."

"Oh, my God," she gasped, her beautiful face flushing scarlet. "How could you be so sneaky? You've been peeking through the keyhole. Lonnie, you're terrible."

"That's right. I have been peeking. I'm glad I did. Otherwise, I wouldn't be here in your arms, like I am now, and you and I wouldn't be going to enjoy a good, old-fashioned bit of country loving."

At that moment, with an extra persistent push, he slid into her all the way.

"Daddy," she screamed, but not loudly, as he began the in and out movements.

Paying no heed to her struggles and pleas, he continued to kiss her passionately, and increase the tempo of his movements. Soon her movements matched his, and her breath came ragged, fast, and hot.

"Daddy," she cried again, in a fainter voice. She clutched him to her tightly. Suddenly, her breath caught in her throat.

"Oh, Daddy," she said ecstatically, pulling Lonnie's face to hers and claiming his lips with her hot, dewy-sweet mouth. "Oh. Oh. Oh. I'm in heaven. I just know I am. I'm floating on a cloud. I'm ahh..."

"Do you want me to stop now?" Lonnie asked in a whisper as nature began exerting itself.

"Oh, God, no," she screamed softly, as she became completely uninhibited. "Never stop this wonderful thing you're doing to me. Go on, and on, and on."

From that night forward, as long as Lonnie was employed by her father, he had access to Esther's bedroom. She seemed to enjoy sexual relations tremendously at the time of contact, but afterwards, she sank into a dark mood. Sometimes she moped around the house for days after she and Lonnie were intimate or burst into tears at the slightest provocation.

Lonnie concluded that Esther's behavior was the result of a deep-seated guilt. Her own mother had succumbed to the love of a man other than her husband and had even abandoned her home and infant daughter for him. Lonnie was certain that Esther felt she was following in her mother's footsteps.

That same wild streak had lain dormant in her. All it needed to bring it into fruition was time, the right place, and a man's all-out lovemaking.

She confided these dark thoughts to Lonnie one night, as she lay in his arms, naked and uninhibited in her response to his movement and touch.

"Let's face it, Lonnie darling," she whispered. "I'm no better than a street-walking slut."

"Esther Woods," he scolded. "What are you saying about yourself?"

"The truth, Lonnie. Only the truth."

"You're not a bad girl. What gave you the idea you was?"

"If I'm so good and pure, like you keep telling me I am, what in the hell am I doing here in your arms, behaving like a blushing bride?"

"You're obeying a natural impulse."

"Sure. Same as the girls in a cathouse are doing. The only difference is they get paid for what they put out, but like a damn fool, I'm giving my ass away."

"Why are you so bitter tonight, honey? Why are you talking like you've lost your best friend and gone to the dogs?"

"I'm no good. That's why I'm bitter. I've suspected it ever since I began getting hot panties from reading love stories. I've had no boyfriends and no prospects of getting one, thanks to my daddy, so I used artificial means to bring about sexual satisfaction."

"That's nothing to be so wrought up about. Doctors say all boys and girls do that at some time in their lives. I have. All the sex books say the same thing. They ought to know."

"I'm a product of heredity," she moaned as she clutched Lonnie's naked body close to her hot, feverish one. "My mother was practically a whore. Now I'm just like her in every respect. Daddy's been right all along. I love sex and everything that goes with it. The only difference between a whore and me is that I try to put up a respectable front. But it's only a front."

No amount of arguing on Lonnie's part changed Esther's outlook. At last, disgusted, he gave up. For two weeks, he refused to have sexual relations with her. When he resumed relations with her again, she insisted they get married right away. That night, he spent his last hours in Esther's arms. She had not the slightest inkling of the plan he had in mind. The next day was the beginning of another month. When Reverend Woods paid him for the previous month's work the next morning at the breakfast table, he asked for the day off.

Lonnie traveled fast and far. By nightfall, he had put many miles between him and Esther woods. It was goodbye.

Chapter 8

The Prostitute

Lonnie's next place of employment was a handle factory in a city. Farm work had lost interest for him since leaving Reverend Woods's employ, and factory work paid better wages.

He obtained board and lodging with an elderly couple who lived close to his work. Mrs. Lee immediately took him under her wing, so to speak, and straightway began fussing over him and bossing him. The good woman was a natural mother, and she exercised the same dominance over all her lodgers.

City life was new to him, with its hustle, rush, and roar. People surrounded him by the thousands. Still, he was often utterly lonely. A familiar face would have been an occasion to celebrate, and there were times he would have given a week's wages for a friend to talk with, laugh with, and do things with. The few girls he had tried to get acquainted with treated him like a green country hick, and maybe he was. They promptly let him know they were not wasting their time on hayseeds. The type of men they preferred, they said, drove sleek automobiles, wore flashy clothes, and sported fat pocketbooks.

One evening, when he was feeling especially low and left out of things, Lonnie was sitting on a park bench in the public square. It was Labor Day weekend. As he sat and watched the people, he mentally cursed himself for vetoing a trip home to see his mother and stepfather. He would have at least had the companionship of his family for a few days.

Suddenly, his attention was drawn to a young woman walking toward him. He didn't know what about the girl had claimed his attention, other than being exceptionally beautiful. She walked with a graceful, free-swinging stride. As she passed the bench Lonnie sat on, she casually glanced in his direction and walked on. She mingled with the people on the sidewalk and was lost to view.

In a few minutes, he saw her coming back up the street. This time, in addition to her purse, she was carrying a package. When she came abreast of him, one of her high-heeled pumps caught in a crack in the sidewalk, and she fell forward on her hands and knees. Her package and purse fell at Lonnie's feet.

He leapt off the bench and ran to her assistance. He gently took hold of her arms and helped her to her feet. She thanked him, began brushing herself off, and rearranged her clothes. Lonnie retrieved her purse and package and tendered them to her.

"That was a nasty spill, Miss," he said sympathetically. "Did you hurt yourself?"

"I don't think I'm hurt too badly." She smiled, brushing a tear from her eyes. "Just shook up an awful lot. I'm more angry than hurt. It makes me mad as wet hen to fall like that. People stare as though you was as clumsy as an ox. I never could walk right with high heels."

At her denunciation, Lonnie threw back his head and roared with laughter. For a moment, she stared at him, undecided whether to be angry or join him. Then, with a broad smile, she laughed merrily.

"Forgive me, Miss," Lonnie chuckled. "I couldn't help laughing. It wasn't because you fell. Heavens, no. It was the way you chastised yourself for being so clumsy that tickled me."

"I don't blame you," she said. "After the spectacle I made of myself, who could blame anyone for laughing? Thanks for helping me up and gathering my belongings. I must be on my way."

"Are you sure you can make it all right?"

"I'm quite sure, thank you. I'll be fine. Thanks again, and goodnight." She took a few steps, but almost instantly moaned and sank down on the sidewalk.

In a flash, Lonnie was at her side. He helped her regain her feet, put one of her arms across his shoulders, and one around her waist. "I insist on helping you home," he said.

She looked up at him gratefully.

"We'll take it as easy as we can. Let's hope you didn't sprain your ankle too badly."

"You're awfully kind," she said as they started down the street with her wincing at every step. "I'm afraid I hurt myself more than I realized. I hope it doesn't swell."

"Put some cold bandages on it when we get you home. Ice will help keep the swelling down. Your mother will know what to do."

"I'm afraid that's impossible," she said with a queer little laugh. "I only work here in town. My folks live fifty miles south of here."

"In that case, you're in the same boat I'm in," Lonnie laughed, tightening his arm around her waist. "My mother and step-father live a good hundred and fifty miles to the east of this burg."

"You're a farm boy, maybe?" she asked hesitantly.

"I sure am. I'm proud of it, too. Come to think of it, the moment I laid eyes on you this evening, you impressed me favorably, but not as a city girl. Are you some farmer's daughter, lost in the big city?"

"I plead guilty to half of that."

"Which half?" Lonnie asked, intrigued by the girl's forthright manner.

"I'm a farmer's daughter, all right, but I'm not lost. At least, I don't think I am. I work here."

"So do I. I work in that big handle factory over on Grant avenue. What kind of work do you do? Factory or office?"

"Neither."

"Oh?"

She leaned heavily on him. "My work is sort of difficult to describe. But mostly I'd say it's entertaining and suchlike."

"You mean you're an entertainer?"

"I guess that's what you'd call me."

"Does that kind of work pay well?"

"Yes and no," she answered, with another queer-sounding laugh. "I suppose it's how a person would look at it."

"Do you work day shift or night shift?"

"When I went to work at this job, I agreed to work any hours they gave me. Mostly, though, I have worked the evening shift."

"Good. I work days. I could come where you work one evening and watch while you entertain. I think I'd like that."

She paused to look up at him, her big eyes clouded. "I work in a club, and it's very exclusive. Only members are allowed in. I'm afraid it'd be impossible for you to see me in my place of employment."

"I'm sorry to hear that," Lonnie said. "I was hoping I could see you again. You're the first girl I've met in this burg that has treated me halfway decent. Seems a shame we won't be seeing each other again. My name's Dolan. Lonnie Dolan."

"I'm Sally Smith." She smiled and offered him her hand. "I'm right proud to have met you, Lonnie, even if I had to almost break my neck to do it."

Taking her small, warm hand in his, Lonnie squeezed it appreciatively and grinned. Laughing up at him, she squeezed his hand in return, her beautiful face flushed and happy.

A few minutes later, they reached the house where Sally said she roomed. When Lonnie wanted to help her up the steps and to her door, she declined.

"I'll be all right," she said softly. "My ankle feels a lot better than it did already. I don't want to frighten my landlady. She fusses over me enough as it is."

"My landlady, exactly," Lonnie laughed. "It's funny how the old ladies who run rooming houses want to take their roomers under their wings. Must be the mother hen in them."

"I know what you mean. Good night, Lonnie. I'll be going in now and tending to my ankle. It's been awfully nice meeting you. Thanks for everything."

"Wait, Sally, please. Surely I can see you again, sometime."

"Do you really want to?" she asked.

"I certainly do. You're the first sociable girl I've met in this burg, and now that I've met you, I'm not going to lose you if I can help it. Not by a long shot."

"I was hoping you'd say that. You're my kind of person, too. I knew it the moment you helped me up when I fell."

"Then we'll see each other again?" he asked hopefully.

"Yes," she laughed, "if you're interested in a cripple."

"How about tomorrow night?"

"That'll be fine, providing my ankle is well enough."

"Gosh, I hope it is. What time can I call for you?"

"Lonnie, please don't feel badly, but I'd rather you didn't call for me here."

"Why not? You're unmarried, I hope, and old enough to have boyfriends. But maybe you already have a steady beau. Most every pretty girl like you does."

"It's that landlady of mine," she said.

"What about her? Doesn't she allow you to have boyfriends?"

"Of course, she does, and she's good as gold about everything, too. It's only that she's so nosey all the time. I can't even mention a boy's name but what she's all up in arms about it and wants to know when I'm marrying him. It's awfully embarrassing."

"Oh, I see," Lonnie grinned. "One of those matchmaker types."

"She certainly is. She doesn't mean anything by it, but try to tell her to tend to her own business. She does the same thing with all her unmarried roomers. Men and woman alike. I'm sick and tired of it, and I don't want her to embarrass you."

"You darling girl." Lonnie grinned happily, pinching her lightly on the cheek. "I was right. You are different than these money-mad city girls. I sensed it the moment I saw you."

"You're not angry because I'd rather meet you somewhere else?"

"Of course not. Just name the place where you want me to meet you, and I'll be there with bells on. The important thing is that we'll be seeing each other again."

"Good. How about the park bench where you were sitting when I fell at your feet? Could we meet there?'

"It's fine with me." Lonnie grinned happily. "What time?'

"Eight o'clock all right?"

"Wonderful, Sally. Now you go in and tend to your ankle. Take your time coming to meet me tomorrow night. I'd rather you was late getting there than not get there at all."

"I'll be there," she said, turning away. "Good night."

"Good night," Lonnie said, watching her cautiously climb the porch steps and slowly turn and wave. He waved in return. Then she was gone.

During the weeks that followed, Lonnie averaged two dates a week with Sally. She was good company and very lovely. He grew quite fond of her and began to devise ways to get her into his arms. However, Sally Smith was not the type of girl who went in for heavy petting, or so she said. Often, she wouldn't even let him kiss her good night when he brought her home from a date. Once, when he threatened to quit her and find himself another girl to court, she gave a choking little sob, melted into his arms, and turned her lips up to his. It was very late at night, and they stood in the shadows cast by the street lamp on the porch of her rooming house.

"Oh, Lonnie," she cried brokenly after he kissed her. "Surely, you wouldn't leave me just because I don't like being pawed and smooched all the time."

"I meant no offense toward you, Sally," he said earnestly, as he gently folded her in his arms and stroked her hair. "I can't help it if I want to crush you in my arms, kiss your sweet mouth a thousand times, and make love to you, all the way. You're a woman, Sally. A damn beautiful and desirable one, too. And I'm a man. I can't change or help it if I desire every wonderful thing about you. That's how it is with me. If I can't kiss you or cuddle you when I want you so badly all the time, what the hell is the use of me hanging around? I may just as well find myself a girlfriend who'll appreciate me. Obviously, you don't. Now you know how I feel."

"Lonnie, darling," she gasped, hurt. "I do appreciate you. Honestly, I do. And I can't believe that you'll leave me. I can't believe that, Lonnie. I just can't."

"But I do mean it. Every word of it."

"It would be sinful for us to give ourselves to each other out of wedlock. The Bible calls it fornication. I'd be ashamed of that relationship between us for the rest of my life."

"I can't help how I feel about you."

"Just how do you feel about me, Lonnie, honey?" she whispered, slipping her arms around his neck and kissing him shyly.

"I'm crazy about you," he growled hoarsely, crushing her to him. "And you're driving me out of my mind from wanting you all the time and all the way. It's getting so bad that I can hardly concentrate on my work for thinking about how much I want you. You've got me in a perfect lather, Sally, girl."

"Want to know how I feel about you?" she asked, her lovely eyes glowing up at him and her winsome body tightly molded to his.

"Yes. Tell me, but tell me the truth when you do."

"I love you," she whispered against his lips. She kissed him long and passionately then she hid her face against his chest.

"Sally, Sally," Lonnie gasped. "I didn't know. I didn't realize."

"It's true, sweetheart," she sighed, lifting a face wet with tears. "Maybe I shouldn't have, but I just had to let you know how I feel about you."

"You darling girl," he said over and over again as he kissed her eyes, her hair, her tear-wet cheeks, her throat, and her eager, waiting mouth again.

"Is that the way you feel about me?"

"Yes, Sally, darling."

"You love me?"

"I do," he whispered.

"Say it, sweetheart," she pleaded. "If you love me, tell me so. Let me hear it from your own lips."

"I love you, Sally Smith," Lonnie said, hiding his face in her fragrant hair and holding her tighter than ever.

"Bless you, my darling. Bless you for having the courage to tell me. Now we can get married."

"Married?" he cried, holding her out from him and looking down into her beautiful face. "Sally, I don't know. I haven't thought about that. I wouldn't want us to rush headlong into something we're not prepared for. I—"

"Don't you love me enough? Wouldn't you like to know I'm yours, all the way?"

"Yes, but—" he stammered.

"Then what are you worried about? It's being together every day. Just think, Lonnie, she whispered, looking up at him. "If I was your wife, we would share the same bed. I would even consent to sleep in your arms naked."

At her bold and shameless promise of love to come, she gasped then hid her flaming face against his chest again. A tremor ran through her body. Lonnie clutched her to him.

"Sally," Lonnie said, "I don't know what to say about us, but I love you more than any girl I've ever known. You're beautiful, sweet, clean, decent, and fine. Any man would feel honored to have a girl like you for his wife, but I've got to think this thing through. I'll let you go in now, dearest. It's cold out here on the porch. I wouldn't want my sweetie catching sick."

"Will I see you again soon?" she asked.

"Of course. Don't look so worried, baby. You'll probably be Mrs. Lonnie Dolan before you're another month older. I've just got to get used to the idea of being married. That's all."

"When will you let me know about us?"

"Next Sunday night. All next week, I'll be thinking about you and how nice it'll be to have you to come home to in the evening. I want you to be thinking about how you'll like being Mrs. Lonnie Dolan. Will you do that?"

"I promise," she said happily, raising her soft, sweet lips to his. "May next week fly by on silvery wings. I can hardly wait. Good night, husband-to-be. I'm so happy, and all because of you. I love you. I love you."

"God bless you, my sweetheart," Lonnie said softly, his voice heavy with emotion. "See you next week. Keep safe and well."

All during the following week, Lonnie wrestled with his decision. He finally confided in his work partner, an Irishman of some fifty years of age who was a bachelor.

"So it's thinking of wedding bells yer doin, eh?" Pat said, grinning broadly as he pumped Lonnie's hand. "Look, laddie, don't rush into this thing half-cocked. When did the idea of takin a wife strike you?"

"Last week. We were standing on the porch of her rooming house. Before I knew it, we was talking about getting married. It hit me like a ton of bricks."

"Uh-huh, I see. Did you bring the subject up, or did the lassie?"

"Come to think of it now, she did."

"Ah-ha. Now I see which way the wind's blowing," Pat grunted. "Don't think I'm prying into yer personal affairs, but did yer sweetheart plant this marryin idea in yer head after you told her how much you loved her and wanted her?"

"Yes, she did," Lonnie admitted.

"Then maybe it's not marryin you want, laddie, but just a good piece of tailin. Tell me true now. How long has it been since you had a good piece?"

"Over two months," Lonnie confessed, shamefaced.

"Let me fix you up with something special. Over on Chancy Street, there's a place that's sort of exclusive. Go there and give them the password. It's Eureka. Once you're inside, ask for Sally. I've topped that little bitch twice myself, and I'm here to tell you she's one hot number when it comes to shaking it up. She's purty as a picture and stacked like a brick outhouse. Promise me you'll do that, laddie. Go there and let Sally take care of you. Then, if it's a wife you're wantin and needin after she's hauled yer ashes, I ain't got no more to say."

"All right, Pat. I'll do as you suggest," Lonnie promised. He picked up his lunch pail and got in line to ring out his clock card for the day.

The following afternoon, he knocked off from work two hours early and went to the address Pat had given him. He had never patronized a house of prostitution before. A beautiful young woman of mixed blood admitted him and asked with a broad smile on her dusky face if there was any girl in particular he wanted to see.

"Dey's all free right now, suh. So y'all can have your pick."

"I was told to ask for Sally," Lonnie said, glancing at her figure admiringly, "but now that I've seen you, I think I'll change my mind. How about you and me getting cozy?"

"I think I'd like dat powerful much, suh," she said, "but I ain't allowed to mess wid any of da customers of dis here house, no way. Dat's the rules."

"Couldn't we overlook the rules, this once?" Lonnie asked.

"I wouldn't dare. If I did, an got caught, I'd be canned f'sure. Want me to tell Sally dere's a gentleman to see her?"

"If the girls aren't busy, why not have them all come out, one at a time? That way I can look them all over. Maybe there'll be one I'd like better than Sally. You can tell me their names as they come and go."

"Whatever you say, suh." The quadroon smiled, her white, even teeth flashing like pearls. "But I'm bettin dere ain't any gal here dat's a hotter number den Sally. She sure purty. Dat gal's got a figure dat'll knock yer eyes plumb out. Wait and see. I'll have Sally come out last."

One by one, the girls came into the waiting room and walked past Lonnie, professional smiles curving their painted lips. All of them were beautiful, after a fashion.

"Sally's next," the quadroon said, disappearing down the shadowy hall between the rooms.

Lonnie's head was lowered, looking at a burlesque magazine on a stand at his elbow. Then the quadroon announced the last girl.

"Dis is Sally," she said softly, her heavy accent falling pleasantly on Lonnie's ears. "An if y'all don't mind my sayin so, I think you is wise to have waited. Dis little gal will take care of y'all real fine. Yes, suh. Just you wait and see."

The room was softly lit, and Lonnie presumed it was done for girls' benefits. Bright light would have shown the lines on their faces too glaringly, lessening their attractiveness to customers. He lifted his head, looked at the last of the prostitutes, and received one of the greatest and cruelest shocks of his life. Sally Smith, the girl he loved and was going to ask to be his wife, stood before him.

"Good god, Sally," Lonnie shouted, springing to his feet. "What in heaven's name are you doing here?"

"Sally works here," the quadroon said, looking sharply at Lonnie's stricken face, then at Sally's pale one. "Dis little gal's our biggest draw. Y'all acquainted?"

"No, I guess not," Lonnie muttered, regaining his composure. "Sally just reminded me of someone I knew for a while. The light in this room fooled me. Let's go, Sally. I'm anxious to see if you'll live up to that hot reputation you've established for yourself."

"Y'all sure won't be disappointed in Sally," the quadroon chuckled as she began tidying up the waiting room.

"I hope you're right," Lonnie laughed mirthlessly as he followed Sally's retreating figure down the shadowy hall.

Not a word did Sally utter as she opened the door to the room she occupied and stood aside for Lonnie to enter. Her face looked chiseled from rock. Once they were inside, with the door closed and locked behind them, her composure deserted her completely.

Sinking down on the edge of the bed, she covered her face with shaking hands and burst into tears. Lonnie looked down on her huddled figure, so miserable and wretched, and felt compassion stir in his breast, but it did not show in his voice when he spoke to her.

"Sally, Sally. How could you?" he said through tight lips. "How could you have had the gall to pass yourself off to me as a clean, decent, working girl?'

"I loved you," she gasped, her sobs shaking her as a tree in a storm. "And I still do."

"Horse manure," he spat, disgusted. "Don't try that love bunk on me again. All the times I tried to hold you in my arms and kiss you, you acted as though you was as innocent and pure as an angel from heaven. And all that time I was making a damn fool of myself, you knew you was nothing but a damned whore. How deceiving can a girl be, Sally? If what you did to me is love, I want no part of it."

"Lonnie, Lonnie," she wailed. "Hear me out. Believe me when I say I love you. After I met you and seen how wonderful you was, and realized how much I loved you, I hadn't the heart to tell you how I was getting along. You wouldn't have understood. What was I to do? Can't you see what a spot my love for you put me in?"

"You would have gone right on and married me, letting me believe you was sweet, clean, decent, and fine."

"I had to appear that way to you, Lonnie. That's what love can do for a woman. I know it's all over between us and you can never forgive me or understand, but I couldn't have been any different with you than I was. Your love and respect meant more to me than anything in this whole wide world. Try to understand that. As God is my judge, I'm telling you the truth."

"Maybe I'll understand someday, Sally, but not now. All I can think of now is the low down trick you was fixing to pull on me. I've wanted to partake of your charms ever since I met you. Tonight, that desire is going to be fulfilled. Skin out of that wrap-around and prepare to give me the works. I sure hope you don't give me a dose of clap."

"I'm clean," she snapped as she rose from the bed and slipped out of the loose garment she wore, "but I don't understand what you mean by 'the works.'"

"We're quite naturally going to screw, Sally, baby. First, though, I think I'd like one of them tongue baths you gals give. Also, I'd like one of them Frenches. They say they're real exciting."

"Nothing doing," she said coldly, drawing her beautiful nude body up regally and looking at him with flashing eyes.

"What's wrong?" Lonnie grinned. "I thought giving Frenches, straights, strips, and tongue baths was all part of a whore's art. What did I ask for that was wrong?"

"I've never given Frenches or tongue-baths, and I don't intend to start with you. I love you, Lonnie, and I would do almost anything for you, but I won't let you shame me more than I'm shamed right now. If you insist on a French and tongue bath, you'll have to get one of the other girls to take care of your needs. I flatly refuse."

"What will you give me?" he asked, admiring her bearing in spite of himself.

"Only a straight," she said lying down on the bed and motioning for him to come to her. "That's all I give any of the customers. I don't even kiss them."

"Let's do it dog-fashioned," Lonnie suggested, slipping out of his clothes and getting on the bed with her.

"Any way you say," she said bitterly, rolling over on her hands and knees and getting her beautiful buttocks in the right position for him. "There it is, Lonnie. Take all the time you want, and take as many pieces as you want. I owe you that. I hope you enjoy yourself. You've wanted it long enough."

Quickly and deeply making the union of their sexual organs, Lonnie momentarily forgot that Sally was a whore and instead considered her the girl he loved and was going to ask to be his wife. Whether she responded differently to him than she did to the other men she had given her body to, he had no way of knowing. However, when their sexual organs fused together, she instantly reciprocated.

Their breathing became hoarse, panting gasps, and their movements became uninhibited. The shadowy room seemed to explode around them. Slowly they separated and fell to the bed, side by side. Sobbing softy, Sally crept into Lonnie's arms. She kissed him with dewy lips and hid her face against his naked chest.

The winter passed, and on numerous occasions, Lonnie went to the house on Chancy Street and enjoyed sexual gratification in Sally's arms. He never mentioned the horrible deception she would have perpetrated on him to a living soul. As time went by, he considered it just one of those things a man comes up against when dealing with a woman.

Gradually, the bitterness he felt toward Sally wore off, and twice during the winter, he drove her home to see her parents and her ten brothers and sisters. He had purchased himself a secondhand car. On nice afternoons, he often drove Sally around the countryside. The day he first drove her home to see her family, she exacted a promise from him that he wouldn't tell anybody how she earned her living.

"Folks out here respect me," she said sadly, brushing a tear away. "I want to keep it that way. It would break my parents' hearts if they knew how low I've sunk. Promise me you won't give my secret away."

"You've nothing to worry about from me, Sally," Lonnie said.

Chapter 9

The Quadroon

Every time Lonnie went to see Sally at the house of prostitution, he held a "gab-fest" with the madam. Her name was Bernice Jackson. She became "Bernie" to him, and he was Lon to her. Bernice was a quadroon, and Lonnie never failed to tell her how beautiful she was or how badly he desired sexual relations with her, but she always declined with a wide smile and her deep, throaty voice softly rebuking him.

"Lon, baby," she said angrily one day, after he put his arms around her and cupped her round breast in his hands. "Y'all knows I ain't allowed to mess wif de customers of dis here cat house. I dasn't."

"What're you scared of, Bernie?" Lonnie asked, pinching her buttock gently.

"Scared? Boy, I'ze petrified. If I was doin dat by one of de man who runs dis joint, I'd be canned, sho nuf. Lands, yes."

"Would you love me up if you could without taking any risk?"

"Now dat's another thing," Bernice grunted. "Right now, I don't think I would. No, sir. I sure don't think I'd lay you."

"Don't you ever lay a white man?"

"Sure, I does."

"What's wrong with me, then?"

"Nuffin, specially."

"There must be something wrong. Don't you find me attractive?"

"Sho do, Lon, honey," she grinned. "It ain't dat at all."

"Then what is it? Level with me, Bernie."

"It's dat Sally gal."

"What's Sally got to do with you and me?"

"Try to understand. Y'all an her was engaged to marry up. Den y'all discovered Sally was a whore. Dat knocked dem nuptial plans of y'all's right into a cocked hat."

"So?"

"Well, it's like dis. I wouldn't feel right screwin y'all knowin how Sally feels bout you."

"What difference could that make between you and me? Sally and I ain't married. We never were engaged, not really. Then it turned out that she and I could never become man and wife. In other words, Bernie, everything's off between Sally and myself."

"Yep, I know dat. Still an all, I'ze not haulin yo ashes long as Sally's here wif her heart in her sleeve every time y'all walks in."

"But Sally's a whore, Bernie," Lonnie growled, exasperated. "I still like her, but it's all over between us. I don't give a tinker's damn who she screws back there in that room she uses. She's in there right now, hauling some guy's ashes. Bernie, it ain't any of Sally's business what I do. She let me down. I didn't let her down."

"Sho, I knows dat. It's eatin dat poor gal's heart out, too. Lon, honey, try to understand. Dere's whores, an den dere's whores. Sally ain't a whore at heart. An she never could be. All de time she's been here, she's held herself above all the other gals in her relations wif de men. All she'd evah give dem cats was straights. Most all dem wanted dat little gal to French em de worst way, but she would have no part of dat. Yes, sir, Lon. Sally's a good gal in spite of workin heah. My heart goes out to dat gal. She was forced into dis kind of doins, an dat is fact."

"Did she feed you that line of junk, too?"

"I ain't saying yes, an I ain't saying no," Bernice replied doggedly.

"At least admit that she tried to tell you she was forced to become a prostitute. Right?"

"She sho enuf did. An de funny thing about it is dat I come to believe dat little gal."

"Horse manure," Lonnie snorted in disgust. "Don't be so gullible, Bernice."

"Us women is funny dat way, lover boy." She smiled. "We learned long ago, de hard way, dat we gotta stick together."

"I'll ask you again," Lonnie said. "You treat me like a sack of potatoes now, but if you and I could do what I want us to do, would you?"

"In a minute," she promised solemnly. "I'd be after you like a house afire. Be patient, Lon, honey. It could still happen."

"I'll remember your promise." He grinned at her, sitting down to wait his turn with Sally. "Don't forget. We've a hot date when the opportunity presents itself."

"I'll keep y'all in mind," she said. "It ain't likely I'll forget, though, seein as how hot y'all been after me evah since y'all first came heah."

One Friday afternoon in early May, he knocked off work early and went to see Sally before going to his rooming house. As usual, Bernice met him at the door with a big smile on her face.

"How's business, Bernice?" he asked, reaching for her.

"Dead, so far," she answered, expertly dodging his grasping hands. "In about two hours, the evening trade'll start pouring in. Den de man who runs dis cat house'll be happy. Not dat it'll make any diff today. Dey's bof outta town."

"Tell Sally I'm here," Lonnie said, settling himself in an easy chair.

"Can't do dat, Lon." She grinned. "Sally quit a week ago. She said she was goin back home to marry up wif an ole school chum. De gals heah all wished her de best of luck."

"So Sally's gone," Lonnie mused, looking at Bernice reflectively. "And the big bosses are out of town. Bernice, here's our opportunity to make whoopee. In other words, the coast is clear for us to let nature take its course. What do you say?"

"Y'all sho do want dat thing I carry round tween mah legs, an I don't mean maybe," she laughed, locking the door.

"The worst way, kiddo. The worst way."

"I'm tellin you, boy, I'ze one gal who's powerful hard to satisfy."

"And I'm one man who can do a powerful lot of satisfying." He grinned, pulling her into his arms.

"Easy, Lon, honey. Dis ain't no place to get fractious. Let's go back to Sally's ole room. Dat way, we get real comfy while we's letting nature take the wire edge offen us."

Lonnie followed Bernice down the familiar hall to the room at the far end. Sally had left this sordid life forever, and he was glad she had had the courage to break away from it. Most prostitutes clung to their trade until they were broken down hags, desired by no one. Sally could still make a good life for herself. She was young, beautiful, and desirable.

As Lonnie walked into the room behind Bernice and looked at the bed upon which Sally had given herself to a host of men, he felt a strange tightening in his chest. For a moment, he felt like turning and walking out of the place, never to return. Then Bernice slipped out of the cotton wrap-around and kay down on the bed. Smiling seductively, she turned her head in his direction and held out her arms.

"Come, honey chil," she breathed softly. "Get undressed an show yo gal, Bernice, what y'all can do when it comes to quilt fightin. I'ze ready an red-hot down tween mah legs. Come put out dat fire, Lon, baby."

"I reckon you're used to them fellers with the big staffs," Lonnie chuckled.

"I like mah men well hung."

"Then it's only fair to tell you right now that you're in for a disappointment. My tool isn't over-sized at all. In fact, it's rather on the small size, or so I think."

"De little one is good, too," she laughed, squirming around in a sexy way as Lonnie undressed and laid down beside her. "Git wif it, boy. Don't let yo pal die of waitin."

"Be patient, Bernice," he whispered, gathering her in his arms and kissing her hot, demanding mouth.

At her instant response, he put his right hand between her shapely legs. He cupped his hand over her mound and began massaging her. Her breath began coming ragged and hot, while her buttocks thrashed from side to side, and around and around, like a snake coiling and uncoiling itself.

"Baby, baby," she gasped in a ragged whisper. "Don't torture yo pal Bernice any longer. I'ze dyin dead fo dat prong of y'all's. Please, baby, please. Give it to me, little as it is. I'ze wantin an needin it real bad. Oh, Lordy, Lordy."

But Lonnie kept massaging, fondling, and kissing until Bernice was squirming all over the bed in feverish desire. Only then, did he comply with her request. She lost control. Crying, laughing, gasping, and screaming softy, she clutched him to her so tightly he could hardly breathe. She bit his neck and shoulders in the intensity of her passion, and he experienced pain and bliss. When it was over, Bernice lay exhausted but happy in Lonnie's arms and looked at him with admiration in her eyes that was almost worship.

"Wowee," she panted, wiping sweat off her beautiful face with a corner of the bed sheet. "Y'all fooled me plenty, Lon, honey."

"Did you like my love-making, Bernice?" Lonnie asked, grinning at her.

"Well, I should smile."

"And did I satisfy you?"

"Man, y'all fractured me."

"I'm happy to know that," he laughed, looking fondly at her as he cuddled her breasts in his hands and leaned over to kiss her nipples.

"Yes, indeedy, Lon, honey," Bernice said, beginning to squirm again under the expert touch of his practiced hands. "Sally was right. Y'all is de most wonderfullest little man I evah did see when it comes to quilt fightin. Y'all done dat job neater, an sweeter, an more completer, an wif less peter, than any man I evah had top me before."

From that day forward, Lonnie had it made with Bernice Jackson. They worked out an arrangement, whereby they could indulge in sexual relations to their hearts' content, without fear of interruption. Lonnie would go to the house on Chancy Street just before closing time then wait around until all of the customers had gone. After Bernice took care of the cash for the day's business, she locked up, did a quick check of the rooms to see that everything was in order, and locked all the doors. Then she and Lonnie retired to one of the rooms, put clean sheets on the beds, stripped off their clothes, and engaged in love-making so passionate and unrestrained that they were exhausted but satisfied afterwards.

This arrangement went for three months. One day in late summer, he went to the house on Chancy Street, and she did not greet him. Instead, an old woman with a sagging figure and straggly grey hair admitted him.

"Who you wantin to see?" she asked, eyeing him as she swished a snuff stick around between her discolored lips. "Bernice Jackson?" She looked him up and down.

"That's right. Tell her I'm here."

"You Lonnie?"

"Hell, yes," Lonnie snapped, exasperated. "Now get a move on and tell Bernice Lon's here to see her. I ain't got all day to stand around and answer foolish questions. I need some nooky in the worst way."

"Then you better let one of the other girls fix you up," the woman said. Lonnie felt she took a certain malicious enjoyment in her words.

"What're you talking about?"

"Bernice Jackson is not here anymore," the woman replied with a toothless smile.

"Bernice isn't here?" Lonnie repeated.

"That's what I said."

"Then where the hell is she?"

"Deep in Dixie."

"Talk sense, woman. What the hell are you trying to tell me?"

"Bernice went back to her folks in Georgia."

"When did she leave?"

"Last week."

"How come?" Lonnie asked, hating the creature more every minute he talked with her.

"She was expecting," said the woman callously.

"What?" Lonnie rasped. "Expecting? Expecting what?"

"A baby, you dope."

"A baby?" Lonnie mumbled, still not comprehending. "What a baby got to do with this? Why can't people take care of their own brats instead of pawning them off on somebody else?"

"Listen, you stupid son-of-a-bitch, and try to get this through your thick skull. I'm trying to tell you—"

"Watch your tongue when you're talking to me," Lonnie roared. "I don't take that kind of bull crap from anybody, let alone an old screwed-out bag like you. One more crack like that, and I'm liable to knock your two eyes into one—woman or no woman."

"You scare me to death," the old woman sneered, spitting a stream of tobacco juice into a can by her chair.

"Now what's this junk about Bernice?" Lonnie demanded. "And this time, give it to me straight."

"I'll tell you everything I know about that quadroon if you'll park that big ass of yours and stop shaking your fists under my nose. Otherwise, to hell with you."

"All right. Let's have it," Lonnie grumbled. He sank into an easy chair and laid aside his hat. "Only make it short and sweet."

"It'll be a pleasure." She gave him another toothless grin. "Bernice Jackson quit her job and went back to her folks in Georgia because she's expecting. In other words, she's pregnant, knocked up, going to have a baby. Does that ring a bell in that blockhead of yours?"

"So that's it," Lonnie whispered, his face grey. "Bernice is going to have a baby. My baby. I'm going to be the father of child of mixed blood."

"Hell, yes," the crone cackled, her snuff stick wobbling crazily between her loose lips. "What else could you expect after all that   pun-jabbin she told me you two've been doing for the last three months? She was bound to get knocked up sooner or later. Be thankful you got to screw her as long as you did."

"And now she's gone," Lonnie mumbled, dazed, as he reached blindly for his hat.

"Long gone, and no mistake. Ha. Ha."

"Why didn't she tell me of her condition?"

"What good would that've done? She's of a different race. She knew you would never marry her, so she just stepped out of your life and closed the door behind her. It's better that way."

Lonnie jammed his hat tightly onto his head and lurched away, completely ignoring the madam's hurried statement that there were plenty of girls available who could take care of his needs. Bernice had affected him in a way no other girl ever had. She was of mixed blood. A quadroon, but she was also a wonderful woman. Every inch of her. With mixed emotions and bursting heart, Lonnie drove away. He never went back to the house on Chancy Street again.

Chapter 10

The Girl of the Roller Rink

Time and hard work healed Lonnie's aching heart after the loss of Bernice Jackson. For a while, he thought of never becoming emotionally involved with the opposite sex again, but the great healer eventually dulled fond memories, and since his blood ran hot, there came a day where the images of his lost loves were fragmented shadows in his mind, and he found himself looking forward to possessing some lovely girl's beautiful body. In order to mix freely with young men and women every weekend, he took up roller-skating. It was becoming a fad. After Lonnie joined a group of skaters, the instructor informed them that they could dance on roller skates.

In the weeks that followed, Lonnie had some nasty spills on the floor of the roller rink. Innumerable bumps and bruises followed, but practice makes perfect, and his awkwardness on the skates soon left him. He could whirl and glide across the polished floor of the skating rink as lightly as a bird on the wing.

As Lonnie's skating improved, so did his popularity with the girls. Never a week went by but he had his pick of a dozen young lovelies to take to the Saturday night dance. Sometimes he went stag. By the time the evening's dance and skating broke up, he had himself a girl to take home. He began to notice a very beautiful young woman who came to the rink with a girlfriend almost every Saturday night. Very seldom was she accompanied by a boy.

She had a beautifully proportioned body and was an accomplished skater and dancer. Often, as she flashed by Lonnie and his date for the evening, her luxurious raven hair waving and tumbling about her shoulders, she gave him a look challenging him to…something. Then she would toss him a sparkling smile.

Before long, Lonnie began speculating on the best way to meet her. He appealed to the instructors for an introduction, but none of them knew her. He pointed her out to several of the girls he brought to the rink, but by chance or choice, none of them knew her. At last, in desperation, he approached her one evening.

"Hello, there," Lonnie said, sinking down on the bench beside her as she adjusted her skates. "My name is Lonnie Dolan. Would you do me the honor of dancing the midnight waltz with me tonight?"

"What?" She smiled up at him, her lovely face dimpled and flushed. "No girlfriend this evening?"

"Nary a one," he said with a grin.

"Why not, big boy? Are you slipping?"

"I don't know as I am. Tonight I purposely came stag. I hadn't asked any girl to dance or skate with me, until you."

"I am honored, Lonnie," she laughed.

"Then how about the waltz tonight?" he asked, intrigued more and more by her sensuous way of talking and looking at him.

"I think that can be arranged," she said, softly patting her hair into place and adjusting her snug sweater and skirt. The garments fit her as though she had been poured into them, and she wore them beautifully. They showed off her full breasts, slender waist, rounded hips, and symmetrical legs advantageously.

"Why don't we skate together once or twice before the midnight waltz begins?" Lonnie suggested. "That way, we'll know whether or not we skate well together. What do you say?"

"I'd love to." She smiled, looking up at him and holding out her hands. "Shall we give it a try? The floor is almost empty. We'll have it all to ourselves."

"Good," Lonnie chuckled, taking her by the hands and leading her out to the polished floor.

As they whirled and sped around the rink, Lonnie realized he had never held a more accomplished skater in his arms. Her every movement, as she kept step with him in time to the music, was a thing of symmetry.

"Gee, that was fun," she bubbled as they skated up to the bench. "Let's sit and rest a while."

"Anything you say," Lonnie agreed, sinking down beside her. "What did you say your name was when I introduced myself to you? I didn't catch it."

"How thoughtless of me," she giggled. "Please overlook my idiotic manners. My name is Nina, Nina McKnight."

"I'm very happy to make your acquaintance, Nina," Lonnie said, clasping the hand she held out to him. "I've wanted to meet you since the first night I saw you skate by with your girlfriend."

"You want to know something?" she asked.

"What's that?" he asked, giving her hand a squeeze as he released it.

"I've wanted to meet you for a long time, too."

"Well, I'll be dog-gone," he said, smiling into her lovely eyes. "Why didn't we try to get acquainted sooner?"

"Better late than never. I guess it was just one of those things."

"Where's your girlfriend tonight? I haven't seen her all evening."

"She has a heavy date and couldn't come with me."

"Anybody with you this evening?" Lonnie inquired, hoping she had come alone.

"No," she grinned, dimples decorating her beautiful face. "I also came stag."

"Gosh, I'm glad. Perhaps I could take you home after the midnight waltz."

"I think that could be arranged, Lonnie. Have you a car?"

"A puddle jumper," he laughed.

"Will it run okay?"

"Like a song, uphill and down."

"That's all the best of the cars can do," she said. "Big flashy cars might be all the rage for some girls, but I look more at what's behind the wheel of the car I ride in than the car itself. After all, that's more important in the long run. At least, I think so."

"You're my kind of girl," Lonnie said happily, as he hooked his arm in hers and led her toward the refreshment stand. "Let's fuel up. It's close to midnight. We can dance better if we have something to eat and drink first."

That midnight waltz was the most enjoyable one he had danced since he learned to roller skate. The music was especially soft and sweet, and Nina melted into his arms and seemed to become part of him, so beautifully did they dance together. While they whirled and swayed to the music in an especially dark corner of the rink, he bent his lips to one of her ears.

"You're wonderful," he whispered, tightening his arms around her.

"Thank you," she whispered in return, snuggling even closer. "You're not so bad yourself, big boy."

Later that night, when Lonnie drove her home, she sat very close to him in his old, rattletrap car. He bade her goodnight at her married brother's home, where she was staying, and she surrendered her lips to him in a long goodnight kiss. Her lips were soft and sweet as a baby's cheek, only much warmer and demanding in their need for masculine attention. Lonnie drove away with her promise to see him at the rink again the following week ringing in his ears.

During the weeks that followed, Lonnie met Nina at the skating rink many times. In the middle of the week, when he had to work the following day, they would skate until a reasonable hour then he would drive her home. She always kissed him good night, her beautiful body molded to his as tightly as she could press it, her arms wrapped around his neck.

Nina became more passionate and demanding when she was in his arms. Soon, every time he kissed her, she insisted it be in the French style. As he claimed her lips with his, and thrust his tongue deeply into her mouth, she groaned ecstatically, closed her eyes, clutched him to her wildly, and writhed all over the car seat. Then, when he released her lips, she gave a great gasping sigh, her breath coming ragged and hot, and fairly collapsed in his arms.

One Friday evening, she asked to leave the roller rink earlier than usual. "It's about time you met some of my family, Lonnie, baby," she said as they drove toward her brother's home. "My brother Jim and his wife, Ethyl, want to meet you. I've told them a lot about you, and today I promised I'd bring you in for a while when you drove me home this evening. Anyway, it'll be a lot cozier for us on their living room couch than it is outside in this old car of yours."

"So now you're knocking my car," Lonnie growled in mock anger, giving her a one-armed bear hug.

"No, I'm not, sweetheart," she giggled, grabbing his free hand and biting his fingers playfully. "You know I like your car. It's only that it's so cold outside now. Why should we freeze our fannies off while we're kissing good night when we could have Jim and Ethyl's living room couch all to ourselves? It doesn't make sense."

"I agree with you wholeheartedly," Lonnie chuckled, leaning over and kissing the top of her head. "I hope your folks like me."

"They will. If they don't, I'll just tell them to go pound salt. You know where I mean."

"What about your mother and father? Have you told them about me?"

"My parents are dead," she said sadly.

"Oh, I'm sorry, Nina," Lonnie said. "And you're so young, too. I don't want to sound nosey, but how did you lose your parents at such a young age?"

"There's nothing much to tell, really. It happened two years ago, about now. They were killed in an automobile accident. We lived out in the country. Dad worked for a large power company. His regular day off from work was Wednesday. I left for school that morning, and Dad and Mother intended to drive into town here for some shopping. A huge trailer truck forced them off the road. They were killed instantly. Later, the truck company said the brakes on the truck had failed and the driver had lost control of it. Jim and I collected some insurance from them, but not half enough, considering our loss."

"And since then you've made your home with your brother and his wife."

"That's right. Jim and Ethyl treat me well. Someday, though, I hope to have my own home."

"I'm sure you will," Lonnie said, his heart going out to her.

"Well, here we are," Nina said brightly, as Lonnie drove up to her house and cut his motor. "Come right on in. They're expecting us."

She dashed out of the car, pulling him after her. In a moment, they were inside the bungalow, and Nina was making the introductions.

"Jim and Sis, this is Lonnie," she said, leading him proudly into the living room. "Lonnie, this is my brother Jim and his wife Ethyl."

Lonnie shook hands with a dark-haired, well set-up young man of medium height and a curvaceous blond. She was beautiful in a baby-faced way, with big, innocent blue eyes.

"I'm right proud to make your acquaintance, Lonnie," Jim McKnight said, wringing Lonnie's hand in a vice grip. "My little sister has told us a lot about you."

"I hope it has not been all bad," Lonnie replied, flexing his fingers to bring the circulation back.

"Oh, nothing like that. You rate higher with her than any boyfriend she's had so far. I take that as a good sign."

"Welcome to our home," Ethyl McKnight said softly, giving him a hand that was soft and smooth, but strong, like steel covered with velvet.

"Thank you, Mrs. McKnight. I've looked forward to meeting you folks."

"It's our pleasure, Lonnie," she smiled, her white even teeth and full red lips drawing his gaze like magnets. "Make yourself comfortable. Jim, entertain our guest while Nina and I go out to the kitchen and prepare some refreshments."

"Please, don't put yourself out on my account," Lonnie hastened to say, covertly watching Ethyl McKnight's walk as she turned on her high heels and tripped lightly toward the kitchen. "I can't stay too long. I've got to work half a day tomorrow. Ordinarily, I don't work on Saturday, but they asked me to come in for four hours in the morning. I'd hate to stand them up."

"Nonsense," Jim McKnight laughed, waving Lonnie into a chair. "We refuse to let you rush away. You're young and full of vinegar, yet. The loss of a couple of hours sleep won't kill you, and anyway, I'm positive my little sister has oodles of things she wants to talk about, right, Sis?"

"I certainly do," Nina giggled happily. "So I'd appreciate it if you and Ethyl would retire early or go out to a late movie, or something. Lonnie and I would like an hour or so of privacy before he has to leave."

"Don't fret, Sis," Ethyl McKnight laughed, boldly giving Lonnie a knowing wink. "Jim and I will hit the hay within the hour. You and Lonnie will have plenty of time to talk or what have you before he kisses you good night."

After the sandwiches and coffee were served, an hour of conversation ensued. Then Jim and Ethyl calmly announced they were retiring for the night. As they disappeared into their bedroom off the living room and closed the drapes that served as a door, they insisted Lonnie stay as long as he wished and cordially invited him to come again, anytime.

"Be good to this boy, Nina," Ethyl whispered loudly, pausing in the entrance of her bedroom and smiling at Lonnie, "but don't do anything I wouldn't do. Nighty-night."

Ethyl had scarcely disappeared through the drapes when Nina plopped herself on Lonnie's lap. "Kiss me," she breathed against his lips. "Please, kiss me. You know the way I want it. I was beginning to think Jim and Ethyl would never go to bed."

Lonnie threw discretion to the wind and kissed her with wild abandon. She reciprocated unreservedly. A rhythmic squeaking began in the bedroom where Nina's brother and his wife had gone. One end of the couch upon which Lonnie and Nina sat jutted up to the draped doorway. Soon Lonnie heard hoarse breathing from behind the drapes.

He clutched Nina tightly to him, gave her another sizzling French kiss, and whispered, "Hear that? Sounds like your brother and his wife are having themselves a ball."

"I knew that would happen by the way Ethyl kept looking at you this evening. She likes you, and she gets hot panties every time I bring home a boy she likes the looks of."

"It sounds like your brother is taking care of them hot panties of hers," Lonnie chuckled, grinning broadly.

"I can't stand this," Nina whispered as the squeaking from the bedroom increased in tempo and soft sighing scream sounded. Then all was quiet. "Excuse me a moment, darling. I'll be right back."

She turned out the lights in the living room until only one small floor lamp remained on. It cast a soft, shadowy glow over the room and left the couch in shadow. Pausing a moment at the bathroom door, Nina turned, blew Lonnie a red-lipped kiss, and flashed him a dazzling smile.

"Don't go away," she breathed. "Close your eyes, and I'll be right out with a surprise for you."

Lonnie leaned back against the couch, closed his eyes, and wondered what the surprise would be, but more than anything else, his mind was on Jim McKnight's wife. Ethyl McKnight impressed him as a sexpot of the highest degree. Her way of talking, walking, acting, and using her eyes, together with the way she showed off her beautifully developed figure, proclaimed this fact as though she had shouted it from the housetops. Ethyl also impressed Lonnie as possessive, passionate, and hot-blooded. "I'd bet a week's wages that that blond bitch would put out if given half a chance," Lonnie thought as he leaned back against the couch with his eyes closed. "I wonder if she ever cheats on Jim? She certainly looks the type. Hotter than a fire cracker between those pretty legs of hers; that's what she is, and no mistake."

"Oh, Lonnie, baby," said a honeysweet voice.

He looked and nearly fell off the couch. Nina stood in the doorway of the bathroom, silhouetted against the bright light within, and she was completely naked.

She flung her nude body into Lonnie's arms. In the twinkling of an eye, her hot, feverish lips found his. She grabbed hold of his hands and cupped them over her luscious breasts.

"Nina," Lonnie gasped. "What in the world do you think you're doing?"

"Getting set to have some fun," she giggled against his lips. "Take off your pants."

"What?"

"We'll have more freedom of movement with your pants off, and you won't get them smeared up any, either."

"What about your brother and his wife?" Lonnie asked frantically. "Suppose one of them gets up to go to the bathroom? Your brother would beat me to death if he caught us in here naked, and I couldn't blame him, either."

"Shh," she breathed seductively against his lips, putting one of his hands between her lovely legs. "Never mind them. They're in for the night. What else could you expect? After that hot piece Ethyl gave him, he's dead to the world. Come on, Lonnie, honey. Take off your pants. Ethyl and Jim had their fun. Let's have ours."

With his heart in his throat, Lonnie partially disrobed and made all-out love to Nina on the couch within ten of where her brother and his wife lay sleeping. Nina seemed insatiable. Once, twice, thrice, Lonnie brought her to climax, but still she wanted more. For the next two hours, he concentrated on conserving his energies and bringing satisfaction to Nina. He found that by centering his activities on her clitoris, he could bring her to climax without himself discharging. At last, with a gasping, panting sigh, Nina pulled his head down, kissed him with lips that were dewy with love, and whispered that she had had enough sexual relations for one evening.

"Gee, but that was heavenly," she said ecstatically, cradling Lonnie's head against her full breasts. "We must do it again soon. Did you enjoy it, darling?"

"I sure did," Lonnie assured her, kissing and nibbling at her breasts. "You're quite a girl, Nina. Quite a girl. You're pretty as a picture, with a knockout figure, and I honestly believe you've a furnace down there between your lovely legs. You're better than a two-dollar pistol, sweetheart, and I love every ounce of you."

"I love you, too," she whispered possessively, lifting his head from her luscious breasts, and claiming his lips in a kiss that left him gasping for air. "You're mine now, and I don't like the way that hot-assed bitch Ethyl kept ogling you this evening. Promise me you won't have anything to do with her, darling, no matter what she tries."

"I promise," Lonnie said, his blood racing at the thought that Ethyl McKnight desired him. "Ethyl is sure beautiful," he ventured, wondering what it was about her sexy sister-in-law that Nina didn't approve of. "Are you and she peeved at each other about something?"

"Her way of throwing her ass around every time I bring a boyfriend home has got me pissed off."

"Ethyl makes plays for your boyfriends?"

"She does and she don't, if you know what I mean. Jim says she is only being a good hostess, but I think it goes deeper than that."

"Do you think Ethyl cheats on Jim?" Lonnie whispered as he pulled on his trousers and rearranged his shirt and tie.

"I don't know," Nina said, getting up from the couch and stretching easily and deliciously, like a beautiful feline, "but I sure wouldn't put it past her. She's unpredictable. Sometimes Ethyl acts so good, pure, and true that sugar would have a hard time melting in her mouth. Other times, she's vulgar, like a girl in a whorehouse. Take a tip from me, sweetheart. Keep clear of her. From the way she looked at you this evening, I think she has designs on you. Remember, you promised."

"Scouts' honor," Lonnie said easily, his tongue in his cheek. He had learned through bitter experience that a woman gives her word of honor easily, and breaks it just as easily. He had long since adopted the same policy.

"I've got to go, Nina, baby," he said, pulling on his top coat. "It's after midnight, and five-thirty comes awful early."

"Nighty-night," she whispered seductively, slipping inside his topcoat with him and molding her beautiful body to his. "Kiss me quickly, the way I like. Go straight to your boarding house from here, and be extra careful on the street. Don't have any wet dreams unless you're dreaming about me. You're mine now, you know."

Wrapping her snugly in his arms, Lonnie tasted the sweet fire of her lips and mouth, and she acted as though she was trying to drink him down.

"I love you with every ounce of me," she breathed as she let him out the door. "See you tomorrow night at the roller rink."

It became a weekly habit for Lonnie to spend one night a week with Nina at her brother's home. Every time he went there, Ethyl let him know that she knew what he and Nina were doing after she and Jim retired for the night. After his third visit, she got into the habit of putting a hand on his arms or shoulders every time she had an occasion to speak to him.

If a joke was told, and she was within reasonable distance, she laughed freely and sometimes put her arms around him. She didn't seem to mind where her hands touched him, either, and she completely ignored the dagger looks Nina threw her way and the strained look on Jim's face. Every night he was there, Jim and Ethyl's bed fairly danced a jig after they said goodnight to him and Nina and disappeared behind the drapes of their bedroom.

"That dirty, hot-assed slut," Nina fumed as she lay in Lonnie's arms and he made love to her. "She's trying to get you between them wicked legs of hers. I know it. I've got that bitch figured. She might not think so, but I have."

"Forget Ethyl, my love," Lonnie would say to her reassuringly. "She's a married woman and means nothing to me. I think she's only teasing. If she wasn't, Jim would've ordered me away from here long ago. Surely you know that."

"Teasing my fanny," Nina always scoffed. "She might pull the wool over yours and Jim's eyes, but I'm not so easily fooled. Mark my words, Lonnie, boy, she's on the make for you. Remember your promise."

"Oh, sure," was Lonnie's reply every time Nina reminded him of his promise, and his tongue was in his cheek every time he gave his word to her.

On Wednesday before noon, the machine he ran at the handle factory broke down, and the foreman told Lonnie to ring his clock card out at noon and go home for the rest of the day.

"I'll phone Nina," he said on his way out of the shop. "Perhaps we can take in a movie this afternoon."

He hurried into a drug store, slipped into a phone booth, and dialed Nina's brother's phone number. The phone rang twice, and then Lonnie heard the receiver lifted off the hook. A woman's voice said, "Hello."

"Nina?" Lonnie asked.

"No, this is Ethyl. Who's calling?"

"Lonnie. May I speak to Nina?"

"Oh, hello, Lonnie." Ethyl's voice took on a more intimate note. "So nice of you to call. Nina isn't home now. Can I give her a message?"

"It's nothing special, Ethyl. I'm off from work this afternoon, and I thought she and I could get together and do something, like go to a movie. Do you think she would be interested?"

"She'd love it, I'm sure. Look, Lonnie, why don't you get cleaned up and come over right away? Jim just phoned that he'd be home in an hour. Before he left for work this morning, he said there was something he wanted to talk to you about."

"Did he say what it was?"

"No, he didn't, but he seemed plenty excited about it, whatever it was. I think it has to do with a deal he expects to make a lot of money by. Be a good boy and come on over within an hour. That way, you and Jim could have your talk by the time Nina gets home. I'm planning an early supper. After you and Nina eat, you'll still have time to take in a double feature. Okay?"

"That sounds fine, Ethyl, but I don't want to impose on your hospitality."

"Nonsense. Think nothing of it. The pleasure will be all ours. Jim will be awfully disappointed if you don't come."

"I'll be right over as soon as I shower and shave. See you soon."

"Bye, now," she said.

In less than an hour, Lonnie rang Jim McKnight's doorbell. At the second ring, he heard footsteps inside, and Ethyl McKnight opened the door.

"Hi, there, Lonnie," she said softly. "Come in. Jim's expecting you." She was a picture of loveliness as she ushered him into the living room and took his hat and topcoat. Her abundant hair was piled high on her head like a golden crown. She wore high-heeled pumps and a dress. An intoxicating aroma of expensive perfume lingered about her.

"Jim here yet?" Lonnie asked casually as he sat on the couch.

Instead of answering, Ethyl McKnight walked over to where he sat and plunked herself on his lap. Her full red lips claimed his, sending a tingling sensation clear down to his toes.

"Ethyl, for heaven sake," Lonnie spluttered, flabbergasted. "Are you out of your mind? Suppose Jim or Nina was to walk in just now? What would they say and think?"

"But they aren't going to walk in just now, lover boy," she whispered against his lips, while the tip of her tongue flicked in and out of his mouth like a serpent's.

"How can you be so sure?" he gasped, overcome by the intensity of her advances. "You told me on the phone Jim would be home within an hour. According to that, he's due any minute. I better go. My face would be a dead give-away if he was to walk in. I couldn't face him if my life depended on it."

"Silly boy," she laughed, a gay trilling sound. "Sure, I told you that, but I only did it to get you over here so we could be alone together."

"Level with me. You've got me here, and we're alone. Now tell me the reason for this skullduggery."

"I've wanted you to make love to me from the first evening Nina brought you here."

"But you're a married woman. Jim's a nice fellow. He looks healthy enough to give you all the loving you need."

"Horse manure," she spat. "Sure, my husband's a nice fellow, and I know it. He's plenty sexy, too. But that doesn't alter the fact that I want you to screw me. A woman gets mighty tired of having the same old joy-prong between her legs year after year. At least, that's the way it is with me."

"Tell me the truth about Jim and Nina. Are they due home soon?"

"No. They drove to Huntington this morning. Jim phoned just before you called this afternoon. He said he and Nina wouldn't be home until bedtime. So stop worrying and fidgeting. We've the whole afternoon to ourselves. We can make it very interesting, if we try."

"Look, Ethyl," Lonnie said. "Jim's my friend, and you're his wife. I wouldn't feel right coming in here and seducing you in his home. I've got my principals, too, even if you doubt it."

"Isn't it a little late for your conscience to be bothering you?"

"What do you mean?" Lonnie asked weakly, putting his arms around her seductive body, in spite of himself.

She smiled knowingly. "Every time you came here to court Nina and screw her on this very couch, I've paid close attention to the way you've looked at me. What do you think I've seen, Lonnie?"

"What, Ethyl? What did you see?"

"Desire for my body. That's what I saw. It showed as plainly as though you had printed it on a slab of wood and hung it around your neck. You've wanted to possess my body all this long while. Why are you so squeamish, now that I've laid the opportunity right in your lap? Are you a red-blooded man, Lonnie Dolan, or are you nothing but a two-legged make-believe?"

"Ethyl, it don't seem right for this to happen between us."

"Hush your mouth, you silly boy, while I show you something. Then deny me, if you can."

With a graceful, flowing movement, she disengaged herself and stood before him. A beautiful smile curved the cupid bow of her ripe red lips, and she licked them with the pink tip of her tongue, making them wet, dewy, and oh, so inviting. Her lovely hands busied themselves with the fastener that held her wrap-around dress in place. It resisted her grasping fingers, but not for long. With a swishing sound, she whipped it from around her and dropped it to the rug at her feet. Her half-slip went next, very slowly, giving Lonnie time to feast his eyes as she pushed it down over her beautifully rounded hips and thighs.

"I need your love, Lonnie, baby," she whispered, her hands going to the clasp between her breasts that held her brassiere in place.

Lonnie waited expectantly while she took off her brassiere. And when it was gone, and she stood straight and slender before him, he was not disappointed. The luscious hemispheres of her breasts with their pink nipples quivered invitingly, and when she stretched her arms above her head and began unpinning her golden wealth of hair, Lonnie could scarcely contain his desire to crush her to him and bury his face against the soft, sweet, wonderfulness of her beckoning breasts.

"Soon we'll be in each other's arms, Lonnie, darling," she purred, smiling as her magnificent hair tumbled over her shoulders in a golden tide.

She wore only her panties now, and she hooked her thumbs behind the elastic top and pulled them down. She was a natural blonde. She stepped out of her silk panties delicately and daintily, as though stepping out of a bathtub. She bent her legs at the knees, and began to sway in a seductive dance. In a trance, Lonnie watched her, powerless to resist her, and she knew it.

She stretched out her shapely arms and walked toward him, lightly running her tongue over her lips. The smell of her luscious body was like an exhilarating perfume. She sighed softly while her breasts quivered then leaned forward and kissed him, her lips as soft as rose petals.

"Stand up, darling," she urged, her arms going around his neck. "Stand up and take me in your arms."

Lonnie came off the couch like a tiger. He swept her into his arms and loosed an avalanche of pent-up hunger and desire. Ruthlessly, he kissed and fondled her until she squealed with delight.

"I want all your love, darling," she panted, looking at him through half-closed eyes, "but how can you give it to me with so many clothes on?"

She thrust a hand below his belt buckle, unzipped his trousers, and reached inside. That did it. Scarcely conscious of his actions, Lonnie slipped out of his clothes, except his shoes and socks. He picked Ethyl up and sank down on the couch, never relaxing his hold on her. Moments later, her voice broke in a gasping, passion-laden entreaty.

"Oh, darling, darling, you're killing me. Oh, no. No. Don't stop. I'm in heaven. That's where I am. Please, oh, please, if you keep doing this wonderful thing to me, I'll go completely out of my mind, but if you stop for just the littlest while, I know I'll die dead. I can't stand it any longer. Something is going to happen. Oh, I'm going to— I'm about to— I'm com—Ahhhh."

An hour later, Lonnie took his leave of Ethyl McKnight. She escorted him to the front door and insisted he taste the sweet fire of her lips again before she let him go.

"You're my kind of man, sweetheart," she cooed, pressing her full breasts against his chest.

"When will we see each other again and do what we just did?" she asked, kissing him possessively and nibbling at his lower lip.

"Look, Ethyl. Suppose we let this episode today wrap it up?"

"But why? Darling, you can't mean what you're saying. We just got together. I believe I'd actually shrivel up and die if I thought I was never going to experience your love again."

"What about Jim and Nina?"

"What about them? It's none of their business what we do. You could still come here with Nina, as though nothing had ever happened between us. When the opportunity presents itself again, we could have a moment together. It'll be hell for me to watch Nina lovey-doveying over you, but I'll make up for it when our time comes."

"A thing like that can be dangerous," Lonnie stammered, beginning to feel trapped. "As it is, I'll feel like seven kinds of heel around Jim and Nina. That sort of double-dealing is mighty hard to carry off successfully, Ethyl. All it takes is one word or look at the wrong time, and in the wrong way, and everything comes crashing down. Then there's hell to pay. Can't you see how impossible the situation would become? We'd be caught like two rats in a trap."

"But we can do it, lover of mine," she said confidently, unlocking the front door and stepping behind it to hide her nakedness from anyone passing on the sidewalk outside. "Go now, baby. I'll be counting the minutes until we're in each other's arms again. I love you, need you, and want you. Good-bye."

In the weeks that followed, Lonnie felt the tension in the air every time he was with Nina at her brother's home. Ethyl carried her part of the farce off extremely well, all things considered. Nevertheless, there were times he felt her eyes fairly burning holes in him. When she began slipping notes in his pockets, urging him to phone her from the shop where he worked, he realized the situation was getting out of hand. The thought of Nina in his arms was working on Ethyl's mind like a drug, and she began to show signs of cracking.

One night, about a month after he made love to her, Ethyl became so upset that she came to the boarding house where Lonnie lodged. His heart in his throat, he hurried her out, but she refused to let him drive her home until after he had parked in a secluded spot and been intimate with her.

"Why have you avoided me, darling?" she asked, her voice bordering on hysteria. "Don't you know it's driving me mad to watch Nina kiss you every time you come to my home to see her? Isn't there some way we could get together at least once a week?"

"Honestly, I don't see how we could manage it. Pull yourself together, Ethyl. We're sitting on a power keg. What we're doing is dynamite, and I don't mean maybe. Suppose Jim followed you tonight. If he did, we could be looking down a gun barrel any minute. I believe he's beginning to suspect something between us. He gave me a funny look the other evening. He's been putting two and two together. When he comes up with the right answer, look out."

"I know it's dangerous," she sniffed, cuddling close to him in his old car and laying her head on his shoulder. "The way I feel about you, I don't care how dangerous the situation is. I belong in your arms, not that damn pissy-assed bitch Nina."

"You're a married woman, Ethyl. Get that fact through your head. We've no business horsing around like this. It's time you woke up and faced the facts of life before something bad happens. Forget about me and shower your love on your husband. It's far safer that way."

"I don't love Jim McKnight," she hissed. "I realize now that I never did. You're the one I love. We belong together."

"Stop talking that kind of nonsense. Get your panties back on and your clothes in order. I'm driving you home. Don't forget to button your blouse. If you go dragging in looking like this, Jim will swear that some man raped you."

Lonnie found the courage to carry on from day to day. He expected his world to come crashing down upon his head at any moment. Ethyl McKnight was turning his life into a nightmare with her constant hounding. Nina, also, made demands that he found increasingly difficult to fulfill. Every time they had sexual relations, Nina reminded him that it would be nice to marry her, should she become pregnant as the result of their intimacies.

"Lonnie, baby," she pointed out to him, smiling prettily, "the least we could do would be to get married of our own free will, should anything come of all this pun-jabbin we've been doing. I'd hate awfully to have my brother step into our affairs and come up with a shotgun wedding. He's like that, though. He'd do it in a minute if he thought I was in the family way and in danger of being left in a lurch. I guess I'm glad my brother is like he is. Having a baby out of wedlock is the last thing I want happening."

Considering the precarious position he was in, Lonnie decided it was high time for him to leave Charleston, as quickly and quietly as possible. If he chose to remain and pay court to Nina, one of two things was bound to happen. Either he would get Nina pregnant and be forced to marry her, or Ethyl would blurt out the sordid story of their illicit love affair in a moment of hysteria. Either way, Lonnie knew he was skating on very thin ice.

The following Friday morning, a telegram was delivered to him at the boarding house where he lodged. His stepfather was very ill, the telegram said, and his mother begged him to come home as quickly as he could. The next day, Lonnie collected all the wages due to him at the handle factory and turned in his badge. That evening, he boarded a train going east. As the train rolled away from the station, he heaved a great sigh of relief. His dealings with Nina and Ethyl were over, and he knew he would never return to them.

Nina and Ethyl were the type of women who would soon transfer their affections and desires to another man. Whoever that man might be, Lonnie sincerely pitied him.

Chapter 11

The Divorcee

Upon arriving home, Lonnie learned that his stepfather had suffered a paralytic stroke. He had not seen his mother in more than a year and was appalled at the change time had wrought in her appearance. He took her in his arms and kissed her faded cheeks, and the lines in her face and the silver in her hair told him plainer than words that his mother was no longer a young woman. She was fast approaching the evening of her life, and it saddened him.

She had always been so hale and hearty, so full of the joy of living and doing things, but now, as she moved about the familiar kitchen, preparing him something to eat, her shoulders drooped, and her steps dragged.

"It's so good to have you home again, son," she said in a tremulous voice as she brushed a tear from her eyes and hovered over him like a mother hen guarding her brood.

"How is John, anyway?" Lonnie asked sympathetically. "Does the doctor say he's in serious condition?"

"Your stepfather isn't a bit good, Lonnie," his mother said sadly. "The doctor tries to tell me he'll be all right, but I know different. He's getting weaker and more helpless every day."

"Does he know everything and everybody?"

"Lordy, no. He's been this way more than a week now, and there's times he's positively looney. I sure need you here now, son. Once he fell out of the bed, and I had to phone one of the neighbors to help me get him back in again. It was awful. While he was on the floor, his bowels moved, with us wallowing around, trying to get him back in bed. He smeared himself up like he'd been rolling in a pigpen. You've got to help me take care of him, son. He's so heavy, he's got me all tuckered out."

"Relax, Mother, and let me take over," Lonnie said. "I'm young and strong. I'll stay with you and take care of John as long as you need my help. I want to go into the bedroom and see him. Maybe he'll recognize me. Then I want you to lie down and take a nap. If you keep driving yourself, you'll soon be in bed, too."

"I'll do whatever you say, Lonnie," his mother said wearily, leading the way into the bedroom.

John McVay mumbled incoherently and his eyes rolled wildly as Lonnie bent over him. His right hand clutched convulsively at the bedclothes, but his left hand was a leaden weight. It appeared swollen and discolored.

"The stroke paralyzed his left side," Lonnie's mother whispered as she straightened the quilts covering her stricken husband. "He's out of his head again. He don't know you. John was sorry you and him couldn't hit it off. After you went away last year, he realized he'd made a mistake. He wanted you to come back, Lonnie, only being a grown man and set in his ways, he couldn't break his pride and write you how he felt. You've got to forgive him, son. If anything bad was to happen now, I'd—."

"Hush, Mother," Lonnie soothed as he led her from the bedroom. "I hold no ill will against him. It was best I leave as I did. When a man marries a woman, he wants and needs privacy with her for a while. I wouldn't want a grown stepson underfoot all the time if I was to marry his mother."

"You're a good boy, and I'm so relieved to know you understand. Most children don't, you know."

"Well, I do," Lonnie chuckled. "When I marry, I want to be able to take my bride to bed in the middle of the day or anytime the urge strikes me. It's better that way. Right, Mother?"

"Oh, Lonnie, how you talk," his mother cried, while her faded features blushed rosy red.

"But it's the truth, isn't it?"

"Son, in that respect, you're wise beyond your years. I take it as a good sign. One of these days, I hope to see you make some good girl a good husband. Have you ever thought seriously of marrying?"

"Once or twice."

"Why didn't you?"

"Aw, Mother, reckon it's one of them things that's hard to explain and harder for someone else to understand."

"I'm your mother, Lonnie. You can open your heart to me. Since you've been gone from home, has some girl caused your heart to ache?"

"It's a long story," Lonnie grunted, "and one I'm ashamed to admit, even to myself. You've enough troubles of your own without being burdened with my sob story. Anyway, Mom, you'd think me a fool."

"Tell me, son," the good woman pleaded. "None of us are perfect. We all make mistakes. If you've done something you're ashamed of, I'll understand."

"All I did was fall in love with a girl who almost played me for a prize sucker."

"I'm listening, Lonnie."

"Sally Smith and me hit it off wonderful, right from the start. She was everything I'd ever wanted in a girl. I loved Sally so much I couldn't keep my hands off her, no matter how hard I tried. I meant no disrespect by my actions, and she never took offense. All she asked was that we wait till we were man and wife before giving ourselves to each other. You understand, don't you, Mother?"

"Perfectly, son, go on."

"Well, Sally and me got so serious about each other that I set the date for when I was going to ask her to be my wife. She claimed she done entertaining work, but always insisted I couldn't come to her place of employment and watch her work because it was an exclusive club and only members and their close friends were permitted. What a fool I was."

"What happened, Lonnie, boy?" Mrs. McVay prompted, concern replacing the weariness on her face. "I'm old and bent and don't have too many winters and summers left. Let me share this with you. You'll feel better when you unburden yourself. Try it and see. I know. I ain't lived all these hard years for nothing."

"All right, I'll tell it all," Lonnie whispered hoarsely, reaching across the kitchen table and taking his mother's timeworn hands in his. "The week I was going to ask Sally to be my wife, some of the fellows at the handle factory where I worked told me of a cat house on one of the back streets. After they'd razzed me for several hours about my coming engagement, I finally promised I'd give this place a whirl. You know how men are. It was to be a last fling before promising myself to Sally. I'll never forget that night."

"Tell it, son. Please, tell it."

"The only way I could get in this place was by a password. The men at the shop had tipped me off, so I got in, easy as pie. The woman running the place brought the girls out one by one. She kept telling me about a girl Sally who worked there. She claimed Sally was the hottest draw they had. I decided to wait for Sally. I was looking at a magazine when she came into the waiting room. When I looked up, I thought my eyes was playing tricks on me. The girl I was going to ask to be my wife that weekend stood before me. My Sally was a whore, Mom. What in the hell is wrong with girls now-days? Why can't they be honest?"

"Lots of girls are that way, Lonnie, boy," Ms. McVay said, squeezing her son's hands. "It's not only women, though. Some men lie faster than a horse can run. Look at it this way. You found out what Sally was before you married her. It could have been worse."

"I don't think I'll ever trust another girl again as long as I live. Now all I mess with them is to get what they can give me. Do you blame me?"

"What can I say?" she sighed. "The best advice I can give you is to let time heal your heart, and don't pity yourself. One of these days, you'll meet a wonderful girl who'll make you wonder what you ever saw in any other."

"I doubt that," Lonnie said bitterly. "In the meantime, what am I supposed to do? Keep looking for that special girl?"

"No, son. Relax and trust in the good Lord to see you through. When the time comes for you to get married, the right girl will come into your life. It always works out that way."

"Okay, Mother." Lonnie smiled grimly. "I'll try your advice, but enough of my troubles. Tell me some local news. Has John been doing all right with the farm?"

"Yes, he has. It's why he's where he is right now. That poor man worked like a horse. I told him to take it easy, but he wouldn't."

"What about the Hamricks? Do they still live on that ten acres up the road?"

"No, they don't. They sold out about six months ago to a divorced woman with a little boy."

"Oh?"

"Folks around here say she's a bottle blonde and always on the make around the men."

"What kind of a looker is she?"

"I can't tell you, but some say she's pretty. Others swear she is brassy and hard, and as ugly as homemade sin."

"Did you ever see her?"

"Only once, but she was wearing sunglasses and had a scarf tied over her hair. She came down to tell us that some of our cattle had broken through the fences and were up there around her house. She didn't come in. Just stood out in the front yard while she talked with me. From what I could see of her, I'd say she's young and has a nice figure."

"Good," Lonnie chuckled. "Perhaps I should cultivate the lady's acquaintance. We might find we have plenty in common. Who knows?"

"Go easy with Verna Monroe," his mother cautioned. "From what I hear, she's on the look for a man who can make love to her morning, noon, and night. Imagine that. That kind of woman is more dangerous than a coiled rattler. A snake is a snake and treated accordingly, but to this little lady, the snakes have to take a back seat. You'll do well to steer clear of her."

"I can take care of myself. Don't you worry. I've had experience with the fair sex."

"Don't be over-confident. Now, Lonnie, you listen to me. I'm your mother, and it's my duty to keep you out of trouble. I've been told Verna Monroe has convulsions in bed at night, just thinking of all the loving she's missing. You'd be out of your mind to become involved with a woman like her. She'd cheat on you and lie to you, and do everything to make your life miserable. I've seen her kind before."

"It's been done before," Lonnie growled.

"Yes, but not like she'd fix you up. This woman works in the bank in Valley Head. She always has men on the string. Married and single alike."

"So?"

"Can't you see what she'd do if you took up with her and she became pregnant? No doubt, she would give herself to you, but when trouble came, she'd forget all about them other men she'd went to bed with while you was seeing her. She'd nail you as the father of her baby, no matter what, and Lonnie, you'd have one dickens of a time convincing the court you wasn't the father. If you just want to play with the girls, get yourself a decent one to mess with. That way, if anything happens, you could marry her and not feel ashamed of your wife for the rest of your life."

"All right, Mother." He laughed hollowly, reaching across the kitchen table and patting her drooping shoulders. "I don't want to sound mean or ungrateful for what you're told me. I guess only I can look out for myself. I'm not interested in the girls right now. Verna Monroe would have to be some pumpkins to hook me."

"It's good that you're leery, son, but never underestimate the power of a beautiful woman. She can squirm her way out of a straitjacket with her eyes closed. Mark my words. I don't know this woman, but I'd think long and carefully before I'd put myself in a position where she could gig me. It ain't that I don't want you to have your fun, as you young fellows put it, but I'd hate awful bad to see you father another man's child."

"Stop preaching, Mother." Lonnie grinned. "I know you mean well. I'm not promising anything where this neighbor of yours is concerned, though. The first chance I get, I'll look her over. Relax and take it easy. You've got a sick husband to worry about. I'll look out for myself."

"All right, son," Mrs. McVay said wearily, as she rose from the table and began clearing the dishes. "Your old room is ready and waiting. Everything is the same as it was when you left."

"That's fine. I'll take my suitcase right up and unpack. Do not worry anymore about running the farm. I'll see that everything is kept in order, and I'll help you take care of John. You just take it easy. I'm here to help you anyway I can."

In the days that followed, John McVay's condition did not improve. The weather turned bitterly cold, and even though he kept the big wood burning heater in the living room stocked twenty-four hours a day, John's bedroom was icy cold. One winter day, Lonnie had cut and hauled wood all day long. When the shadows of another frigid winter night followed the setting of the sun, he was ready to drop in his tracks. The stars were shining by the time he completed the evening chores. After supper, he carried in enough wood for the night and soon was dozing in an easy chair before the huge heater.

At ten o'clock, his mother roused him to say she was retiring for the night. Lonnie had taken to spending his nights on a day bed in one corner of the living room. He kept an alarm clock on a stand by his bed, so that he could replenish the fuel in the heater.

"Set the clock and lay down, son," his mother pleaded. "You're so tired. John is resting better tonight. Maybe he's taking a turn for the better. Wake up now, Lonnie, and do like I say. You can't rest all doubled up like you are in that rocker. Good night. Get me up at six."

Lonnie stoked the heater again and removed his trousers and heavy shoes. More asleep than awake, he picked up the clock and set it with fumbling fingers. Stretching out on the daybed, he pulled the heavy patchwork comforters over him. The next thing he knew, his mother was shaking him violently and calling his name.

"Get up, Lonnie. Oh, please, get up," she cried. "Something terrible has happened."

"What'sa matter? What'sa matter?" Lonnie mumbled, sitting up on the daybed and rubbing the sleep out of his eyes. "Did the clock go off? If it did, I didn't hear it."

"It's John. He fell out of bed again. It's cold as ice in here. Heaven only knows how long he's been on the floor."

Staggering erect, Lonnie rushed into the bedroom and bent over his stepfather. John McVay lay doubled up on the hard cold floor. His breath came in ragged gasps, and his bare feet and hands were as cold as chunks of ice. Scooping his stepfather off the floor, Lonnie placed him on the bed and tucked the bedclothes snugly around him. Then he rekindled the fire in the wood heater. He picked up the clock and looked at it closely. It said four o'clock. He had been asleep six hours, instead of the two he had intended. Twenty-four hours later, John McVay had a relapse and pneumonia set in. Within a week, John was in his grave.

All the doctor's efforts to save his life were for naught. The congestion in his lungs, combined with the paralysis of his left side, choked him to death. A fortnight after his stepfather's funeral, Lonnie met Verna Monroe. It was a Friday evening, and he had just finished the chores for the day. As he and his mother sat down to supper, a knock sounded on the kitchen door.

"I'm Verna Monroe, your neighbor," a voice said.

Mrs. McVay opened the door wide. "We were just sitting down to eat."

So this is the sexpot I was warned to steer clear of, Lonnie mused, as he waited expectantly for Verna to enter the kitchen.

Verna Monroe came in, her laughing brown eyes giving Lonnie a quick appraisal. She stepped out of her fur-lined galoshes and set them by the door.

"If you don't mind, Mrs. McVay, I'll take off my coat, too." She smiled, and Lonnie noticed that her eyes looked into his as she spoke.

"It's so cold that if I leave it on while I'm inside, it won't do me a bit of good when I go back out."

"Let me take your coat, please," Lonnie said, rising from the supper table and holding out his arms.

"Oh, thank you," she said in a throaty whisper. Her sparkling white teeth flashed an appreciative smile as she slipped out of the heavy woolen garment. She handed it to him then removed the scarf that covered her hair. This she also handed to him. Lonnie could not have said whether Verna Monroe's hair was dyed or not, but he openly admired it as she shook her head and it tumbled about her shoulders in a glossy, golden wave.

"Verna, this is my son by my first marriage, Lonnie Dolan," Mrs. McVay said reluctantly. "And Lonnie, this is Verna Monroe. She bought the place up the road where Cindy Hamrick and her parents used to live."

"I'm glad to make your acquaintance, Miss Monroe," Lonnie said as he took the small, well-shaped hand she extended.

"Same here, Lonnie." She grinned, giving his hand an intimate little squeeze. "Only, please, call me Verna. All my friends do. I've been looking forward to meeting you, but gosh, I never thought you was so tall and well built. I'm five-foot-two, but I only barely come to your shoulders. How's the weather up there, handsome?"

"The same as it is down there, beautiful," Lonnie laughed, completely ignoring the thundercloud that had settled over his mother's face. Verna Monroe was a fine looking specimen of young womanhood. Her oval face had a flawless complexion, and she had wide-spaced, dark eyes. Her beautifully proportioned figure was clad in tight-fitting black slacks and a white pullover sweater.

"Won't you have supper with us?" Lonnie asked, pulling out a chair and getting a plate, cup, saucer, and silverware from the kitchen cabinet. "I'm sure Mother cooked enough food for one more."

"Since you twist my arm, what can I do but accept?" she said, gracefully sinking into the chair he held for her and thanking him when he poured her a cup of coffee.

If Verna sensed the restrained attitude of Lonnie's mother, she gave no indication of it. Instead, she ate with the appetite of one who is genuinely hungry, and even asked for a second cup of coffee.

"Please excuse my shameless appetite," she apologized, shaking her wavy blond head and placing one of her well-cared-for hands on her full bosom. "Mrs. McVay, it tastes so delicious I just can't help myself."

"You're perfectly welcome," Mrs. McVay said graciously. "Don't push back your chair, yet. I baked a pumpkin pie this afternoon. I'd be mighty pleased if you'd try a piece of it."

"How can I refuse?" Verna smiled, dimpling prettily, and spread her hands in resignation. "A piece of homemade pumpkin pie will be a rare treat for me, Mrs. McVay."

When they finished eating, Verna insisted on helping with the dishes. Then she sighed. "I'm practically out of firewood," she said hesitantly, giving Lonnie the full benefit of her expressive eyes. "I was wondering if you would come up to my place tomorrow and help me. I'll pay you well for your time and trouble."

"Who supplied you with firewood till now?" Lonnie asked.

"That old man who lives on up the road. He's got the flu. Not bad, but his wife told me he wouldn't be able to cut me any firewood for quite a while. I'm in a fix, Lonnie. I need your help bad."

"Looks like I'll have to come to your rescue," he laughed. "Do you have timber to cut fuel from?"

"I have a patch of second-growth trees that will do nicely. Don't bring a lunch bag. I'm not working tomorrow, so I'll feed you."

"Okay. I'll not be able to get there early, though. I have a lot of chores to do. When I come, I'll bring the mules and an axe."

"Good." Verna smiled happily. "I have to get home. It's dark outside, and I never feel safe on the road by myself at night. Good night, Mrs. McVay. Thanks a lot for the supper. I'm sorry to hear about your husband. Come up and see me sometime. Good night, Lonnie. I'll be expecting you in the morning."

"Not so fast, neighbor. What kind of man would I be to let a beautiful woman walk home alone at night? Nothing doing. I'll see you safely to your door."

"What about your mother?" Verna asked guilelessly. "Will she be all right?"

"Mother will be fine," Lonnie said quietly, as he brought Verna's coat from the bedroom and held it for her. "You go on to bed, Mother. I'll be back before long."

"Do be careful, son," Ms. McVay said meaningfully. Lonnie read the emphasis in her words and noticed the sharp look she bestowed upon Verna, but he ignored them.

"Just like a mother to put her two cents in," Lonnie mused as he put on his heavy fleece-lined coat and fur-lined cap. "They always want to keep their sons tied to their apron strings. I'm not about to let that happen. I've been my own man for years, and I intend to keep it that way. Besides, friendship with this neighbor gal has definite possibilities."

On the way up the road, Verna was talkative and gay. Most of the time, she walked quite close to Lonnie. Once, when she apparently stumbled on the uneven road, she clutched his arm.

"I'm sorry, Lonnie," she said softly. "I seem to have two left feet tonight."

"You're doing fine," he said matter-of-factly, slipping his right arm around her waist. "There now. Isn't that better?"

"It's wonderful," she whispered, leaning against him as they walked. "I don't want to make nuisance of myself."

"You could never do that, honey," Lonnie said gallantly, tightening his arm around her waist.

"It's good to hear you say it, even if you don't mean what you say."

"Never was more serious in my life. If you're not cold, let's not walk so fast."

"Why not, Lonnie? Aren't you anxious to get home quickly?"

"Not that anxious. I'm enjoying this walk. I hate to see it end so soon."

"I'm pleased that you enjoy being with me," she purred. "I'd be delighted if you'd come in for a cup of coffee or something, when we get there. You're by far the handsomest neighbor I've got, and I want to treat you right."

"Verna, I might as well be as honest with you as you're trying to be with me. You're the prettiest neighbor I've got, and no mistake. I hope we get to know each other real well. I believe we've got a lot in common. What do you think?"

"I'm sure we have. Nothing would please me more than to have a friend like you, Lonnie."

"Look, Verna, baby," Lonnie said, stopping in the middle of the dirt road and wrapping his long arms around her. "Before I kiss that sweet mouth of yours, let me say that you're a very beautiful and desirable woman, and I'm a red blooded man. My blood is on fire from the nearness and sweetness of you. Forgive me for saying this to you on such short acquaintance, but your hair isn't the only thing I hope you'll let down when we get to know each other. It would be heaven to make love to a girl like you."

"Oh, Lonnie," Verna whispered happily as she pressed against him and raised a pair of soft, sweet lips to his kiss. "Forgive my shamelessness. It's been a long time since a man I could respect has told me that. It's music to my ears to hear you say you find me desirable."

For a long moment, she permitted her mouth to cling to his. When she drew away, a throaty laugh of joy welled up out of her throat.

"You're my kind of man, Mr. Dolan," she said, standing on tiptoe to claim his lips again. "It's too cold outside tonight to smooch this way. Besides, we just met this evening. You don't waste any time getting to the important things when you meet a girl, but that's what I like in a man."

"Never could see any sense in dilly-dallying," Lonnie chuckled. "Mostly, though, it depends on the attractiveness of the girl whether I waste time or not."

"You big flatterer. I'll take that as a compliment and thank you for saying it. Let's go on before I freeze. My hands and feet and nose are beginning to feel like they're made of ice, instead of flesh, blood, and bone."

In a few minutes, they were at Verna's front door. Taking a key from her coat pocket, she unlocked the door. She turned to Lonnie and graciously invited him inside.

"Perhaps I better not come in tonight," he murmured.

"But I expected you to."

"I understand. Right now, I might not act like a gentleman at all. More like a wolf, I imagine."

"That could be interesting," she laughed, stepping inside. "Come on in, 'fraidy cat. I won't eat you up."

"I don't expect you would. But one never knows."

"Still tied to your mother's apron strings? Is that it?"

"Hardly," Lonnie laughed. "I'll see you tomorrow. We'll talk then. Somehow, I think it'd be better that way. Good night." Turning away, Lonnie walked out of the yard, ignoring Verna's protest.

"Whew," he chuckled as he strode homeward. "If I'd gone in there, steamed up like I am, I'd have been behind that sexy bitch's panties in ten minutes. From the way she was acting, I'd say she expected me to, and really wanted it. That Verna is sure a looker, and what a figure she's got. Stacked like a brick shithouse, and on fire for attention.

What a combination. Mother was right. She is on the make, not that I discouraged her any. Got to watch my step with that little lady. If I don't, I'll knock her up with the first load I shoot into her. Then there'll be hell to pay."

Lonnie was surprised to find his mother waiting up for him at home. He braced himself for a sermon. "Mother, still up? I expected to find you in bed. What's the matter? Aren't you sleepy?"

"Of course, I'm sleepy," Mrs. McVay snapped, rubbing her eyes, "but the way that woman threw herself at you tonight, it knocked the sleep out of me."

"Look, Mother," Lonnie said patiently. "You're worrying needlessly. As far Verna Monroe is concerned, I can take care of myself. I've met more than one like her. I just got home after being gone almost a year and a half. Remember?"

"Sure, I remember, and I don't have to tell you how happy I am to have you here, but I don't want to see my only son get mixed up with a woman I honestly believe is no better than a whore. Now, Lonnie boy, can you blame your old mother for feeling that way?"

"Of course not," Lonnie soothed, placing an arm around his mother's shoulders. "I'd probably feel the same way if I had a son of my own and a woman like Verna was eyeing him. That's natural. But let's go to bed now. I promised to cut and haul wood for this designing neighbor of ours tomorrow. Sally Smith was a whore, and all set to deceive me into marrying her, but it didn't work. Verna Monroe won't have any better luck with me than Sally did."

"I sure hope you're right, son," Mrs. McVay said. "Only remember that that brassy bitch will stop at nothing to put her hooks into you. Her kind are noted for that sort of thing. Good night. Wake me in the morning before you go up there. I'll pack you a lunch. I'll feel better if you don't go into her house at all tomorrow. The way I see it, there's no need to borrow trouble."

The stars were still shining the next morning when Lonnie ate his breakfast and commenced doing his chores. With an hour, he was on his way to Verna Monroe's, his mother's admonition to watch his step ringing in his ears.

When he reached his destination, he was not surprised to find a note from Verna tacked to the kitchen door. The note said she was a late sleeper when she didn't have to get up early. "See you at noon," the note read. "Please don't work too hard, and be careful. Verna."

All that morning, Lonnie cut wood. Only once, at about ten o'clock, did he catch a glimpse of Verna. He glanced at the kitchen windows as he drove the mules into the wood yard and saw her peeping out. He waved casually and was gratified to see her wave gaily in return.

When he brought in another load of wood at eleven-thirty, he unhitched the mules, tied one on either side of the wagon, and fed them. He walked to the kitchen door and knocked.

"To hell with eating a cold lunch," he muttered, waiting for Verna to answer. "I'd be crazy as a loon if I did. I look forward to a hot lunch with a beautiful woman. And while I eat, I expect to entertain the thought of cuddling her a bit when time and opportunity present themselves."

"Hi, Lonnie," Verna said warmly as she opened the kitchen door and stepped aside for him to enter. "Come right in out of the cold. Dinner will be ready in about ten minutes. I hope you like what I prepared. Gosh, but you look big and outdoor-sy. I'll be disappointed if you're not as hungry as I anticipated. It's always more satisfying to cook for a man who's hungry."

"Don't worry your pretty head about me not being hungry," Lonnie said, grinning into her upturned face. "I could eat a horse, if someone had it already skinned for me. But you look good enough to eat yourself. Don't stand so close to me. I might lose control and take a great big bite off some sweet, tender, juicy spot."

"I dare you," she said, grinning impishly as she stepped close and placed her hands on his arms.

Lonnie swept her into his arms and hungrily sought and found her waiting mouth. It was full of sweet fire and demanded his in a kiss that rocked him back on his toes.

"Lonnie, Lonnie," she cried softly, as she tore her lips loose. "I actually believe you would eat poor little ole me up if I gave you half a chance."

"You can just bet your life I would," he growled good-naturedly.

"Be patient, dear boy. Everything in its own good time and place. Right now, if you'll be kind enough to let me out of this bear hug, I'll put our dinner in the table."

As they ate and talked, Lonnie learned much about his beautiful neighbor. She was twenty-two and divorced. She had one child, a boy, who lived with her parents in Elkins. When Lonnie asked why she had never remarried, Verna looked at him thoughtfully then asked a surprising question.

"Did you ever feel that there's a perfect physical mate for each of us in this old world, if only we are fortunate enough to find him or her?"

"I never thought much about it, but some people swear by such things. Is that the way you feel?"

"It certainly is," she declared with flashing eyes. "I always did feel that way. After one lukewarm try at marriage, I'm more convinced than ever."

"How so?" He grinned across the table at her. "Go ahead. Lay your cards on the table. Tell me anything you like. I'm not a school boy anymore. I've been around. I'll understand."

"I was right last night," she breathed, excited. "You are my kind of person. I feel it more with every minute I'm with you."

"Good," Lonnie laughed. "Now tell me more about this conviction of yours. It sounds interesting."

"It's like this, Lonnie," Verna said softly, leaning across the table and taking one of his hands in hers. "All this might sound terrible wacky to a non-believer, but there's any number of married couples in this world who are no more rightly mated then a square peg trying to fit a round hole. It just can't be done successfully. I ought to know. My ex-husband and I were two such people. He's big and strong, and exciting to be around, but right there is where his good qualities end, as far as being the proper husband for me is concerned."

"Go on," Lonnie encouraged. Her intense manner and speech intrigued him in spite of himself.

"It'll embarrass me something awful to tell you this, but I feel sure you'll understand the reason for our breakup after I lay my cards on the table. My ex-husband had the twisted idea that he was the cat's whiskers when it came to love making. But I'm here to tell you he stunk as a lover, and I do mean stunk. There I'd be, lying in bed with hot panties, waiting expectantly for him to come to bed and make love to me. And when he did come to bed, what do you think my big, virile husband did?"

"I'm listening. Please go on."

"He'd sweep me into his arms, give me an unexciting peck on the lips, and without waiting to see if I was ready or not, plunge his penis all the way into my vagina. Then he would peck, peck, peck away, fast and furious, blow his load, pull his privates out of mine, give me another dry peck, roll over, and in two minutes be sound asleep. That was my sex life with my ex-husband. In more than two years of being married to him how many times do you suppose I felt satisfied with our sex life? I mean really satisfied. How many times do you think I came, as you men put it?"

"You tell me, Verna," Lonnie said, thinking of Ethyl McKnight. He got up from the table and walked around to her side. Cupping a hand under her chin, he raised her face to his and kissed her soft, sweet lips then moved into a French kiss.

"Thank you, Lonnie," she whispered huskily. Her usually pleasant voice became even more bitter as she resumed her denunciation of her ex-husband. "In all the time I was married, I never had one single satisfactory sexual experience. He never brought me to climax, or even near one. When I tried to talk to him about it, he got angry. I even went so far as to get some books on sex. These books described how to do the sex act to the complete satisfaction of both parties, but my husband called me a sex-fiend and burned the books. After he began calling me whore and other bad names, and after he began slapping me around, I decided to call our marriage quits. I divorced him. That happened three years ago."

"In the three years since you've been divorced, have you found the type of man you feel would make you an ideal mate?" As he asked the question, Lonnie pulled her to her feet and began passionately caressing her. He kissed her lips, eyes, nose, and throat, and came back to her eager, hungry mouth again.

"I'm sure I have," she gasped, giving herself over to the magic of their intimate embrace. "Make love to me, darling. Prove that our reactions are the same. We're ideally suited for each other. I'm positive we're compatible."

"Look, Verna, honey. I'm quite sure it'd be heaven on earth to make love to you, but I came up here to cut and haul wood, not lollygag around. I'm not saying we don't have plenty in common. I sensed it the minute I laid eyes on you yesterday evening. There's much for us to learn about each other. As for my being able to satisfy you sexually, I honestly believe I can do it to your complete satisfaction. I've had lots of girlfriends. None of them has complained about my love-making so far."

"Forget about the wood this afternoon," she pleaded. Taking one of his hands in one of hers, she placed it on her full bosom. "See what I mean, sweetheart? All of me can be yours this day if you let yourself go. Have no fear. I'll pay you for all day."

"What about protection? If we become intimate, you could get pregnant. I don't have any rubbers with me. Have you thought of that?"

"Sure," she whispered against his lips. Her beautiful eyes resembled pools of crystal water. "If you had a hundred of those things with you, I wouldn't let you use a one on me. When we give ourselves to each other, I want it to be as nature intended. Skin to skin, honey. That's the way I want you."

"Skin to skin, huh?"

"That's right."

"Suppose you get with child?"

"It's worth the risk, just to enjoy your love all the way, as nature intended, without anything separating us."

"We'll talk some more on this subject later," Lonnie said firmly, as he disengaged himself from her embrace. "It's almost one o'clock. I should already be out there cutting and hauling wood. After all, that's why I'm here today."

"But, Lonnie, what of our lovemaking this afternoon? I want your love. I need it so badly. I'll pay you for the whole day like I promised. I'll even—"

Lonnie grabbed his top coat off the back of a kitchen chair and dashed out of the house. That evening, he didn't stop to collect his money for the day's work.

"She'll find a way to pay me in her own good time and in her own good way," he said to himself on his way home. "Damn it all to hell, but she's an eyeful. I must be getting soft in the head to turn down such a red-hot piece. Maybe I'm more cautious than I used to be, or it could be I'm leery because of the way she's throwing herself at me. Many a man's been caught in the kind of trap she's setting. I guess you could truthfully call it one of them tender traps. The kind with hair on it. Haw, haw."

During the next three weeks, Lonnie avoided contact with his beautiful neighbor. However, in the fourth week of his exile, she waylaid him as he drove the mules past her place on his way home from a day of winter plowing.

"Lonnie," she called gaily from her front door as he was abreast of the yard gate. "Please, wait a moment. I've wanted to see you all day."

"Hello, Verna," Lonnie replied as he halted the mules and she came skipping down the front walk. "You're looking as pretty as ever."

"You big fibber," she chided, stepping up to the wagon. "If I was half as desirable as you try to make out, the men would beat a path to my door. Where have you been hiding? It's been almost a month since I've seen you."

"Oh, I've been busy whipping the farm in shape," he said lamely.

"Sure you haven't been avoiding me?" she asked softly, leaning close and putting one of her gloved hands on his left arm. Her full lips pouted just a little as she waited for his reply.

"Of course not, Verna," Lonnie said, but he knew he was not deceiving her. Verna Monroe might be the picture of girlish innocence, but he knew from experience with her type of woman that she was as discerning as a fox, and just as crafty.

"Good," she said, "then I'll not take no for an answer to a proposal. It's Saturday, and I just got back from a shopping spree in Elkins. I bought lots of goodies, and I am in the mood for company tonight. I'll be expecting you at seven-thirty, Lonnie. Don't try to beg off. Anyway, I've yet to pay you for the day you cut and hauled wood for me."

"But I'll—" he spluttered, at a loss for a reasonable excuse.

"See you at seven-thirty then." She laughed and went back up the walk.

That evening, after lying something scandalous to his mother, Lonnie was at Verna's front door by ten minutes to eight. At his knock, she answered the door, and he had to admit that she was as beautiful and desirable a young woman as he had seen in a long time. A deliciously intriguing perfume lingered on her trim figure, and the wrap-around dress enhanced her loveliness.

"So good of you to accept my invitation," she said happily, taking his topcoat and hat. "Just make yourself at home before the fire. I'll only be a minute in the kitchen. I've some refreshments to serve. I hope you like them."

"I'm sure I will," Lonnie replied, drinking in her beauty. "Can I help you?"

"Oh, please, no. You're my guest. It won't be too long."

Verna served tasty sandwiches and expensive wine. Lonnie threw discretion to the wind and drank a generous portion of it. The wine burned through his body with a slow, invigorating warmth. As the minutes ticked by, his desire for Verna grew.

"It's real nice having you here," she sighed contentedly, as she cleared away the remains of the refreshments. "Now, if you don't mind, I think

I'll show you my Christmas present. The president of the bank in Valley Head gave it to me. I work there. It won't take long."

In a few minutes, she came out through the bedroom door clad in a luxurious fur coat. She held it around her trim figure very tightly. As she turned this way and that for Lonnie's approval, she kept it wrapped close around her. Only once did she flare the coat out wide, and that was when her back was to him.

"Like it?" she asked, sweetly stepping up to him.

"Sure do," Lonnie said, getting to his feet and taking her in his arms. "That muskrat coat probably set the old boy back a couple of C notes or more. Does his wife approve?"

"Oh, he's a widower. He says he likes me ever so much and wants to get real serious, but I'm leery of an old stag like him. After one good night of pun-jabbing, he'd be popped out for a month. I had enough of being unsatisfied with my first husband. I don't want a return engagement. Do you blame me?"

"Hell, no," Lonnie growled, claiming her lips in a long, passionate kiss. "You're too much on the ball, Verna, baby, to get yourself tied up with an old duffer like that bank fellow. Why he must be sixty, if he's a day."

"He's sixty-three," she said as she looked intently into his eyes.

"Gosh, but you're sweet, lovely, and desirable tonight. You may not know it, but I'm putting up one hell of a fight with my better self to keep from raping you. I better be heading home before I really misbehave."

"The evening's just begun for us, Lonnie. I hoped you'd forgot this malarkey about taking advantage of me. I'm a woman who needs love made to her. You're a man, aren't you?"

"If you don't stop gigging me, I'll prove it to you enough."

"Wonderful," she breathed, leading him to the smoldering log fire that flickered in the fireplace. "Let's set down here on this big throw rug. I even have two large cushions for us to get real comfy with."

Sinking down upon the soft, thick rug, Verna stretched out with her feet away from the fire and her head on one of the cushions. All the while, she kept the fur coat wrapped tightly around herself.

"Come to me, darling," she said in a throaty whisper as she held her arms up to him.

Lonnie flung himself down beside her, and her arms went around his neck. Pulling his head down to hers, she French kissed him, sending a tingling message of love and desire. Then, taking one of his hands in hers, she slipped it inside her fur coat.

Lonnie's questing fingers contacted bare flesh. Verna's eyes were full of heaven's promises. Laughing softly, Lonnie flipped the fur coat open and feasted his eyes on Verna's naked body. From head to toe, she was physical perfection. The flickering firelight created devastatingly beautiful outlines over the sweep of her breasts, her delicately rounded abdomen, her slender waist, and the perfection of her hips and legs. Verna Monroe was a beautiful woman.

"Make love to me, sweetheart," she implored as she wiggled out of her fur coat, tossing it onto a nearby chair. Lonnie could not deny her longer, and he did not try.

Fairly panting in his desire for her, he slipped out of his clothing except his shoes and socks. Then she was locked in his embrace and he was showering her nude body with hot, eager kisses. In haste, they found the place of love and parts thereof, and fused them together. Then their movements became violently intense, their breathing hot, ragged, and gasping.

A little longer they kept up their frenzied action. Suddenly, with a gurgling scream, Verna acquainted Lonnie with the fact that she was having a climax. In the moment of her release, as she kissed him wildly and with feverish passion, nature exerted itself with him, and after a few more rapid movements, he sank into her loving embrace, exhausted, but happy and satisfied.

Twice more that evening, Verna and Lonnie sought and found sexual gratification in each other's arms. Each time, much to Lonnie's surprise and delight, she reached her climax before he had his release. When he departed at two o'clock in the morning, they agreed to spend many more exciting and satisfying evenings together.

"Oh, Lonnie, darling," she whispered happily against his lips as she let him out her front door. "I was right all along. You're wonderful, just like I knew you'd be. Tonight, you made love to me like I never had it done before. It was heaven in your arms. You're mine, sweetheart, mine alone. Surely, you must realize that. We was meant for each other. I won't let another man touch me the rest of my life. I promise. I swear it. I belong to you now. I'll be true to you and you alone. Oh, I'm so happy we finally found one another. We're soul and body mates. Good night, my lover."

The weeks slipped by, and within sixty days, spring had come to work its magic on the countryside. The trees and shrubs that had slept for many months shook winter's icy grip from their branches and came alive with racing sap and swelling buds. Easter flowers and tulips bravely shot up out of the earth and brought forth their fragrances. Day by day, the grass took on a greener hue as the migratory birds came back from the southland and began feverishly mating and building nests.

In the marshy spots and along the creeks, frogs lifted their voices in raucous discord almost every night and, heeding nature's call, began their age-old ritual of reproduction. The winter had passed, and spring, with her soft winds and beautiful flowers, had come; soon, the voice of the turtledove was heard in the land.

During those many weeks, Lonnie and Verna held their trysts as frequently as they could. Somehow, they kept his mother unaware of their activities. Lonnie was positive that sooner or later, she would discover their carryings-on, and then she would fairly raise the roof with him. Each time they met and made love to each other, Verna swore her fidelity to Lonnie.

"I'm yours, darling," she would whisper softly and sweetly, as she lay naked in his arms, giving herself to him with wild abandon.

"Is any other man sharing you with me?" Lonnie would ask, and always she reassured him that he was the only man in her life and her heart.

"You're the man I love, sweetheart," she insisted, her big, dark eyes looking fondly into his. Nevertheless, despite her reassurances, Lonnie felt that Verna Monroe was untrue.

When she began urging that they marry, Lonnie began spying and eavesdropping on her. When he had proof of her perfidy, he would confront her and make a clean break between them. Almost every night, unless he had a date with Verna, he laid in his bed until his mother's snores assured him she was asleep. Then he slipped noiselessly out of bed, dressed quietly, and silently approached Verna's home.

As silent as a shadow, he glided to her front door and glued his ears and eyes to the keyhole. Many nights, a strange car was parked in her driveway, her blinds were tightly drawn, and a man's voice mingled with hers in muted conversation and laughter until midnight, and later. Lonnie familiarized himself with the bank president at Valley Head, and his automobile. The banker drove an expensive, shiny black car. Thereafter, Lonnie kept a sharp eye out. Few men, especially professionals, gave young women like Verna Monroe expensive fur coats without expecting and receiving something of equal value. What better way to pay for such gifts than with her own beautiful body? Lonnie was positive that such was the relationship between Verna and her employer.

One chilly night in late May, he was once again listening at Verna's front door. The blinds were tightly drawn, but a dim light filtered through them. Occasionally, the flickering shadows cast by a fire in the huge open fireplace played against the blinds. From the deep tones of a man's voice, he knew she was entertaining a visitor, but no car stood in her driveway, so he decided to look for it.

He looked up and down the road for a hundred yards or more each way, but saw no parked automobile. Then he returned to the house. The garage housed her small roadster, but when he examined the barn, his search ended. The banker's new Packard was parked in the barn, the doors tightly closed behind it.

"A-ha," Lonnie chuckled grimly. "So my true lady love is entertaining old money-bags himself. I'll bet a plugged nickel he's collecting a good-sized payment on that fur coat."

With all the finesse and cunning of a general, Lonnie planned his campaign to expose Verna. First, he got a key to her kitchen door. Then he bought a camera with a flash bulb attachment and waited for the banker to pay her another visit. The following week, Verna again gave herself wantonly to Lonnie, and while they lay on the bed of love, she tearfully whispered to him that she was with child.

"I'm sorry, darling," she whispered softly, "but it happened in spite of all the things I did after we gave ourselves to each other. We'll have to get married. You understand, don't you, sweetheart?"

"Everything will be all right, baby," he said. "Don't you worry your pretty head one bit. I'll take care of it."

"Oh, Lonnie, Lonnie. You're simply wonderful. What did I ever do to deserve a fine man like you for a husband?"

"You loved me, that's what. You've been mine, and mine only, since we met. Right, dearest?"

"Oh, yes, lover. Yes, yes. I swear it on my honor as a woman in love. No other man has as much as held my hand since we met and fell in love. My conscience is clean, darling. Trust me."

Three nights later, the banker paid Verna another visit. Smiling grimly, Lonnie haunted her front and back door until he knew they were reclining on the thick throw rug in the living room. He had his flash camera and intended to wait until the most opportune time, make his presence known, and denounce her before the banker for the lying, cheating, two-faced person she was.

Lonnie heard Verna plead with the banker to undress her and hurry a little with his lovemaking. Slipping quietly to the kitchen door, he let himself into the house like a shadow. He removed his shoes and set them outside the door. Then, in his sock feet and on tiptoe, he quietly eased towards the living room. At the living room door, he paused in the shadows and peered inside. A dim light cast a soft, pale glow over the room, enough to reveal Verna and her guest engaged in sexual relations. His blood boiling in silent rage, Lonnie watched their rhythmic movements and listened to their labored breathing.

He adjusted his camera and felt for the light switch alongside the door. When he found it, he took a firm grip on the camera, raised it level with his eyes, and tensed for action.

"Put it to her, old boy," he yelled as he flicked on the living room light. A stifled scream of fright and a muffled curse of amazement met his intrusion. The instant Verna and the banker turned their faces his way Lonnie snapped the picture. A blinding flash of light flooded the room. His camera had not failed him.

"Sorry to barge in and break up your little nooky party, folks, but I just couldn't pass up the opportunity," Lonnie said harshly.

"Lonnie, for God's sake," Verna gasped, fear, embarrassment, and anger flashing across her face. "What is the meaning of this? What are you doing here?"

"Merely checking up on your behavior, my true, honest lady love. So this is how you've been true to me and me alone, eh? This is how you've let no other man touch you. Right?"

"I can explain everything," she cried, tears streaming down her face as she disengaged from the banker and slipped into some of her clothes.

"Who is this man, Verna?" the banker growled, scrambling to his feet and pulling on his trousers.

"A neighbor," she whispered, white-lipped apprehension all over her face as the two men faced each other.

"You young lout," the banker roared, facing Lonnie with a baleful glare. "How dare you barge in here and invade my fiancée's and my privacy? I've a mind to break you in two. As it is, I intend to see that it costs you plenty. You've committed a serious offense, young fellow. Breaking and entering carries quite a penalty. I shall see to it that you spend time over at Moundsville for this evening's shenanigans."

"Sit down and shut your big yap, you pot-bellied old jerk," Lonnie roared. "And you sit and stay put also, Verna, love. I've something to say, and I want to do it without interruption. So this little lady is your fiancée, eh?" Lonnie asked, turning back to the fuming banker.

"She is," was the tight-lipped reply. "And I'm proud to say I intend to make her my wife within the next thirty days."

"Good. Then you won't mind my telling you that she's already knocked up."

"What?" the banker gasped, his face turning a dirty grey. "Verna, is there any truth in what this madman is saying?"

"No. No. Not a word," she whispered desperately. "Don't believe a word he's saying. It's a lie, I tell you. It's a lie."

"Lying, am I?" Lonnie said, laughing harshly. "Have you told this old stag of the many times you and I have screwed each other over the past three months? Have you told him that?"

At Lonnie's words, Verna burst into tears, sinking even lower into the divan on which she was sitting. She covered her guilt-stricken face with shaking hands.

"What a terrible thing to say about me just because I won't let you court me," she cried, sobbing brokenly. She turned toward the flabbergasted banker, raised a tear-stained face, and gazed into his eyes. "Oscar, darling, please believe me and ignore his outrageous lies. It's you I love. You know that. And it's your child I'm going to bear. I've been pestered something awful by this plowboy ever since he come crawling home to his mother's apron strings the last week of January because I wouldn't have anything to do with him. I've been true to you, dearest, so help me I have. But this boy's constant pestering has been well-nigh unbearable at times."

"Why didn't you tell me this fellow was causing you trouble?" the banker asked, his florid face taking on a stony look. "Why didn't you tell me you were expecting a child? If you are expecting, Verna, I have every reason to believe I couldn't possibly be the father."

"Why not, dearest?" she asked, the look of a trapped animal settling on her fear-twisted features. "We've given ourselves to each other wantonly on several occasions since we became engaged last fall. Maybe we shouldn't have, but being in love like we've been, and going to marry next month like we've planned, I didn't see much wrong in what we've done."

"I know we've been indiscreet," the banker muttered, "and I've made allowances for our actions because of our love for each other, but I don't see how I could be the father of your child. My doctor told me five years ago that I was hopelessly sterile. If you're pregnant, Verna, that changes everything between us. I'm a respectable businessman. I might act a bit fractious at times, but I'll be damned if I'll let myself be played for a fool."

"Listen to me, sweetheart," Verna cried hysterically as she jumped up from the divan and flung herself into the banker's arms. "That doctor's report was five years ago. Our bodies change with the passing of time. I'm going to bear your child. If you turn against me now, you'll be against your own flesh and blood. I can't believe you'd be that heartless. I'm yours, darling. I love you. I've been true to you. I—"

"All right, you two," Lonnie snapped, his voice like the sudden lash of whip. "I'll be on my way now. Sorry I disturbed your nooky party. If you try any monkey business with me in the future, Verna, I'll show this picture I snapped in court. As for you, mister moneybags, I leave this two-faced little bitch to you. Take her and marry her, if you want, but I wouldn't have her for a wife on a bet. All the time she was screwing you, she was also screwing me. On top of that, she's had plenty of other men here. For the past two months, I've been keeping close tabs on our ladylove. I've seen at least a half dozen different cars parked in her driveway on different nights. Callers came to sample her wares at different times, and all of them stayed until after midnight. I'm sure your future wife will have a reasonable explanation for all those cars and men. Ask her about it. You'll see what I mean. Goodnight, folks, and good luck, mister moneybags. You'll need it."

Turning away, Lonnie left the house. He pulled on his shoes and began walking down the driveway. As he went, a smile touched his lips. Inside the house, he heard the banker's rage filled voice raised in strident tones, intermingled with Verna's sobbing replies. As he walked home, he muttered to himself bitterly, "Well, reckon that puts the finishing touches on another chapter in my life with a two-faced, two-timing woman. Man alive, will I ever find one that'll be honest and true? Will I ever find a girl I want to make my wife?"

Chapter 12

The Fortune Teller

After Verna Monroe, Lonnie did not seriously consider romancing any girl until the summer of his twenty-fifth birthday. It was on a Saturday afternoon in June when he met the young woman destined to become his next heartthrob. The weather was exceptionally warm and sunny, and the first carnival of the summer season had come to Valley Head. Knocking off from his farm duties at noon, Lonnie had gone to town to do some trading. His first stop was Brady's General Store. That was when it started.

"Look, Lon," the talkative old merchant said as he filled Lonnie's order. "There's a one-horse carnival in town this weekend. Got in yesterday, just ahead of that downpour. They've pitched camp in back of the high school. The boys tell me this outfit is mostly gypsies. Are you planning on taking in the show this afternoon?"

"Reckon not." Lonnie grinned. "Gypsies are bad luck for me."

"Hog wash," Old Amos scoffed. "That's pure superstition."

"I wouldn't say that. Folks say they are noted for their light fingers. With the kind of luck I've got, they'd pick my pockets as clean as a whistle. I ain't got any money to be trifling away. Too much expense on the farm this past spring. Besides, I'm in a hurry. Be right back, Amos. By the time I get some stuff at the drug store, you'll probably have my order filled."

"Sure will," Amos agreed. "But listen to this, boy, and maybe you'll take interest in this carnival what's in town. The boys also told me there's a young woman telling fortunes in this outfit. She's a gypsy, they say, but a pippin for looks and figure, if you know what I mean."

"Not interested," Lonnie grunted, turning to inspect a stack of new bib overalls.

The old merchant chuckled under his breath. "Maybe you're not interested yet, Lon, but I'm inclined to think you will be when I tell you everything the boys told me about this fiery-eyed little prevaricator."

"Spill it, Amos, only make it short and sweet. I know you're determined to tell me about this gypsy queen, so let's get it over with. I haven't got time to stand here all afternoon and listen to you spiel about some female."

"She's worth making a play for. That is, she's worth it, unless the boys have been ribbing me, and I don't think they have. Listen to these vital statistics before you decide to pass up the show. A person only lives once in this life, I say."

"Cut the hogwash, Amos, and get on with it," Lonnie growled, heading for the door.

"The boys said this gal has an hourglass figure and a face that'd put an angel to shame. Blood-red lips, even white teeth, thick lashes, long hair as black as midnight, and such eyes. It's the truth, I'm telling you, so help me. Why, bald-headed and ugly as I am, if I was thirty years younger, I'd—"

Waving his arms in disgust, Lonnie strode out of the store and out of earshot.

"Old men are all alike," he muttered, walking toward the drug store at the other end of the street. "She can be homely as homemade sin, but to them she the most beautiful creature the sun ever shone on. Bah. They're all half-crazed. That's what they are. Every last one of them."

About midway between the general store and the drug store, Lonnie realized his shoelace was undone. Pausing a moment, he stopped and tied the rawhide lace. When he straightened up, Lonnie stopped short.

Less than a dozen yards in front of him, coming closer with each dainty step, was a perfect vision of femininity. She was young and strikingly beautiful, with an olive complexion. Coming abreast of him, she halted and looked a question at him.

"Pardon me, sir," she said, her voice a low, throaty alto. "Would you be kind enough to direct me to the general store of this village?"

"By all that's holy," Lonnie breathed as he took in the lovely young woman before him, from her daintily shod feet, to the top of her head with its crown of raven hair. "I'd bet my bottom dollar that this innocent-eyed filly before me is the gypsy gal Old Amos was raving about. He is right. She's sure a knockout. Wowee."

"It's a pleasure to be of your service to you, lady," he said aloud, doffing his battered felt hat and smiling down at her. "The general store is just a few doors ahead of you. I'd be happy to accompany you."

"Oh, thank you, kind sir," she sighed happily, her foreign speech falling pleasantly upon his ears. "That won't be necessary, but does the general store have a good line of things for women?"

"Practically everything a person would want or need, but let me warn you. Old Amos Brady is a bachelor, and he has a terrible weakness for a beautiful young woman like you."

"Have not all men?" she asked, smiling and flashing him a look as old as time.

"We men plead guilty," Lonnie laughed.

"Perhaps it's better so," she returned, smiling prettily. "I'm Rosetta. My folks and I are with the carnival that stopped here yesterday. We're putting on a show this afternoon and evening. I tell fortunes. Please come. You've been so kind. The least I can do is give you a reading."

"You owe me nothing, Rosetta. I won't promise to take in your show, but if I do, I'll be sure to look you up."

"Are you married?" she asked, her big eyes searching his.

"No."

"Then Granny Marie won't object too strongly should you ask to see me."

"Suppose I come to your tent, but your grandmother refuses to let me see or talk with you? What then? They tell me your people aren't overly pleased when outsiders call on their young women."

"It's an old custom, and strictly enforced, even today," she sighed. "Please, come anyway, and see the rest of our show. Good day to you, sir. I must be on my way. I have to start telling fortunes as soon as the show starts. Granny will be fretful if I'm not back in an hour."

"Call me Lonnie."

"Is that your name?"

"Yes. Lonnie Dolan. Rosetta, us here in the mountains also have a custom when a young man meets a beautiful, unmarried, young woman like you. If I come to your show tonight and have a chance to talk to you privately, maybe I'll show you what I mean. Goodbye for now, little dark eyes."

"Good bye," she whispered as she turned away. "I hope we see each other again."

Lonnie hurried on to the drug store, made his purchases, and sped back to Brady's General Store in the hope of seeing the gypsy girl again, but she was nowhere in sight.

"Great day in the morning, Lon," Old Amos said excitedly as he rubbed his bony hands together and danced a gig. "You just missed her."

"Missed who?" Lonnie asked innocently.

"That gypsy gal I was telling you about."

"So?"

"Aw, hell, Lon. From the way you're talking and acting, people might get the impression you're dead from the waist down. You're just a boy yet. Why, when I was your age, I had more lead in my pencil than I could find gals to use it up on. Don't tell me you're burned out already."

"Never mind the lead in my pencil. Believe me when I say it's working satisfactorily."

Lonnie knew from past experience that if he told the old merchant about his meeting with the lovely young fortuneteller and her invitation to come and see her, Old Amos would spread it like wildfire. He wisely chose to keep quiet. Amos Brady was a gossip, and Lonnie knew it.

"Before you rush out of here like a ninny, young feller, get an earful of this. That olive-skinned little bitch would be hot as a firecracker. She wants it the worst way, all right."

"How do you know, Amos?" Lonnie asked casually as he gathered his purchases.

"Experience, boy, experience. As I was waiting on her, I watched her like a hawk, not that I expected her to swipe anything—just cautious, you know. Anyway, they don't usually try that when they're alone."

"So far, Amos, you haven't told me a damn thing about this girl that'd excite my interest. All you've done is flap your lip. Do you think I never saw a pretty girl before today, or had my fun with them? What's so special about this one?"

"She's a gypsy. That's what I've been trying to impress upon you. Gypsy women are known the world over for their hot-bloodedness and their love for a good jab in that hot spot between their legs."

"What healthy young woman is any different? They all like it."

"Scoff if you want, but I believe this babe could be laid if a feller like you was to get her alone in the dark after the show. It's worth a try. Man alive, she bought two brassieres with the biggest, deepest cups I had in the store. Then, after she had held them out and looked them over,   she gave me a wicked smile and said they'd probably be too tight for her. I also sold her six pairs of the skimpiest black silk panties I carry. The kind these jazzed up teenagers wear. She said she wanted the kind that was small waisted and full in the hips. Get it, Lon, boy?

"So the girl has a nice figure. Is that anything to get steamed up about? Lots of girls has nice figures. Very nice figures."

"Damn you, Lonnie Dolan, for a clod-hopper." Old Amos spat in disgust. "If you want to pass up an opportunity at a once-in-a-lifetime piece of nooky, don't come crawling to me later, whining that I didn't put you next to it."

"So long, Amos, old friend." Lonnie grinned, enjoying the storekeeper's discomfiture. "Thanks for trying to leg for me. So far, I haven't needed it."

"The show starts at eight o'clock tonight," Old Amos called as Lonnie passed out of the store. "Be there."

That evening, Lonnie did the chores an hour earlier than usual. Afterwards, he bathed and shaved with more than the usual concern for his grooming. At the supper table, he informed his mother that he was going back into town that evening for an hour or two.

"Got a date lined up, Lonnie?" his mother asked.

"Could be." He grinned, giving her a big wink.

"Let's hope she's a nice girl."

"All my girlfriends have been nice," he laughed.

"Sure, I know, but men are so blind to the opposite sex, and you, my son, I sometimes believe, are blinder then most when it comes to a pretty face and a well-turned ankle."

"If I am, mother dear, it's a weakness I'm not ashamed of," Lonnie chuckled. He drank the last of his coffee and rose from the table. Stepping to his mother's side, he bent and kissed her on top of her head. "Don't fret about me if I'm a bit later than usual getting home tonight. Some girl is bound to snare your loving son sooner or later. That's how it's been since this old world began, and you mothers wouldn't want it any other way."

"Of course, we wouldn't, but us mothers want our children to marry well. That's what I want for you, son. When dating girls, a good rule to remember is never date one you'd be ashamed to have for a wife."

"I'm not wife hunting tonight, mother," Lonnie laughed, wondering what his mother would say if she knew he was going to town to try for a date with a gypsy girl.

"Even if you aren't, it's good rule to live by. I'm not trying to be nosey, my son. I just have the best interests of my only child at heart. Have a good time on your date and be a gentleman. She'll respect you if you are."

"That's something to look forward to," he chuckled. "There's nothing like having a girl respect you for not trying to make her. I'll help you with the dishes before I go. That way, you can sit on the front porch and relax."

The sun had sunk behind the bold thrust of Point Mountain when Lonnie climbed into his old car and started for Valley Head. Twilight was at hand when he reached his destination. He parked close to the high school building and loafed around town until two hours after the carnival had started, then entered the brightly lit section where the tent shows were in progress.

It was after eleven when he finally meandered over to the gaudily adorned tent of the fortuneteller. At the entrance sat a gypsy woman in a cloth-bottomed folding chair. She was old and bent, with a face that was a maze of wrinkles, but the eyes she raised to Lonnie as he stopped before her, were as bright as polished diamonds.

"Step inside, young man," she cackled, giving him a toothless smile. "Rosetta is waiting to tell you many strange and wonderful things."

"Suppose I don't want to hear about those strange and wonderful things?"

"Ah, but you do." The old crone rose from her chair and laid a claw-like hand on his arm. "Us mortals have great curiosity about ourselves, our successes, our friends, and the future."

"That's a bunch of hooey," Lonnie grunted. "And I don't believe it."

"Ah, but it's true, my son. Fortune telling is a gift from the powers that rule the universe. The good book tells of it being practiced thousands of years ago, and it's the same today. Rosetta can foresee the future."

"I don't think I'd better go in," Lonnie growled, pretending to turn away. "Something tells me it's nothing but a waste of time and money. I better be on my way. It's getting late."

However, the crafty old gypsy woman was not to be denied. Business had not been very rewarding that evening, and she was determined to sell Lonnie on the idea of having his fortune told. Lowering her voice to a confidential whisper, she brought into play the greatest and oldest attraction that females have for males.

"My son," she whispered slyly, smiling up at him. "This balmy June night is perfect for learning Life's greatest mysteries. Forget the hour. Heed, instead, the call that is churning in your blood. I know, for I can see it in your eyes."

"But," Lonnie said, "if Rosetta can't, or won't, tell me all I want to know tonight, what then? Am I to be left dangling?"

"Definitely not, young man. I will see to it that you are not left in doubt. Come back to see Rosetta every night of the two weeks we will be here. She will tell you many of life's most closely guarded secrets. And in the future, you will look back upon this meeting with her with gladness and thanksgiving."

"Rosetta might not want to talk to the likes of me. I am an uneducated farm boy. What can I say to her that will help her understand my problems, my needs? Knowing my shortcomings as I do, what can she say to me that will be of lasting benefit? Really, I'd don't know about this. I think I'll—"

"Hush, my son," the old gypsy woman counseled. "Forget all your doubts and fears. Go in to Rosetta. She will understand. You are young and handsome. Rosetta and you have that in common. She is young and very, very beautiful. She is very sweet and desirable, and wise in the mysteries of life. Look deep into her knowing eyes and pour out the problems of your heart. She will comfort you, help you, and make you happy."

Bowing his head, Lonnie permitted the old woman to usher him through a heavily draped doorway and into the dimly lit interior. A shaded lamp cast a weird glow over the back portion of the tent. Exotic perfume assailed his nostrils. At the far corner of the tent sat a shadowy figure behind a small table, upon which a large round ball rested. Chuckling triumphantly, the old gypsy woman gently pushed Lonnie toward the small table.

"Rosetta," she cackled. "Here is a young man full of doubts and fears. He scoffs at the gift of fortune telling. Before he leaves, show him that you have the gift. I know you can help him. Charge him to secrecy on everything you tell him. Nobody is waiting, so you can take plenty of time."

"Yes, Grandmother. I understand."

At the sound of that intimate, seductive voice, Lonnie's heart leaped.

"Leave us alone together, Grandmother," the shadowy figure said. "I will do my best to help this young man. You, who doubt, please come forward and be seated at the table."

Lonnie hesitated until the old woman had retired to her chair beyond the draped doorway then cautiously moved forward and sat at the small table. He peered around the large tent. From what he could see, he and Rosetta were alone. The dim outline of a cot showed on one side of the tent. Seeing it, his blood turned to fire in his veins. That cot might have possibilities in the future visits he planned to make.

"Rosetta," he whispered. "It's Lonnie. I came. I'm here."

"Lonnie," she whispered, reaching across the table and lightly touching one of his hands. Instantly, he took possession of her small, warm hand and imprisoned it in his. She did not move to withdraw it. Instead, she trapped some of his fingers with some of hers and squeezed them in a way that thrilled him clear down to the tips of his toes.

"I was beginning to think you were not coming," she reproved gently, again squeezing his fingers. "And even when I heard you talking outside to Granny Marie, I began to doubt you were coming inside. Why did you argue with Granny so long?"

"I had to play it that way," he explained, speaking in a hoarse whisper so as not to be heard by the old woman outside the tent. "By arguing and stalling like I did, she said if I wasn't satisfied with what you told me tonight, I could come and see you every night of your stay here. I was trying to pave the way for us to see each other in the future without folk getting suspicious."

"Do you really want to see me again?" she asked softly.

"Again, and again, and again, little dark eyes," he said fiercely, reaching across the table and throwing back the heavy veil covering her face.

"I'm very happy you feel that way," she sighed happily, while her big, expressive eyes glowed with an intense light. "But it's better that you put me out of your mind at once."

"Why, Rosetta? Don't you want me to like you an awful lot?"

"Yes, oh, yes," she whispered sadly. "It's only that nothing but pain and sorrow can come from such an attraction, for the both of us. You see, Lonnie, I am betrothed to one of our people."

"Do you love this man you are engaged to?"

"I loathe him," she hissed.

"I don't understand. Why did you promise to become his wife?"

"I had nothing to do with it. The whole shameful thing was arranged by him, my father, and my grandmother when I was only twelve years old. That was six years ago, almost seven now. Lately, he has been frantic for me to marry him, but I keep putting him off, hoping he'll drop dead or something. As it is, it's only a matter of months until I must take this hated man as my mate. Now you know why it's useless for you to come here again. Much as I'd like you to, it'll only cause us both a lot of trouble."

"Tell me about this man you're betrothed to," Lonnie urged. He half-rose from his chair, leaned across the table, took her face in his hands, and before she could pull back, claimed her upturned mouth in a long, searching kiss. When he released her, she gave a shuddering gasp and covered her face with her hands. Even in the dim light, Lonnie saw that they were shaking.

"I'm sorry, Rosetta," he hastily whispered, "but I could no more keep from kissing you just then than I could stop breathing. You are so beautiful, so sweet, and so very, very desirable. I had to do it. Please, say you forgive me."

"I forgive your rash act," she whispered. She raised her head and looked at him with shining eyes. "Though I beg of you not to torture me further by doing it again. You're the type of man I would choose to pay court to me, if I had anything to say about it. The man I'm promised to is older than my father. He has had three wives already. He now has a housekeeper, whom I am certain is his mistress. All of his wives left him because of his cruelty and his misbehavior in bed. I shudder at the thought of my life with such a man. Now be good boy and let me try to tell you something by gazing into the ball here. I hope I can concentrate."

Turning the strange looking ball, the gypsy girl gazed intently into its shadowy depth. She began to speak softly, in a low monotone. "I see you standing with a pained expression on your face, your arms outstretched. Now I see you smiling. A young woman has come running out of the shadows, straight into your arms. I see you kissing her, and she is holding you tightly. She is smiling. Her face turns more into the light. She looks very familiar. Surely, there's some mistake. But there isn't. The ball never lies. Oh, no. Oh, no. The girl I see is—"

Suddenly, the gypsy girl stopped speaking and covered the glowing ball with a cloth from edge of the table. Raising her head, she looked at Lonnie with eyes dark with pain, sadness, and frustration.

"Who was the girl?" Lonnie asked, though he somehow knew what her answer would be.

"I saw myself," she gasped. "I was so happy. It can't be true. It just can't. I'll look again. There's some mistake."

Twice more, Rosetta gazed intently into the mysterious depths of the huge ball. Each time, the result was the same. She confessed to Lonnie, in a quavering voice, that she saw only herself in his arms.

"It's no use looking longer. This strange, wonderful, and terrible thing between us is far too powerful for me to dispel. This is a force over which I have no control. I'm very sorry, Lonnie. I'm unable to tell you anything of value tonight."

"Oh, but you have. You have, my darling," he said joyfully. "I will come again tomorrow night."

He pulled a five-dollar bill out of his pocket and dropped it onto the table. As he rose to depart, she also rose and stepped around the edge of the table to his side.

"I'm sorry I'm such a flop as a fortuneteller," she breathed sadly, looking into his eyes in a way that set his pulse to pounding. Throwing caution to be the wind, he swept her into his arms. Bending his head, he began raining kisses on her face, her eyes, her neck, her hair, and especially her fiery, sweet mouth.

As fierce as a tigress, she resisted him, but not a whisper of an outcry did she make. Then it was a though a miracle happened. Trembling from head to foot, the gypsy girl ceased struggling against him, threw her arms around his neck, and began returning his kisses. Several times, her tongue probed his mouth deeply, like a hot, sweet rapier. She began to moan softly against his lips and gently tried to disengage from his embrace. Lonnie released her slowly and reluctantly. Lonnie begged her forgiveness and understanding.

"It's all right," she sighed happily. Reaching up, she gently touched his lips with the tips of her fingers. "I understand how you feel. I feel the same, wonderfully, unexplainably. Go now, and let this be good-bye between us. It's better so."

"Never," Lonnie growled fiercely. "I'll come again tomorrow night."

Without waiting to hear her protests, he stalked out of the tent. As he emerged, the aged gypsy woman fastened her bright eyes upon him. At the sight of his disheveled appearance, she cackled joyfully and rubbed her boney hands together.

"I'll be back tomorrow night," Lonnie muttered, dashing away into the shadows.

"Rosetta will be waiting to give you additional readings," the old woman called after him. "Have faith in what she tells you, and true happiness will be yours. It never fails."

"Old woman," he muttered as he drove home, "your type of foretelling will continue to please as long as the victim's money holds out. When the money is gone, the crystal ball goes blank. I wonder if Rosetta really did see herself in my arms. She seemed very upset about it. She'd be a wonderful person is she only had a half a chance. How beautiful she is, and how sweet, but a regular little bundle of dynamite. I know I shouldn't, but I've got to see her again. Damn it all to hell. I only met this girl today, and already she's under my skin. I wish I could turn my back on this, but I can't, damn it, I can't. I ache all over with my desire to know Rosetta's love, all the way. Son of a bitch. Old Amos Brady was right. That gal is a knockout. And I love her, heaven help me. I'm a goner this time, sure as hell, if I don't watch my step. That old grandmother, her father, and intended hubby would slit my throat quick as a wink if they caught me fooling around with her. I'm skating on very thin ice with that little bundle of TNT. Oh, Lordy, I ain't got the backbone to turn away from her now that I know how wonderful she is. Maybe I'll be able to look at this whole thing with a clear head and some common sense tomorrow. I sure hope so. One misstep and yours truly could be in one hell of a pickle."

Feeling miserable, Lonnie cursed himself for being a spineless rat and swore by the stars shining over his head that he wouldn't go see the gypsy girl again, but he knew he was lying to himself. Once again, he had fallen victim to one of the greatest attractions this old world has to offer to a hot-blooded young male—sexual attraction. And so, the next night, close to midnight, Lonnie found himself approaching the fortuneteller's tent again, where waited the beautiful Rosetta. The old gypsy woman greeted him toothlessly and joyfully, with greed shining in her eyes like a beacon.

"Young man, you are wise to come back for more knowledge, but why did you wait until so late an hour? Rosetta would have seen and comforted you hours ago."

"I know, I know," Lonnie muttered, feigning embarrassment. "I had to wait. You see, my folks and friends don't believe in fortune telling. I can't rightly say I believe in it, either. If anyone saw me coming here they would never let me forget it. Even so, I have to settle a thing in my mind, once and for all. I hope you understand."

"Of course I do, but be not ashamed of your thirst for knowledge. Only good can come of it."

"May I go in and see Rosetta now?"

"Certainly. Go right in. Take plenty of time with her, only accept and believe what she reveals. That is the key to your future happiness."

"I find myself wanting to argue what she tells me. I know I did last night. Is that bad?"

"Think nothing of your reluctance to accept those things that are revealed. It's natural to fight the power that Rosetta is demonstrating. However, she can be most persuasive. Rosetta is strong willed, my son. You will attain peace of mind by bowing to her superior knowledge. It is the only path to happiness for you."

"Thank you for your patience," Lonnie said in what he hoped was a convincing act of mental confusion. "Here is a dollar for the trouble. I'll go in now. When I leave, I'll pay Rosetta the usual fee."

"You're very kind, my son." The old woman smiled up at him from the depths of her easy chair. She pocketed the money he gave her and gazed greedily at the bills still in his hands. "Be not impatient with Rosetta if she is unable to tell you all you wish to know tonight. Other visits may be necessary. However, we only wish to help you."

"I understand. I'll try to be patient."

Still smiling, the gypsy woman nodded and waved toward the heavily draped doorway of the tent. Bowing his head, Lonnie stepped forward. Dividing the drapes with his hands, he stepped inside, his heart in his mouth and fire in his blood. He scrutinized the interior of the tent before walking to the little table in the far corner and spoke softly to the shadowy figure behind the table.

"Rosetta," he said hopefully. "Is it you?"

"Yes," she replied, in a voice no louder than a breathless whisper. "Why did you come? Why must you torture me more?"

"I had to come. I hope you understand. You know how I feel."

"Do you wish me to try to give you a reading?"

"I wish only one thing, my darling," he whispered fiercely across the table. "And that is for you to be in my arms and for us to make love to each other."

"Let me look me look into the crystal," she pleaded. "What I see might drive this madness from your heart."

"Go ahead and look, little dark eyes, only don't look too long. My arms ache to hold you close."

With a sob of protest, the gypsy girl flung back her veil and gazed into the murky depths of the ball on the table. For long minutes, she gazed, as motionless as a sphinx. Suddenly, she gave a low, moaning cry, covered the ball, and turned her face away.

"What did you see?" Lonnie asked. Reaching across the table, he imprisoned both of her hands in his. She made no protest, but averted her eyes. "Sweetheart, please tell me."

"It was the same as last night," she gasped. "Only this time, we were making love to each other as only a husband and wife should."

"My darling," Lonnie said huskily. Stepping behind the table, he laid pulled her to her feet and began to kiss her in a way that brought forth an impassioned response, but while she kissed him in wild abandon, she moaned protests.

"Please, oh, please, Lonnie," she said. "This all wrong for us. Can't you understand we live in different worlds? Our relationship is more dangerous than playing with fire. If my people found out what was going on, they would beat me within an inch of my life and do something terrible to you."

"But they're not going to find out. Your grandmother says it's all right for me to come and see you as often as I feel I need to. So you see, the coast is clear."

"I know she said that. I was listening while you talked to her. But she meant for you to come and see me professionally. Not to make love to me like you're doing now. Lonnie, please believe me when I say it's not safe for us to do this here."

"Then slip out and meet me tonight after the show."

"How? Granny sleeps on that cot over there by the wall of the tent."

"Where do you sleep, little dark eyes?"

"In a small tent behind this one."

"Then it would be easy enough for you to wait until Granny's sound asleep. Then come and meet me behind the schoolhouse. That way, we could talk freely, and we could kiss each other without fear."

"I tremble with excitement at the thought of meeting you secretly. Only, it would be unwise for me to do so, in more ways than one."

"Why do you say that, my darling?"

"We're far too attracted to each other to trust ourselves alone together in the moonlight on a night like this. I keep remembering what I saw in the crystal ball. It never lies."

"Rosetta, Rosetta," Lonnie groaned as he kissed her in the French style. "I love you. I know it sounds wacky, when I only met you yesterday, but such things happen between people. And I can't help myself if I ache all over from wanting to make love to you. Don't you want me to hold you tightly in my arms and caress you?"

"Yes, oh, yes," she whispered against his lips. "It's pure hell to feel this way about someone and be afraid to do something about it. I want to come to you, oh, how I want to, but my knees knock with fear at the thought of what my folks would do to us should they get wise to what we are doing."

"What your folks don't know won't hurt them," Lonnie muttered, gently disengaging himself from her embrace.

"Must you go so soon?" she asked.

"Yes, my love. But I'll wait for you each night behind the schoolhouse. Somehow, I feel that you will come to me. Until you do, my heart will ache. Good night, little dark eyes."

"I love you, too," she cried softly, her eyes like fathomless pools. "I won't promise to come to you, though. I won't, darling. I know I won't come. This has to be good bye for us."

"Aw, yes, you will," Lonnie whispered as he moved out of the reach of her arms and out of the tent.

The next night and the one following, Lonnie waited for Rosetta in the shadows by the schoolhouse until the eastern sky heralded the approach of another day, but she did not come to him. A third night, he kept his lonely vigil until long after the merry-makers at the carnival had departed, but still Rosetta did not come.

On the fourth night, he waited with heavy heart and fading hope. Midnight came and went, and a violent thunderstorm rolled over his head. Shivering, half soaked from the summer storm, Lonnie crouched in the doorway of the schoolhouse and watched the stars come out as the clouds rolled on. It was far past midnight. Hope of Rosetta coming to him had been washed out of his heart by the rainstorm. He accepted that she was lost to him in that dark and lonely hour of his vigil. The knowledge was bitter, and it tore a groan of anguish from him. Bowing his head in defeat, he turned away. Plodding to the end of the schoolhouse, he took a last look at the gypsies' darkened tents.

"Good-bye, little dark eyes," he whispered regretfully, and blew a kiss toward her tent. "May your future be brighter and happier than you hope."

He began walking away. A sound fell upon his ears from the direction of the tents. Crouching, Lonnie peered intently into the dark. Pattering footsteps came to his straining ears, and his heart leapt with joy. Someone was out there under the trees, coming closer with every heartbeat.

He saw a girl clad in a long coat running toward him. A girl with dark, flowing hair, hair as dark as the breath of midnight. The girl paused in the shadows at the corner of the schoolhouse.

"Lonnie? Where are you?"

At her cry, Lonnie sprang forward. "My darling little dark eyes," he said as he swept her into his arms. "You came. You came."

"Oh, my love," she sobbed. "I had to come to you. I just had to. I kept telling myself that I wouldn't, but my love for you overruled all resolutions to the contrary."

"Hush, my sweetheart," Lonnie cautioned. "We are too near the tents, and our voices will carry far on the night air. Come. My car is nearby. Let us get in and drive to a more secluded spot, where there will be no danger of discovery. Come, little dark eyes. I will bring you back safely in an hour or so. You do want to go with me, don't you?"

"With all my heart," she replied, clinging to him. "I gladly place myself in your hands. I trust you, Lonnie, darling."

Twenty minutes later, Lonnie and Rosetta were parked well off the main highway and she was pouring out her heart to him.

"My promised husband came into my sleeping tent last night as I was about to retire," Rosetta said, her voice harsh and full of fury. "He was awful, Lonnie, darling. I believe he intended to force his love upon me right then and there. To save myself, I lied. I told him I was having my monthly sickness. Oh, the beast. I despise him and loath the thought of his touch. And I love you, my darling, and keenly anticipate your every touch. What am I going to do? How am I going to live with that terrible man as my husband?"

"It's horrible to even think about," Lonnie roared. "I'll tell you what I'd like to do. It'd do my heart good to knock that bastard's block off. That's what he needs."

"That would never do," she moaned. "He would only make my life more miserable as payment for his embarrassment."

"But what about us, sweetheart?"

"What do you mean?" she whispered.

"Remember what you saw in the crystal ball?"

"How can I ever forget? Every time I look into the ball and think about us, and our love for each other, it tells me the same thing, only more. My darling, would it be wrong?"

"Would what be wrong?" Lonnie asked.

"Would it be wrong for us to make love to each other?"

"What kind of love do you mean, sweetheart?"

"The kind of love I saw us making to each other in the crystal ball."

"I don't think it would, but tell me about it, my love. Tell me everything you saw. That way, I'll know exactly what you mean. Don't be embarrassed. We love each other, and we belong together. It's only natural to express our love for one another in every way." Sensing her hesitation, Lonnie took her in his arms and covered her beautiful face with passionate kisses. She reciprocated, her lips hot and demanding, as though she would eat him up.

"There now, my little dark eyes," he said. "Just relax and tell me everything you saw. I know you want to tell me."

"All right," she whispered against his chest. "I was shameless, but so very happy. We had met somewhere and were passionately kissing each other. You put your hands all over my body, and I loved your touch. You took off my clothes, and I assisted you. Then you undressed. We were so eager to get into each other's arms. It was positively shameless, the way we acted, but it was heaven to realize the fulfillment of our love."

"Then what did you see us do, sweetheart?" Lonnie urged.

"Oh, my love. Need I go on? You know the rest. It was impossible to deny the fulfillment of our love. Some might say it was wrong, but it doesn't seem so to me."

"I love you. I love you," Lonnie whispered hoarsely, his face buried in the fragrant glory of her hair. "I want you so much so very much. Say you want me, too."

"I do. I do," she panted. "Tell me it's all right."

"It's all right, baby," he said gently, tightening his arms around her. "Come. Let us deny our love no longer. Tonight is ours. Tomorrow may never come for us. Let's you and I live this hour to its fullest."

That which followed was something only true lovers should experience. As gently and quickly as she would permit him, Lonnie disrobed the beautiful Rosetta. Her dress, her slip, her brassiere came off in a rapid succession. Then he paused to kiss and fondle her luscious breasts. Trembling and gasping ecstatically, but never protesting, Rosetta clung to him. They lay down upon an old blanket Lonnie took out of the trunk of his car.

"Please be gentle with me, darling," Rosetta pleaded. "I'm a virgin. No man has ever touched me as I am going to let you touch me now."

"Have no fear, sweetheart," Lonnie reassured. He commenced to fondle her lovingly from head to toe.

"Oh, Lonnie, Lonnie," she gasped, her breath coming hot and thick as she strained against him. "Hurry and give yourself to me. Only be gentle at first. Don't make it hurt too much the first time. I can't stand this torture any longer. I'm on fire from wanting you."

Gently, firmly, Lonnie complied with her request as best he could. After her panties were removed, and they were in the right position, he gently pushed, trying to begin the intercourse. Rosetta strained against him, rotating her hips. She screamed softly, then clutched him tighter than ever and accelerated the intensity of her movements and the speed of her gyrations.

Giving herself over completely to the passionate release she was experiencing, Rosetta became uninhibited in her movements and response to Lonnie's touch. Lonnie and Rosetta shared their first climax simultaneously. Gasping and clinging to each other, they sank into their embrace, and Lonnie pulled a portion of the old blanket over their naked bodies.

The balmy night wind sighed softly around them, and the stars shone brightly upon this fulfillment of nature's plan for reproduction. However, the recuperative powers of young lovers are amazing, and before Rosetta would consent to Lonnie driving her back to her tent, they enjoyed nature's greatest experience twice more.

During the week that followed, Lonnie and Rosetta shared many stolen hours under the stars. From the very first, she would not consent to him using contraceptives of any kind when they gave themselves to each other.

"I want your love, my darling, as nature intended it should be received," she whispered intimately against his lips as she lay in his arms. "Do not deny me this, my right, as a woman."

The young lovers continued to meet in secret and make love to each other in any position, way, or manner. Rosetta was the most satisfying love partner Lonnie had ever had. She made every effort to be cooperative in speech and action. Lonnie truly and deeply loved Rosetta, the gypsy girl, but when he asked her to marry him, she burst into tears and hid her face against his naked chest.

"Why do you weep, my darling?" he inquired.

"Don't ask me to explain," she sobbed brokenly. "I love you, too, more than my life."

"Then say you will marry me," he urged. "I will take you away from this life you hate."

"I can't marry you, my lover, and I can't tell you why, but let us not fret over that which can never be. Instead, let us enjoy to the fullest the stolen moments."

No amount of urging or pleading could sway her in the slightest.

On the last night of their meetings, before the carnival was scheduled to move to another town, Rosetta was moody and silent, but more demanding than ever in her desire for Lonnie's love.

"Tomorrow we move to the next town down the river," she said as he kissed her good night behind the schoolhouse.

"How far away is it?"

"Twenty miles. Will you come to see me there, also?" she asked softly, a queer little break in her voice.

"Wild horses could not keep me away, little dark eyes," Lonnie assured her as he kissed the sweet mouth she raised to his.

"Then I can go to sleep tonight knowing that I will be in your arms again tomorrow. I am happy now. Goodnight, my lover."

She slipped reluctantly out of his arms and sped away under the trees, back to the tents she called home.

The following afternoon, a cloudburst swept the Target Valley. Four days passed before the valley road was open again to automobile travel. His heart in his throat, Lonnie drove to the town down the river where the carnival had gone.

When he arrived, he learned that the carnival had moved on that morning, but the gypsies were not with them. A wedding had taken place in the gypsy camp the evening before. The beautiful young fortuneteller had married one of their own, a man to whom she had been engaged since she a little girl.

With aching heart and tear-filled eyes, Lonnie turned away. It would be useless and cruel to try to see Rosetta. She was lost to him, and he accepted it. He never saw her again.

Chapter 13

The Widow

*F*or many months after Rosetta's loss, Lonnie grieved as only one who has truly loved and lost will grieve. He lost weight and interest in everything and everybody. He became short tempered. His mother suspected that her son's trouble was the result of a bitter disappointment in an affair of the heart, and she wisely refrained from asking useless questions and giving a lot of unwanted advice. During those days of painful readjustment, Lonnie vowed that he would never permit himself to become romantically interested in a woman again. Two years passed, and Lonnie maintained his unnatural withdrawal from the opposite sex. He had been burned, so he shied away from a repetition. Time is Mother Nature's healer, and so it was with Lonnie Dolan. He was a strong, healthy, normal young man, and his sexual urges were the same as any male.

He became disinterested in farming and eventually persuaded his mother to rent out the farm. Coal mining paid handsome wages and had regular hours, so Lonnie secured himself a job in a mine. He and his mother lived in a three-room house near the mine where he worked, but the dwelling was too small.

After Lonnie saved up several hundred dollars, he decided to go house hunting and learned of an attractive, well built, six-room bungalow on a five-acre lot that could be purchased for a reasonable piece. It was also near the stores of Valley Head. After talking the matter over with his mother, and knowing her love of a good garden, he went to view the property near the end of March on a Saturday afternoon. On his way, Lonnie did something he'd never done before. He stopped at the local tavern and had a few drinks with some of his mining friends. When   he arrived at the bungalow, he was more intoxicated then he had been in many a long day. As a result, he was unprepared for what confronted him when he knocked on the door.

A beautiful, auburn-haired, brown-eyed young woman of medium height stood in the door. Two bright-eyed children, five years or younger, clung to the hem of the plain housedress she wore.

"Did you knock, sir?" she asked pleasantly.

"Yes, I did," he replied.

"May I help you? Are you looking for someone?"

"No, ma'am. I'm not," Lonnie replied, grinning up at her foolishly. "I'm looking for a house for sale."

"Yes, it is."

"May I look at the property?"

"Certainly. Mind if I make a suggestion first?"

"Not at all," Lonnie said, gallantly sweeping off his hat and trying to bow low. He staggered a bit then straightened. "Anything your little heart desires. I'm always ready to listen to suggestions from the fair sex. Especially from one as pretty as you are."

"Thank you for the compliment." She smiled, her white even teeth sparkling. "However, in your condition I'm inclined to doubt you can rightly tell how pretty I might be. Why not look at the outside of the property first? Then look at the inside."

"On my word of honor, I meant every word I said. I'd have to be blind not to see how pretty you are," Lonnie vowed solemnly. "If you don't mind, I would like to take some time looking at the outside and the acreage."

"That'll be perfectly all right. Just knock when you're ready to come in."

Twenty minutes later, Lonnie stood at the front door of the bungalow again. He had liked the looks of the land that went with the property and was anxious to see the inside of the house. When he heard footsteps approach the door in answer to his knock, he kicked off his four-buckle overshoes and made himself ready to enter.

"Come right on in," the lovely young lady said as she opened the door. "Oh, that's fine. I see you've kicked off your Arctics. That mud sure plays bob with the floors."

"It sure does," Lonnie muttered, his eyes drinking in her trim figure as he brushed past her on his way into the house. "I'll do my best to not mess up anything up."

"There's six rooms. Come. It'll only take a couple of minutes. I'll show you the rooms."

Muttering his thanks, Lonnie followed the young woman through the house. The living room first, then the dining room, then the kitchen. When he looked at the heavy four-poster bed in the master bedroom, his blood leaped excitedly through his veins as he envisioned the hours of passionate love making this young wife had doubtless spent with her husband on that well constructed bed.

"There's also a small bath off the kitchen," she said, seemingly oblivious to the naked desire in Lonnie's eyes as he followed her about. "No toilet in the bathroom. That's outside. Just a tub with a drain to it. If you wish to bathe, you'll have to heat the water on the kitchen stove or out in the backyard in a big iron kettle."

"I understand," Lonnie mumbled, following the young woman back to the kitchen again. "I have to heat my bath water the same way at home."

"Well, that's the way with most rural property." She smiled, busying herself about the kitchen. "Sit down for a while if you want. I have to start a bite of supper. It's getting late, and the children are used to having their supper at about this time."

"That's perfectly all right," Lonnie said as he pulled out one of the chairs at the kitchen table. "I'll have to be running along soon. If you don't mind, though, I'd like to stick around for a few minutes. Maybe I could talk with your husband about the property when he gets home. I hope you don't mind. I'll try not to get in your way."

The young woman swung away from the sink where she was slicing potatoes into the pot and faced him squarely. Her beautiful face took on a strained look, while her big, brown eyes went dark with pain.

"It's all right for you to sit there for a while, sir," she said slowly, sadness dominating her words. "But if you plan to wait for my husband's return, you'll have a long wait."

"I don't understand," Lonnie said.

"I have no husband."

"Divorced?"

"No."

"He walked out on you? Is that it?"

"He's gone," she whispered, as though talking to herself. She turned back to the sink.

"Now I get it," Lonnie said, still too intoxicated to grasp what the young woman had tried to tell him. "The worthless lout took off with another woman. Of all the nerve. A man that'd walk out on a beautiful wife and his own kids ought to be horsewhipped. Why—"

"Stop it," she screamed. She faced him again. This time, her lovely eyes were blazing. "Listen, you drunken so and so. My husband is dead. He was the best man on the world, too. He lost his life cutting timber. A tree fell on him."

"I'm sorry, ma'am," Lonnie apologized. "I didn't know. You only said—"

"What I said is my own business," she blazed. "Bill never would have left me and the children. We loved him terribly, and he loved us just as much. How dare you insinuate such a degrading thing?"

"Please, accept my apologies," Lonnie said miserably. "I meant no offense. I am bit tipsy this afternoon. I don't ordinarily go in for this sort of thing, but when I stopped at Blake's Tavern for a sandwich on my way here, I ran into some of the fellows I work with at No. 3 Mine up on the Point. They insisted I have a few drinks with them."

"And you got hog drunk," she said scornfully.

"Not hog drunk, ma'am. Just more than I ought to be. I'm sincerely sorry I came to your home in this condition. It won't happen again. I'll go. First, though, I'd like to ask a couple of questions about your husband."

"The subject is painful to me, and it's none of your business."

"I know that, and I don't mean to pry. I'm wondering how you support yourself and the children. The only man I knew about that got killed around here in the woods was Bill Bronson. That was a year and half ago. Was he your husband?"

"Yes."

"Did he leave you an insurance policy?"

"No."

"Then how do you get along with two small children? Living costs are high right now."

"We subsist on the workman's compensation the lumber company carried on my husband. The children and I get so much every month. We'll get it until the twins are sixteen, maybe older."

"Good. Do you and the children live alone?"

"Most of the time. Last summer, one of my sisters came up from Virginia and stayed with us for three months. She left the first of

September. Had to go back to school. It's been awful lonesome here since my husband's gone, but I manage. Elsie promised to come back this summer, just as soon as school is out."

"How about your husband's relations? Don't they come see you and the kids?"

"Not any more. My husband only had one brother in this part of state. He came for a while, but not for over a year now."

"Why not?"

"He began to get some fancy ideas about him and me. I put him in his place, however. Since then, he hasn't pestered me."

"How about boyfriends? A beautiful young widow like you should have a handful hanging around."

"Sir, I don't like what you said, or the way said it. My social life is my own. As for men, I don't need any of them hanging around my door."

"Then I take it you don't have a steady boyfriend just now. Right?"

"That's correct."

"Well, neither do I have a steady girlfriend. I'm unmarried, but available to a lovely young woman like you. We should get together. I think we'd be good for each other."

"What do you mean?" she asked as she paused in setting the table to look at him. "What are you trying to suggest?"

"Only something that's perfectly normal, according to the laws of nature," Lonnie calmly said, watching her beautiful face. "I'm a normal, healthy, young man. And you're a normal, healthy, young woman."

"So?"

"I need what a woman like you could give me, and you, lovely lady, need in the worst way that which I would enjoy giving you. Do I make myself clear?"

"Perfectly," she snapped, her voice icy cold. "Now listen, you drunken bum, and listen well. When I want to shack up with a man, it won't be with the likes of you. Get out. If you ever show your ass around her again, I'll have the sheriff on you for molesting me. Does that answer your filthy questions?"

"Sure. Hell, woman, I was only saying something I'm positive you've thought about many times since you started sleeping by yourself. It's against nature for healthy men and women to deny the desires they feel for each other's bodies. It might not be right according to the rules of social etiquette, but it's true. I have urges. We all do. Why, I'll bet at night in bed you even—"

"Get out of here with your indecent ideas and suggestions," the young widow cried in rage and frustration. She grabbed a wicked-looking butcher knife from the kitchen cabinet and waved it menacingly. "I'm a lonely, sad woman," she said slowly, her voice pregnant with pain. "I'm also a God-fearing Christian, but if you lay one of your dirty hands on me, I'll cut you wide open. Now, for the last time, get out."

"All right, all right," Lonnie grunted, scooping up his hat and making a dash for the front door. "There's no need to get yourself all worked up." He yanked the door open and stepped outside. "We all have to live with our sexual needs. I still think you and I could—"

"To hell with what you think!" the enraged widow screeched, throwing the butcher knife on the table and picking up a stick of firewood. She flung the wooden missile with amazing accuracy. With a sodden thump, it bounced off Lonnie's buttock as he bent over to draw on his rubber overshoes.

"I ought to come right back in there and screw you for that," he said angrily as he felt his injured rear gingerly, retreating down the driveway, overshoes in hand.

"Oh, beast," she gasped, her face scarlet. "Heaven help the unfortunate woman who falls into your clutches. Depraved wretch. Go find yourself a fur-lined knothole. Even that is better than you deserve, you drunken lout."

Lonnie's next meeting with the beautiful, fiery young widow came about quite unexpectedly, at the elementary school on Point Mountain, the night before the last day of school. The tenth of May. School was later than usual in closing that spring due to heavy snows the previous winter that had forced the school to close its doors for more than a week. Those days had to be made up. On the night of the school social, the weather was ideal. A cloudless sky prevailed, with a great round moon, bright as a new silver dollar, shedding its mellow light over the countryside.

"A perfect night for romance," Lonnie mused as he parked his battered car and casually strolled into the dark shadows cast by the weather-beaten old school.

Memories of bygone years flooded over him as he pushed through the crowded doorway and sank into a seat at the back of the room.

"It's been ten years since the last winter I was here," he said, gazing around the room at the many unfamiliar faces. Some few he recognized, but only because they worked at the mine. He saw nobody, however, that he remembered as a school chum.

"Time sure changes things, and people," he mused as he nodded to the men from the mine and looked their dates over with an appraising eye. "Wonder where all my old school chums have drifted to? If any of them are here tonight, I sure don't recognize them. That last teacher I had. Betsy Blake. That little gal was one luscious armful. I was only a kid then in years, but I was enough of a man to tom her for a fare you well. I did such a good job of it that I knocked her up. Even so, she loved every jump I gave her. Betsy might have a pack of kids now, but I doubt it. That jerk she married was nothing but skin and bones. He didn't look like he had enough zip about him to knock up a grasshopper. That was the way he stacked up with me, only I'm no authority in such matters. He could have been a whiz in bed, and then again, he might have had good neighbors. Betsy once said he wasn't much on smooching. Oh, well. What the hell? Enough of this raking through the ashes of the past. All that is water over the dam, and I'm glad. Hello! What's this? From the looks of the greybeard who just walked out on the rostrum, I'd say the festivities are about to begin. Reckon I better bring my thoughts back to the present and pay some attention to what's going on around me. Sure hope I latch onto a box tonight that some hot little babe fixed up, and I hope she doesn't have a boyfriend along. I'm really in the mood for lovey-doveying."

The elderly man on the rostrum held up his hands to command the audience's attention. When the buzz of conversation died down, he began to speak.

"Friends, neighbors, pupils," he boomed. "Welcome, one and all. Tonight, we've decided to depart from the usual way we hold our last day of school exercises. Tomorrow, all the pupils need do is report here at the schoolhouse and pick up their report card. We, the school board, sincerely hope all of our pupils passed. Your teacher earnestly joins us in that hope. After the children have put on the plays, sung the songs, and said the recitations memorized for this occasion, we will auction off the boxes of candy and the lunches the ladies graciously prepared for tonight's doings. Here's hoping everybody has a fine time. Kids, let 'er roll."

For more than an hour, Lonnie enjoyed the dialogues and recitations the pupils had prepared for the evening. Two songs were sung, and the audience was invited to participate. Afterwards, the auction was held. The boxes of candy were sold first. Lonnie listened to the spirited bidding from the young men, and the squealing and giggling cries from the girls whose candy was being auctioned off, and he smiled and decided to bid on one of the lunch baskets.

Bidding on the lunch baskets was also spirited, at first. Soon, however, it began to wane. At last, only three lunch baskets remained. The one Lonnie chose to bid on was a small wicker basket tied with a bright red ribbon. The bidding for the basket climbed to three dollars. Then, after two rounds of ten-cent bids, the basket was knocked off to Lonnie for four dollars.

"Will the lady come forward whose basket was just sold?" the auctioneer called. "Will the gentleman who bought the basket please step forward?"

Wondering whom he had to share the basket with, Lonnie rose from his seat and strode forward. As he did, a young woman stepped out in the aisle about halfway up the room and preceded him to the rostrum.

The woman's steps were quick and energetic. Lonnie looked appreciatively at her poised head, slender waist, and wiggling hips as he strode behind her. When she reached the auctioneer, she accepted the lunch basket and turned around. Lonnie gasped in surprise as he stared into the upturned face and flashing eyes of the widow that he met six weeks before.

"Hello, there," he mumbled, his face going brick red. "That sure is a pretty basket you've fixed up for tonight."

"Thank you," she replied. "I hope you like the food." She walked towards a table. Lonnie followed.

"Mrs. Bronson," Lonnie began as soon they sat and she opened the basket of food. "I'm awfully sorry if I've embarrassed you in any way this evening by bidding on your basket."

"It's all right," she assured him. "How was you to know this was my basket? Every man present tonight has a right to bid on the boxes and lunch baskets. That's the way it is at the box social."

"I know," Lonnie replied. "It's only that I feel badly about the way I acted the first time we met. I didn't even have the manners to introduce myself. Please permit me to do that now."

"All right," she said. "Who are you? I'm Ruby Bronson."

"It's a pleasure to meet you, Ruby," Lonnie said, gratefully accepting the hand she held out to him. "I'm Lonnie Dolan. I'm unmarried and twenty-seven. I live with my mother, who also is a widow. I work at one of the mines up here. I sincerely apologize for my behavior the first time we met. There now. I feel better."

"Good," she laughed softly. "Your apology is accepted, Lonnie. Now eat up. The food is still warm. The people I came with will be leaving soon. I want to be ready to leave when they are."

"May I call you Ruby?"

"I'd like that," she replied slowly, her voice a low musical alto. "That is, I'd like you to if we're going to be friends."

"We're going to be friends, I'm sure," Lonnie said earnestly. "But why must you rush off now that you've discovered I'm not a monster? I have my car outside. It's not the most elegant car in the world, I know, but I'd be honored if you'd let me drive you home tonight."

"That would be nice," she murmured softly. "Maybe I ought not, though. After all, we hardly know each other. The people I came with might—"

"Nonsense," Lonnie said. "I'm sure they'd understand. Introduce me to them as your friend. That's no lie, Ruby. I want very much for us to be friends, if you'll give us a chance to get to know each other."

"That's awfully kind of you to say, Lonnie," she said, gazing into his eyes as though searching for a reason behind his sudden kindness. "Do you mean it in the right way, though? Are you serious? Are you just angling to get me alone with you on one of these mountain roads in the middle of night? Is that it, Lonnie? Is that what you're trying to do?"

"So help me, Ruby, no. On my word of honor, I mean to be perfectly honest with you. If you'll let me drive you home, I'll not say one word against it if you insist on your friends driving behind us, all the way. When we arrive at your home, they can even stick around until I drive away. Is that fair?"

"More than fair," she said, dropping her head and putting the remains of the lunch back into the basket. "I don't know what to say."

"If you'll go with me, and it'll make you feel safer, you can also carry a club on your lap. That way, you can konk me over the head if I try anything funny. Now, what do you say?"

"I'll go with you, Lonnie Dolan," she answered quietly, lifting her head and giving him a long look. "I want to believe you're sincere. Heaven help us both if you're not. Come. Let us go before I change my mind. I'll tell my friends. It'll only take a minute."

With mixed emotions, Lonnie waited while Ruby Bronson told her friends of the new arrangement. The glances the elderly couple shot his way were full of suspicion and distrust.

The miles sped by under the wheels of his old car far too quickly for Lonnie. Occasionally, he glanced into rear view mirror, but no one was following. Ruby Bronson had believed him. She had placed herself in his hands, trusting that he would conduct himself as a gentlemen. When he realized this, he felt humbled.

Ruby was quite talkative. Once or twice during lulls in the conversation, she even burst into song. Once, when Lonnie laughed at something she said, she laughed with him. It made him feel good inside to hear how genuine and carefree her laughter was.

"You're home," he called cheerily as he drove down the last long, winding slope and up the driveway to the six-room bungalow. "The big bad wolf has delivered you back to your doorstep. All safe and sound, I hope."

"As safe and snug as a bug in a rug," she laughed happily. "It was real nice coming home with you, Lonnie. I'm sorry I was so suspicious of your intentions at first. Am I forgiven?"

"I don't blame you. I know I deserved it. There's nothing for me to forgive. I must ask you to forgive me for the shameful way I acted when we first met."

"You're forgiven," she said softly, laying one of her hands on his where they gripped the steering wheel. "Why don't you come in for a while and have a cup of coffee? It's not too late, yet. Besides, the woman I hired to stay with the twins tonight is going to stay all night."

"Let me take a raincheck on the invitation, Ruby. I know it's not too late, but I won't stop in this time. We had such a wonderful time together this evening that I'm afraid I'd wear out my welcome if I went in. I sure wouldn't want that to happen."

"Will I see you again?" she asked.

"I'd like that an awful lot, but are you sure you want to after the way I acted before?"

"Yes, Lonnie, I would. After the wonderful way you treated me tonight, I know I'm safe in telling you that. Come again, anytime."

"Thanks a million, Ruby. Good night now, and may you have pleasant dreams."

"Lonnie," she said slowly, as she bade him good night and started to get out of the car. "You still interested in buying this house?"

"Not after the fool I made of myself the day I came and looked at it."

"What's that got to do with buying?"

"The way I look at it is this. Even though you rent this house, it's still home to you and the kids. My mother and I decided to stay where we're at this summer. I wouldn't feel right buying this place now, not after knowing you and your circumstances."

"You are a gentleman, Lonnie Dolan," she said with a queer little catch in her voice.

"Forget it," he growled.

"Oh, I almost forgot," she said, after he had gotten back into the car and closed the door. "The neighbors and I sometimes have parties. If we have one soon, would you like to come?"

"I'd be very happy to. I'd like to come to the party if you'll be there."

"That's out and out flattery, Lonnie Dolan," she chided him gently, standing distractingly close. Her full red lips were inches from his.

Exerting iron control over his emotions, he grinned down at her and nodded his head. "Flattery or not, Ruby, I meant every word," he said.

"It was music to my ears," she laughed. "I promise that I will personally see that you get invited to every party I'm invited to. Satisfied?'

"Good enough," he chuckled. "Bye-bye, now, Ruby. See you soon."

"Lonnie," she whispered softly, turning towards the bungalow, "if we have a party, I'll get word to you at the mine. Be sure to come."

"I'll come if I have to walk on crutches," he called after her retreating figure. Getting into his dilapidated car, he drove away. His heart was light and carefree for the first time in many months. He had not felt so light-hearted since the day he lost Rosetta, the gypsy fortuneteller.

"I wanted to latch onto some hot-blooded, unattached little chick at the school social tonight," he mused as he drove home. "I sure did. That Ruby is plenty hot, and in the right places, too, I'll bet. She's obviously unattached. She's pretty as a picture, and cute as a speckled pup. And that figure of hers. Boy, oh, boy. But hold on there, Lonnie, old man. That kind of thinking could be dangerous for a single man. That gal is a wide-open mantrap, if ever I saw one. I just know that she's looking for a father for them kids. Now that I've showed her I can be a gentlemen, maybe she's getting ideas about me. If she has, I'll have to watch my step, but while I'm watching my step, I'll slip a stiff prong right square between those pretty legs of hers if she gives me half a chance. So help me, I sure will. And I'll enjoy every minute of it."

Ten days later, Lonnie received word at the mine that he was invited to a party at the Widow Bronson's. The foreman rolled his eyes knowingly as he delivered the message, and as is the way of older men, he gave Lonnie a bit of fatherly advice. Assuming as indifferent an attitude as he could muster, Lonnie shrugged, smiled casually, held his tongue, and walked away.

"What these loose-tongued coal diggers don't know about Ruby and me won't hurt them," he muttered as he returned to his duties. "One thing for certain, I'm not going to give them an ear full."

Ruby introduced Lonnie to all of her nearby neighbors the night of the party. They had come in full force. The six-room bungalow was full to overflowing with men, women, teenagers, small children racing from room to room, and crying babies.

"Holy smoke," Lonnie thought as Ruby monopolized him and turned the duties of hostess over to one of the older women. "If this is what it takes to be a family man, I doubt I'm cut out for it. And with a ready-made family to boot. Wow."

The merry-making, gabbing, and yelling at the children went on until after eleven o'clock. Then the couples began collecting their offspring and bidding Rudy good night. All of them shook hands with Lonnie as they left and expressed pleasure at having made his acquaintance. They all invited him to their homes.

"They liked you," Ruby said happily as the last of the neighbors trooped away and she and Lonnie were left alone. Ruby's children had been tucked into bed since nine.

"I liked them, too," Lonnie said, moving closer to her on the couch and imprisoning one of her hands in his. She gave him a questing look, but made no effort to withdraw her hand.

"It's nearly midnight, Ruby," he said, squeezing her hand gently. "You've had a hard day, so I'd better bid you goodnight. I had a very nice time, and I enjoyed meeting your neighbors. Thanks a million for inviting me."

"Must you leave so soon, now that we're alone and can talk?" she protested, a note of disappointment in her voice. "Tomorrow is Sunday, and you can sleep late."

"I know, little auburn hair," Lonnie replied, looking into her lovely eyes. "But I better go, now. It's safer if I do."

"What do you mean, Lonnie?" she asked, her eyes wide and innocent, but Lonnie knew that she understood perfectly well what he meant.

"You're a beautiful woman, Ruby Bronson," he said with brutal frankness. "And I'm a man who's attracted to you more than I care to admit."

"I'm glad," she whispered, giving his hands a squeeze.

"If I stay longer, I'll offend you."

"How?" she asked softly, moving closer to him on the couch.

"By pulling you into my arms and kissing that sweet mouth of yours," Lonnie said, jumping off the couch and facing her. "I have to be honest with you, woman. That's the way I feel."

"I understand, Lonnie," she said, her throaty voice filled with the knowledge that a virile man desired her. In one sinuous flowing movement, she got off the couch and moved toward him. In her clear eyes was a challenge as old as time.

Cursing under his breath, Lonnie swept her into his arms and crushed her to his chest. She gave a great, whispering sigh, closed her eyes, and flung back her head. Her inviting, partly opened lips were inches beneath his. Bending his head, he claimed that ripe, waiting mouth in a kiss that shook him from head to toe. Her lips were soft, and very warm, and sweet as new honey. From the moment of contact with Lonnie's they clung with a tenacity that left him gasping for breath.

"I'm sorry, Ruby," Lonnie said, releasing her and stepping back. "I didn't mean for that to happen, but it did. I suppose you're angry at me again."

"No," she whispered softly, as she rearranged her hair. "I'm not angry at you, and I'm not sorry it happened. Sometimes a woman wants to be kissed just as intensely as a man wants to kiss her. I'm only human, too, you know."

"You darling," Lonnie cried happily, reaching for her again.

"Please, kind sir," she remonstrated, pushing him away. "Not again tonight. Let's not spoil our first evening together."

"You're not angry?"

"Of course not. Only a bit tired, a lot confused in my mind about certain things, but awfully happy you came to my party. I wouldn't have missed it for anything," she said, smiling very prettily. "When you get home and hit the hay I hope you have pleasant dreams."

"Good night, Ruby," he said, putting on his hat and coat. "I hope we have pleasant dreams about each other. However, I don't only want to dream about you, dear lady. I want to come and see you again. When, Ruby? Tell me when I can come again. Name a date, and make it soon."

"Next Saturday night be all right?"

"Wonderful," he said. "Only it's a lifetime away."

"The days will soon pass, impatient one."

"They always do." Lonnie grinned, wryly. "See you at about eight. Okay?"

"Perfect," she called after him as he turned away, and strode out of the house and down the driveway to his car.

Thereafter, Lonnie had a date with Ruby Bronson at least once a week. However, she kept her emotions under perfect control when they were alone together. Lonnie, on the other hand, tried numerous ways to break down her resistance to his advances, but she somehow managed to thwart his devious schemes and remain her calm, unruffled self, in complete control of her emotions at all times.

Often, when they were in a close embrace, his hands intentionally strayed to her full breasts. At such times, she would quietly, quickly, and unceremoniously remove his hands from her breasts and favor him with a reproachful look.

"Damn it all to hell, Ruby Bronson," Lonnie growled one evening after she had just removed his hands from her bosom and tweaked his nose vigorously in payment for the privileges he had taken. "Can't you get it through that lovely head of yours that I love you and want every wonderful thing about you more than I can say?"

"Do you really mean that, Lonnie?" she asked with a tremble in her voice. "Are you serious about what you just said?

"Hell, yes," he roared, pulling her into his arms. "As much as any man can want a woman."

"Then marry me," she whispered, looking into his eyes. "I love you very much, Lonnie. I'm sure you know now that I've loved you from the first."

"Us get married?" Lonnie mumbled, as he stared down into her flushed face. In that moment, he realized that the quivering creature he held in his arms was a woman in love. A vibrantly alive young woman who needed a mate. A mother, who desperately needed a husband and father for her orphaned children.

"Yes, yes, Lonnie darling," she breathed. She clutched him tightly in her arms and laid her head against his heaving chest. "It's what we both want and need. I know that, and so do you. We belong together as man and wife. Speak to me, sweetheart. Tell me you want that for us as much as I do."

"I do, Ruby. Honestly, I do," he stammered, his head whirling. "But I get the feeling that I was never cut out to be a husband and father. Maybe we better not see each other anymore."

"Why not?" she cried, bursting into tears. "If you love me like you just said you do, how can you say a cruel thing like that?"

"I don't feel like I want to get married just now. Is that so difficult to understand?"

"Lonnie Dolan," she cried, as she pulled herself out of his arms and flopped, full length, on the couch. "I understand only one thing. You don't love me. You never did. How could you, if you don't think we should see each other again?"

"Damn it, woman, stop blubbering, and listen to me. I love you terribly, though you don't believe me. I want your love so much I'm actually in pain every minute we're together."

"I get it now," she said angrily. Sitting up on the couch, she began wiping the tears from her eyes. "You say you love me, but I know now it's not the right or decent way. Your love and need for me is all physical. It's what you'd feel for a whore you picked up out there on the road."

"That's not true, Ruby," Lonnie roared, wroth.

"Oh, yes, it is, and don't bother to deny it. At last, it's been brought out in the open."

"How can you say that?"

"How can I be honest with myself and not face it? All you want of me is to satisfy your physical desires. Nothing else. Just a clean, decent woman to hug, kiss, paw over, and screw whenever the urge hits you. It's the truth I'm speaking, Lonnie Dolan. And you know it as well as I do."

"Maybe it is," Lonnie growled, sitting down on the couch beside her. "Even so, wanting to make all out love to you isn't as shameful as you try to make it sound."

"If I gave in your desires and let that happen between us, we'd be no better than a couple of animals out in the fields," she whispered, moving as far away from him as the couch would permit.

"Hog wash. We'd only be two people in love, doing something about our desire for each other. That's the situation in a nut shell. Nothing more. Nothing less."

"I love you, Lonnie," she said, her beautiful face white and drawn. "I'll marry you in a minute if you'll have me and the children. I want your love, too, in the worst way. I'm red hot for it. But I'll never give myself to you on your terms."

"Time will tell whether you live up to your noble convictions or not," Lonnie growled. Picking his hat up off the clothes tree, he bent down and kissed her. "See you next weekend, honey," he said, turning to the front door.

"Good night, Lonnie," she replied, sadly. "I love you. Don't forget to come and see me again."

The weeks of the summer sped by, and Lonnie continued to court Ruby Bronson. They never spoke of his desire for her anymore, but each knew it was between them like a living flame, every moment they spent together. She never permitted him any liberties with her person, other than passionate kisses.

Her passion for him matched his for her, Lonnie knew. More times than not, she seemed impatient for him to fold her in a close embrace and rain passionate, demanding kisses on her. When he did not meet her response as she felt he ought, she increased the intensity of her kisses in a way that never failed to set him on fire. At French kissing, she was an artist. She liked standing in a close embrace when they kissed each other this way.

"It's better this way, darling," she would whisper. Then she fastened her soft, sweet, demanding mouth on his in a possessive manner that was positively sinful. Her torrid little tongue would dart in and out of his mouth in explorations that were pure ecstasy, while she pressed her beautifully proportioned body to his.

As the weeks passed, Lonnie noticed something about Ruby that he believed would eventually spell success for him. He wanted to possess her so badly that it had become an obsession. The thought of her willingly giving herself to him haunted every waking hour and every dream at night. He at last became willing to employ any unscrupulous method to attain his goal.

Whenever they visited the neighbors and alcoholic drinks were served, Ruby always drank a small glass. She seemed to enjoy the lift the beverage gave her, and after this small indulgence, she was more intense in her response and more demanding when he kissed her good night.

Always, after a nip of wine, whiskey, or hard cider, Ruby insisted on being caressed, long and passionately, before she let him leave for the night, and she always gave her most devastating French kisses after she had had a drink of some alcoholic beverage.

Knowing all this, he decided to lower his standard of conduct. If, in order to have his way with Ruby Bronson, he had to get her intoxicated, then he would get her intoxicated. Such was his decision, though he cursed himself for an unprincipled cad.

A week later, Lonnie bought a quart of expensive, smooth, potent wine. His date with Ruby the following Saturday night went off satisfactorily. They took the children and saw a double feature at the drive-in. It was late when they returned to the bungalow where Ruby lived, but she insisted he come in for a few minutes and have a cup of coffee.

"Why don't we try some of this?" Lonnie suggested, reaching under the car seat and pulling out the bottle of wine. "A friend of mine gave me this a few days ago," he lied. "He said it was good stuff, but I haven't tried it yet."

"It's all right with me," Ruby replied, a strange note in her voice. "We might as well have a couple of drinks together, I guess."

As soon as they entered the house, she tucked the children into bed and brought two small glasses from the kitchen. Lonnie opened the wine and poured her a full glass. Her hands shook as she received it and raised it to her lips. Closing her eyes, she drunk it down without stopping to catch her breath and held out the empty glass to him.

"Pour me another one, sweetheart," she whispered, while a shadow crossed her lovely face. "That's very good wine."

"I'm glad you like it, honey," Lonnie grinned, refilling her glass.

Clutching the wine in both hands, Ruby raised it to her lips, shot Lonnie a queer look across its brim, and drank all of it. Lonnie watched in open-mouthed amazement. The only thing he could figure was that she was desperately trying to get herself drunk.

"Maybe she's ready to give in to me," Lonnie mused, as she lurched off the couch they were sitting on and staggered into her bedroom. "And this is her way of going about it."

In a few moments, Ruby came swaying back into the living room. She gave a strange little laugh and turned out all of the lights in the room, except a small table lamp across the room. As she passed Lonnie, she grabbed the wine bottle out of his hands. Standing spraddle-legged in the center of the living room, she tipped the bottle of wine of her lips and drank deeply.

Ruby handed the bottle back to Lonnie and walked to the couch on legs that appeared to have turned to rubber. Uttering another strange laugh, she flung herself on the couch, turned over on her back, drew up her knees, and turned her face to the wall.

Lonnie realized that his golden opportunity was at hand and sat the bottle of wine on the floor by his chair. In two long strides, he reached the couch and sat down beside Ruby. When he bent and kissed her, and put his hands on places she had forbade him to touch, she trembled like a frightened fawn. Then, when he ran his hands up her legs, she cried out incoherently and covered her face with her hands.

As his right hand slipped under her dress, he gasped in surprise. Her rounded buttock was completely naked. Smiling to himself, Lonnie slipped out of his trousers and shorts. With firm, gentle hands, he separated Ruby's legs. Then, holding them apart, he crawled between them. As soon as he had properly positioned himself, their sexual organs made contact, and Ruby came alive with feverish intensity. With a sharp little scream of surrender, acceptance, and fulfillment, she gave her buttocks a squirming movement. Lonnie's organ plunged into her. Ruby Bronson became a wild woman in her uninhibited participation of giving themselves to each other.

With her breath coming hot, thick, and fast, she gave Lonnie one of the most violent and satisfying sexual experiences he had ever had. Afterwards, they could never recall who attained satisfaction first, not that it mattered. All that the lovers knew was that each had attained absolute fulfillment. From that night on, Ruby asked Lonnie to marry her every time he came to see her.

"Marry me, darling," she would plead, as she lay in his arms, naked as the day she was born, quenching the desire they felt for each other. "Make an honest, decent woman of me. I'll do my best to make you a good wife."

Lonnie always gave her some vague reason why he felt marriage would not work out for them. Then, in October, something transpired that made his reason for wanting to remain single more logical than ever. A law was passed, whereby all eligible men were required to register for a year's training in the United States Armed Forces. Six weeks after Lonnie registered, he reported for his pre-induction physical examination. He passed the physical examination with flying colors, and was promptly put in 1-A, subject to immediate induction into the armed forces.

That night, Lonnie and Ruby shared a tub of hot water for the first time. First, each gave the other a bath. Then they gave each other a rubdown. Lonnie kissed Ruby's beautiful body as he ministered to her, and she sighed in deep contentment at his every caress. When it came her turn to minister to him, she worked over his body for more than an hour. Then, before she let him to put his clothes back on, she gave herself to him, wantonly. Only when he was exhausted and pleaded for her to have mercy on him did she stop stimulating his desire.

"I love you, my beautiful man," she whispered as she wiped the sweat from his brow and covered their naked bodies with a blanket.

The following week, Lonnie received his induction notice. That night, he went to call on Ruby for the last time, only he didn't know it then. As he wheeled his battered old car over the road that led to her home, he didn't know of the many strange lands he would set foot on over the next three years as a member of the United States Army. Nor did he visualize the many strange and beautiful women he was destined to make love to in those strange lands. But that is another chapter in the eventful, tempestuous life of Lonnie Dolan, and it will be told in another story.

The End

1979 – Jane and Harold, his first dance.

1972 – Giving Janice away at her wedding.

Early 1950's – Jane and Harold

Fall 1969 – Nancy, Janice, and Harold at the park.

Harold H. Milton

January 16, 1990 – Janice and Harold on her birthday.

1980 – Janice and Harold.

Janice and Harold on Easter.

Janice reviewing Harold's books for publishing.

June, 1986 – Nursing graduation.

Harold's birthday.

Harold at the fireplace in their Bay Village home.

Janice with Harold on his birthday.

Fall, 1969 – Jane and Harold.

Harold'sgrandparents,AlfredFarleyandLucindaMillerFarley.

House on W. 19th – Cleveland, Ohio.

Harold and dog, Heidi.

Harold's birthday.

1995 – Harold with great-grandaughter, Madison.

Harold and Madison.

Harold and daughter, Nancy.

Orville Blanton

Orville Blanton with baseball.

1980s – Harold and Janice in the woods.

1993 – Harold gets his GED.

1994 – Harold in Vegas.

Jane and Harold after Nancy's death.

Harold with his GED.